Beyond
the Mountains

•

By the same author

THE FOREST OF CHWEDKOWICE (SHORT STORIES)
THE SILENT ARMY (NONFICTION)
REBEL AGAINST THE LIGHT

Beyond
the Mountains

·

BY
ALEXANDER
RAMATI

THE NEW AMERICAN LIBRARY

FOR DIDI

© *1958 Alexander Ramati*
All rights reserved. No part of this book may be reproduced
without written permission from the publishers.
First Printing
Library of Congress Catalog Card Number: 66-24427
Published by The New American Library, Inc.
1301 Avenue of the Americas, New York, New York 10019
Printed in the United States of America

I

THE FREIGHT TRAIN FROM TASHKENT to the border town
of Ashkhabad had been waiting at the small station for two
hours. Marek Sobel sat on the floor of one of the freight cars,
watching the brown-faced, colourfully dressed natives, as with
their brass pots and empty cans they lined up in front of the
station's bubbling hot water tap, keeping an anxious eye on
the train. From the main platform, a small blue-uniformed
station-master leaned out over the rails, peering into the distance for the long-delayed passenger train. Across the wall of
the brick station building that reared up proudly in front of the
mud huts dotting the barren desert, hung a long, linen poster,
its hand-painted letters solemnly proclaiming that the railwaymen of Uzbekistan vowed to Comrade Kaganovich to run their
trains on schedule. In one of the freight cars, three white-
shirted Russian boys made loud jokes about the masculine uniform and red peaked cap of a pretty, round-faced girl conductor,
standing on the tracks nearby. The girl blushed and bit her lips,
intently studying the horizon. Marek, one hand stretched pro-
tectively over two knapsacks, watched with amusement the
boys' efforts to attract the girl's attention. Behind him in the
car he could hear the sporadic exclamations of two Ukrainian
boys playing cards, the staccato snoring of a chubby, uniformed
Russian matron, the click of the white tea-bowls a Turkoman
woman was extracting from a huge bundle with the help of her
barefoot children. The air was thick with the sour smell of
people who had not washed or changed their clothes for weeks.

Marek looked again at the crowd in front of the water fountain, trying to find his brother, who had gone for water half an
hour ago, leaving him to guard their knapsacks. He wasn't
there. Anxiously, Marek's eyes swept back and forth over the
platform, searching for the tall, familiar, quilt-jacketed figure.
A fierce-looking, bewhiskered Turkoman, in an enormous
sheepskin hat, climbed into his car, proudly carrying a full can

7

of boiling water, welcomed by the appreciative whisper of his wife and the contented squeaks of his children. The girl conductor suddenly moved a step forward. In the distance Marek heard the sound of the approaching train. He jumped up quickly, his troubled eyes focused on the station-master walking to the bell. His hands clutched the straps of his knapsack, twisting them nervously. Uncontrollably, a muscle in his cheek began to pull. The bell rang and the crowd, like a scared flock of birds, scampered across the rails. Throwing empty cans and pots inside the cars, the people climbed in feverishly, one over another. The clatter of the running train grew louder, mixing with the shrill rattle of wheels changing rails. The girl conductor exhorted a few stragglers, waved her green flag to the engine-driver, and jumped up on the steps of the train. With despair Marek heard the station-master blow his whistle. The wheels were beginning to turn when he finally saw his brother hurrying to the platform from the station building. 'Victor!' he yelled. 'For God's sake, hurry!' Victor ran across the rails, a pouch and flask swinging from his shoulder. He reached the car easily and jumped in, waving away Marek's outstretched hand. 'Another second and you'd have been left here!'

'No, I wouldn't,' Victor answered confidently. 'I was keeping track from inside.' He wiped the sweat off his face with his sleeve. An amused smile appeared on his lips, as he watched the platform again filling with a new crowd of pot and pan carrying people from the passenger train. 'Look what I've got.' He opened his pouch and pulled out a bunch of long, finger-like grapes.

'You're always so sure of yourself,' Marek said. 'What would I have done without you?' He rubbed his face nervously, as his anger and excitement grew with his words. 'If you do it again, I'm not going through with it, so help me God! I'm not going to risk losing you somewhere on our way.'

'Take it easy. Have some grapes.' Victor divided the fruit into two uneven parts and gave the larger portion to his brother. Marek shrugged and ignored the fruit. Victor happily reached for a cluster. Marek glanced at the grapes and plucked one, but Victor caught his arm. 'Wash them first.' He opened his flask and carefully poured a little hot water over each portion and then rubbed the fruit with his handkerchief.

A wan, self-pitying smile appeared in the corners of Marek's lips. 'I've almost forgotten how they taste.' As he slowly savoured the cool, tart flesh of the fruit, he looked at his brother's energetic profile, the sunburnt, angular, unshaven face, the full lips sucking grapes contentedly, the sharp blue eyes under the heavy brows watching a herd of thin-tailed karakul sheep. Victor looked like a carefree tourist enjoying a sight-seeing trip to Central Asia. It was hard to believe that he had just spent two years felling trees in a Siberian forced labour camp. Marek thought of his own dry, pallid skin, bony cheeks, colourless lips and wary, shadowed eyes. He winced at the comparison, but consoled himself with the thought that Victor derived his self-assurance from his physical strength. He had never been ill in his life, nor even had a day's cold. If he only had his brother's health, Marek thought wishfully, he would be just like him.

The car was filled with the sucking sounds of the tea-drinking Turkoman family. The uniformed woman suddenly awoke and rubbed her eyes. 'We haven't passed Kagan, have we?'

'No,' a square-faced boy answered, his eyes glued on the cards in his hands. 'You've got plenty of time.' He threw a card on the floor. 'Forty!'

'Let's see the King,' his tow-headed opponent said.

'Don't you believe me?'

'Of course, but let's see the King.'

Marek glanced over his shoulder at the boys. 'Want to play sixty-six?' the Ukrainian asked, showing his opponent the King.

'I haven't the money.'

'Then you'd better watch the scenery.'

The Russian woman, completely awake by now, re-tied the scarlet kerchief under her chin, watching the shaven-headed Turkoman children, clad in long white robes, sitting cross-legged on a carpet. They were avidly drinking hot, green tea from bowls almost as big as their heads. The Turkoman beckoned hospitably. The woman nodded agreeably. 'But wash the bowl first,' she said. She accepted the tea, placed the bowl on the floor, unbuttoned her khaki Party jacket, unbuttoned her blouse, and digging deep, came up with a blue kerchief, full of sugar. She took out a single lump, re-tied the kerchief carefully and again hid it in her blouse. She licked the sugar and began to sip her tea loudly. 'My husband is fighting Germans near Moscow. He got a Red Star medal a week ago, but they won't give me a place in a passenger train. I've got to ride in a freight car!' Her high, wheezy voice invited recognition of the railway officials' ungrateful behaviour.

'Shall we make some tea?' Victor asked his brother.

'No, not now. How can anyone drink tea when it's so hot?'

'Why are you going to Kagan?' one of the card players asked the Russian woman, his voice betraying no interest.

'I'm visiting my mother. She's sick. You know Kagan?'

'Yes.'

'My brother-in-law is a manager of the Party dining hall. On Pierwomajskaja Street. You know Pierwomajskaja Street?'

'Yes.'

'You know the Party dining hall?'

'No.' The boy threw his cards down. 'All aces and tens.'

The woman propped her bowl against her jutting bosom. She gave the boys a sharp, measuring look. 'Two healthy young men. Why aren't *you* in the army?'

'What are you—an NKVD officer? Looking for deserters?'

'Why should my husband fight and you—you have a good time playing cards?'

Marek chuckled, thinking of a ribald joke and opened his mouth to tell it, but Victor looked at him warningly and he snapped it shut again.

'Relax!' the tow-headed Ukrainian said. 'We've just been drafted into the Army and have to report in Kagan tomorrow. Satisfied?'

The woman grunted. 'I hope they'll send you to the front

soon, so you can share the privilege of defending our country.'
Marek recalled the posters on the street walls of the Soviet
cities, and the Sunday lectures in the labour camp, and the
daily editorials of the Moscow *Pravda*. The woman finished
her tea in one gulp and self-righteously put the bowl on the
floor. In a moment she was asleep again, her head bent over the
valise, her big bosom surging patriotically under her manly
Party jacket.

Marek looked out of the car. The sky was not marred by a
single cloud. A beturbaned Uzbek, with an upward-pointed
beard, was swaying on a stately camel towards a lonely yurt.
The train threw a long, racing shadow on the yellow sand
dunes. Marek saw Victor finish his grapes and only then realized that his own portion was bigger. 'Take these. You gave
me more.'

'I don't want them.'

'Then let's save some for later. Put them into your pouch.'

'You'd better eat them. They're good for you. We'll get
more in Kermine, don't worry.'

'Maybe we'll get chocolate there. I'd love just one piece of
chocolate, or even a lump of sugar. Something sweet to keep
in my mouth.' He went on slowly eating the grapes, watching
the Turkoman woman who was wearing red pantaloons, a
white caftan and a tall cylindrical hat, with a piece of heavy
cloth at the back which fell in folds over her shoulders. Her
husband's enormous feet brushed against Marek every time
the train jolted.

Victor pulled out some tobacco wrapped in a piece of cloth,
then he took out a shred of newspaper and tore out a square.
He distributed a pinch of tobacco evenly along the centre of
the paper, wrapped it carefully, licked the paper's edge and put
the home-made cigarette to his lips.

'Want to smoke?'

'No.'

Victor struck a match, cupping it against the draught.
'We'll be there soon,' he said slowly. 'Remember, I do all the
talking.'

'Yes.'

'We'll have to be very careful.'

'I know.'

'We'll have to sell my watch, but I'm sure we won't get as much money as we need.'

'I wish we didn't have to sell it. It's the only watch we have now.'

Victor smiled. 'We traded yours for garlic, remember?'

'I made the deal,' Marek said proudly. 'We got twenty heads. That was a lot, wasn't it?'

'Yes.' The wind blew Victor's dark blond hair over his face. He brushed it back with his fingers; his high forehead wrinkled in memories. 'It helped to cure your scurvy.' He glanced at his brother's right leg. Between the boot, the original red colouring of which had mostly been scuffed off, and the turn-up of his linen trousers was a reddish scar, conspicuous on the sockless leg. Victor turned to his brother and patted his shoulder. 'That's all over with. Don't think about the camp. Forget it.'

Marek nodded, but his thoughts slipped back to the huge pine forest, its trees rarely green in the endless winter. He heard again the crisp, crunching steps of the prisoners marching to work in the violet dawn that broke through the peaceful starlit sky. He could almost smell the piercing frosty air spiced with the scents of snow, timber, and sweaty wadded jerkins. Marek shook his head, as if reproaching himself, and glanced at Victor, guiltily. His brother was watching the Turkoman woman pull out some old clothes and wrap them carefully around the empty tea-bowls. The train's draught blew a musty, pungent scent into Marek's nostrils that made him think about the camp's hospital with its four naked wooden walls and people lying on sacks of straw, their open wounds filling the windowless room with an unbearably offensive stench. He saw the little, almost childish face of the hospital's nurse, Anushka, the only woman he had met in two years, bent over him, her cool hand touching his forehead, her gentle eyes focused on his face as if trying to read his thoughts. He remembered the sleepless nights filled with elaborate visions of making love to

Anushka. He recalled the mornings when after restless expectation he would welcome her familiar thick black braids, her small, compressed mouth and her wordless stare; and would finally feel happy, but at the same time miserably helpless, at the thought of his weakened body, of the crowd of people in the hospital, and of the barbed wire separating the camp from the barrack where Anushka lived.

A wan, nostalgic smile appeared on Marek's lips as his memories turned to the afternoon when, released from the camp, he came to say good-bye to the girl. Within the barren wooden walls of the hospital's corridor, he had stopped her. 'I'm leaving the camp,' he said. 'For good.'

She looked at him, 'I was told you're leaving,' she said. 'And I'm very happy for you. Very happy.' A slow gentle smile came upon her lips, she raised her hand and brushed his cheek delicately, then hurried away to her patients. As he heard the soft sliding noise of her felt boots, receding down the dimly lit corridor, he reproached himself for every time he had undressed her in his mind.

The train curved slightly and Marek saw the girl conductor sitting in the next car with the three boys, all gay and friendly. One of the boys was playing a harmonica, and was particularly happy because the girl was holding his arm. Marek looked away, dried the sweat from his forehead and, leaning back against the frame of the entrance, closed his eyes. He didn't know why but suddenly he began to think about his mother. He could see her small and wrinkled face, as she sat on his bed, watching him picking up cherries from a bowl and drawing big letters in his exercise book by the yellow light of a kerosene lamp that had replaced candles in Brest Litovsk after the last war. His stout father was standing at the glazed tile stove, warming his huge hands and smiling at his son's uneasy efforts to master the art of writing. In the door Victor appeared in an Indian headdress. 'Hey you, you're not ill any more! Come on,' he called in a strident voice, that was just changing, 'let's play a man's game! Or would you rather stay tied to mother, eh, softy?'

13

Suddenly his brother's voice deepened. 'Don't fall asleep. We get off at the next station. We ought to be there soon.'

'I'm not sleeping. I'm thinking.'

'You're always thinking. What is it this time?'

'Oh, our parents, the camp, a girl, lots of things.'

'What girl?'

Marek grinned sadly. 'I haven't kissed one in two years.'

'Neither have I. But that's fine, think about girls. Don't think about camp or about our parents. It doesn't help. It only makes you soft. I told myself when we left home that I'd never think about Mother and Father. So if I catch myself thinking about them, I immediately force my mind on to something else.'

'I can't change my thoughts at will.'

'When you start thinking about home, switch to remembering a girl you once made love to. It's a very good method. You'll see how it helps.'

'That's not easy either.'

'It's easier. At least it doesn't hurt.'

'That's what you think.' Marek opened his eyes. 'I wonder how a girl's kiss tastes after all this time?'

Victor smiled. 'About the same, I imagine.' He raised his head a little and said warningly. 'Don't you get into any trouble. We can't afford to.'

'Don't worry.'

'If you meet a girl, just make love to her. Don't get attached and sentimental.'

Marek nodded in annoyance. 'I'm not as soft as you think.'

On the horizon he saw five camels in a single line. As the train drew closer, the figures of the riders grew more distinct. He recognized the white uniforms and peaked hats with the red star in the centre. 'The desert police,' Victor said slowly. 'Watching the borders.' The two brothers exchanged glances.

The camel patrol halted and the policemen saluted the train. An uneven chorus of voices greeted them in response. The policemen grinned, waited till the train passed by, then resumed their routine desert inspection.

'Marek,' Victor touched his brother's arm, his voice low and guarded. 'Never mention the camp. Never say we were in it.'

'No.'

'Always pretend we're Russians.' Marek nodded in agreement. 'And never talk Polish in public.'

'We're talking Polish now.'

'Here it doesn't matter. We're getting off soon and we will never see these people again. But in Kermine we must only speak Russian.' He shifted closer to Marek. 'Remember, we moved south because you needed sun and better food. You know, fruit and fresh vegetables—vitamins.'

'I know.'

'We must avoid suspicion. We'll mix with the villagers just like anyone else.' Marek nodded. 'Of course it's different if the police stop us. Then we can't lie. If we do and they find out, we're sunk.'

The train began to slow down and suddenly a second line of rails appeared. 'I think we're coming to the station.' Victor turned to the Ukrainians behind him. 'What's the next stop?'

'Kermine,' the blond boy said. 'There's plenty of time before we get to Kagan. Want to play?'

'They don't have any money,' his partner said. 'Your move.'

'We're getting out at Kermine.'

The shifting rails squealed under the car's floor. The Turkoman's feet were drumming against Marek's hip and he drew away. The Russian woman woke up. 'Is it Kagan?' she asked in alarm, peering out at the telegraph poles.

The square-faced boy cursed under his breath. 'Relax, Comrade. You've got plenty of time.'

Marek held his long, gaunt hands limply on his knees. He watched the procession of telegraph poles in front of him, his thoughts far away, in the comfortable compartment of a Polish train, with his brother, himself and their parents the only occupants. It was ten years ago and they were going to the seaside for their summer vacation, the only one their father, a municipal bookkeeper, could ever afford.

'Get ready,' Victor said. 'We're here.' The train switched

rails again, rolled past a semaphore, a traffic control booth, and a few white-washed buildings. A station-master waited on the main platform, signalling the train to halt with the wig-wag of his raised hand. The wheels squeaked, the cars jerked and stopped abruptly. 'Come,' Victor said. They hung their knapsacks over their shoulders. 'Good-bye,' Victor waved to their fellow travellers.

The Turkoman saluted good-naturedly, raising his hand to his fur cap. The Russian matron bowed slightly. 'Make some money,' the blond Ukrainian called, 'so the next time we meet, we can have a game.'

2

THEY CROSSED THE RAILS, CAUTIOUSLY, looking right and left, stopping for a moment to let a locomotive adorned with the portrait of Kaganovich go by. They passed a crowd of people lining up at the hot water tap and entered the brick building plastered with the same poster that they had seen at the previous station.

The waiting room was small and overcrowded. A few Russians dozed on wooden benches, Uzbek peasants bivouacked on their carpets on the stone floor. On one side there was a closed ticket window, flanked by a pair of low, narrow doors, a cock painted on one, a hen on the other. The air was heavy with the smell of human sweat and unattended lavatories. In the exit a bulky NKVD man in uniform scrutinized the faces of the new arrivals. 'Go straight ahead,' Victor whispered, and they eased out quickly, mixing with a group of freight train passengers. They heard the NKVD man's imperious voice halting an Uzbek for a routine check of his bundle in search of unrationed food.

In front of the station were several camel-drawn arbas with their two-yard long axles and man-high wooden wheels, loaded with huge cotton bales. Barefoot Uzbek workers, in long, canvas blouses and colourful woven skull caps carried the bales of cotton from the arbas into the train, grunting and groaning as they eased their burdens.

The small town lying before them looked as if it hadn't changed since Tamerlane's rule five hundred years ago, except for a red banner arched across two wooden poles urging the proletarians of all countries to unite. Its buildings were huts made of loam mixed with straw, chaff and the urine of camels, roofed with mud and reeds, patted into shape by human hands and baked by the sun's heat. As Marek and Victor walked along the narrow winding pathway which ran at the side of the earthen road, through clouds of dust whipped up by the iron wheels of arbas and the horses' hooves, the rhythmical sound of the men working at the station floated off in the distance.

A large square on their right opened on a mosque with a pagoda-like dome and long, wooden Mongolian pillars. Marek stopped, shifted his knapsack to the other shoulder and caught a glimpse of mechanics repairing a tractor in front of a wall with scenes in mosaic from the Koran. Over the open gate of the mosque was a sign identifying the place as the Kermine Tractor Repair Base No. 2.

'Come on,' Victor said over his shoulder. 'It's getting late.'

Marek caught up with his brother and they walked quickly past groups of people queuing up in front of shops; an unopened news-stand, a shop selling scissors, its windows decorated with empty tins and bottles, and a bakery filling the air with the fine smell of freshly baked bread. In front of the bakery stood a line of Uzbek women, robed in wide, striped, cloak-like paranjas with floating sleeves, wearing skull-caps on their much braided hair. Enviously they looked at the people hurrying out of the shop with bread, frightened that the supply might not last. Marek's eyes followed a little girl victoriously carrying the brown, disc-shaped loaf. 'I'm hungry,' he said.

'We must see Ulug Beg first. We'll eat later.' Victor critically inspected Marek's face and rubbed the stubble on his own chin. 'We look terrible. Let's get a quick shave and find out where he lives.' He looked around for a barber's shop and spotted one on the opposite side of the street. They waited until an old truck, serving as a local bus, had passed, then they crossed to the barber's shop which displayed Stalin's portrait in the window and a small red flag at the door.

In a little half-darkened room, in front of a mirror, a white-aproned barber was sitting in the chair reserved for customers, trimming his whiskers with a pair of scissors. He sprang up when he saw the two and motioned them to the chair invitingly. 'Go ahead,' Victor said in Russian, as he pushed their knapsacks, pouches and flasks into the corner of the room.

Marek lowered himself into the uncomfortable chair. 'A shave,' he said, unhappily scrutinizing the dark patches under his eyes. Cauldron 'C', he thought, grinning sadly to himself in the mirror, watching the barber sharpen his razor on the long end of his belt. A tin mess-can of soup and half a pound of black bread per day. As the barber went about his business, smiling at his customer with professional friendliness, the vision of the camp's three lines in front of the cauldrons returned to Marek's mind. Again he saw men in fur caps with flaps over their ears, their feet and legs wrapped in rags and tied about with string. He spotted Victor in the line in front of cauldron 'A', waiting for his ration and additional spoonful of thick barley and a piece of salted fish—the reward for good, hard labour in the forest. The picture dissolved to one of a shack with a small fire sizzling and hissing in the iron stove between the wooden bunks. They were both sitting on a bench, dividing his brother's extra-ration in one of the rare times that he managed to smuggle it past the watchful eyes of the camp guards.

Someone entered the shop. The barber paused for a moment. 'Good day, Comrade Kisielev,' he said. In the mirror Marek saw the pleasantly smiling, tanned face of a young man wearing an upturned peaked cap and an olive-green Konsomol uniform with a medal of distinction on his chest. He returned the greeting by raising his newspaper to his ear. 'I'll be through in a moment,' the barber said, pointing to the empty chair near Victor.

'I'll have tea across the street,' the young man said cheerfully. 'Call me when you're through.' He gave Marek a friendly smile in the mirror, glanced at the knapsacks in the corner, smiled at Victor, and left.

'Comrade Kisielev,' the barber said, admiration and respect in each syllable, 'is the local secretary of Konsomol, a town councillor, chairman of the draft board. . . . He has many functions. A very important man. You'll get to know him if you stay in town much longer.' In the mirror Marek saw Victor lift his head, watching him. Marek said nothing. The barber started to massage the fresh foam into Marek's skin. 'I was new here myself fifteen years ago. I came from Yerevan in Armenia. Ever been in Yerevan?'

'No.'

'Armenians are fine people. Where did you come from?'

'Chkalov,' Marek answered and saw his brother's slight confirming nod in the mirror.

'Oh, I've passed through there. Never got out of the station though. It's a very nice town.'

'Tell me,' Victor interrupted, 'do you know where Ulug Beg lives?' He paused before the name and pronounced it hesitantly as though he had difficulty in recalling it. Marek held his breath, waiting for the Armenian's answer.

'Of course,' the barber said. 'You turn left after the open air movie-house. It's one of the last huts on your right. What do you need him for?' he asked with the inevitable curiosity of a barber.

Marek studied the brushes and combs on the counter in front of him, avoiding Victor's face in the mirror, listening to his calm even voice.

'We were told he sells skull-caps. We don't want to expose our heads to this fierce sun.'

'Of course not. His wife makes nice skull-caps.' He massaged toilet water into Marek's face and hair, parting it on the left. He beckoned to Victor. 'Your turn, Citizen.'

Marek examined his face in the mirror, rubbed it complacently and then walked to the door. The sky behind the mud huts had turned to golden-red. The shops were closing down and he saw the remaining women in the bakery queue leave dejectedly with empty netbags. A group of children in the red neckerchiefs and khaki shirts of Pioneers passed by proudly carrying the scrap they had collected for war factories. Across the street Marek saw the tea-house with its three clay walls, filled with Uzbeks sitting cross-legged on their dusty carpets, sipping green tea from bowls and drying the sweat from their necks with towels provided by the management. In the shop he heard the barber humming a Russian military march under his breath and telling Victor that the Soviet Union was a big country and that no matter where you went you felt at home. A pretty, blonde Russian girl passed by. There was something about her face that attracted Marek. He looked after her till she turned into a side street. Then he realized what had struck him. She was wearing lipstick.

The barber had finished and Victor paid him. Marek went back into the room and hoisted his knapsack to his shoulder. 'Is there an hotel here?' Victor asked.

The barber chuckled. 'No, we don't get many tourists.'

Victor's eyes measured the cupboard in the corner. 'Could we leave our knapsacks with you until tomorrow? As soon as we find a room we'll pick them up.' He held a rouble in his hand.

'Of course,' the Armenian said. He opened the cupboard, partly filled with ragged barber cloths. 'Just put them there, Citizen.' Victor and Marek threw their knapsacks, pouches and flasks inside. Victor gave the rouble to the barber. 'If you don't find anything,' the Armenian said, 'come back. I could inquire from my customers. People should help each other, shouldn't they?'

'You don't have to bother. We'll find something.'

They left the shop. 'Now let's find Ulug Beg,' Victor said.

'When will we eat?'

'After we see him.'

'All the shops are closing.'

'We'll get into some dining hall.'

'Then let's hurry before it gets dark and we lose our way.'

Shopkeepers were pulling down the shutters over their windows. In the middle of the empty street, three dogs sat quietly, watching with serious faces the closing of the business day. A street lamp went on, throwing off a sickly glow. As they walked, a string of lights lit up the sky ahead of them and they knew that they were approaching the open air movie-house. Even though it was much too early, a queue had already formed before the closed box office, next to the poster of a robust king sitting on his throne below the golden sign 'Peter the Great'.

They turned into a narrow sand street, walking between two winding mud walls, the doorways of the various courtyards overhung with ragged blankets. Over the walls, the roofs of the huts glowed a deep violet for a few moments, then began to fade quickly. A light breeze suddenly rose bringing with it the far-off howling of dogs, the secretive murmurs of voices behind the walls, the clatter of wooden sandals on a stony courtyard, the noise of an iron can against the side of a well. The air was filled with the smell of onions and animals and women's daily washing. A lonely street lamp was burning ahead, throwing a streak of light on the roadway, dim and flickering like the gleam of a candle at the head of a coffin. In the middle of the hard dirt road, a cat sat, licking his paws, watching them calmly. 'We'd better ask where it is,' Victor said as he saw they were approaching the end of the street. He looked over his shoulder. On the curve of the road an Uzbek girl appeared, but at the sight of the two men, she withdrew quickly. They took a few more steps, and heard the quiet monotonous rhythm of an oriental tune, floating up towards them from behind the wall. Victor lifted the blanket and ducked inside the courtyard. A young man was sitting on the doorstep of his hut, strumming a long, shovel-like instrument. 'Hello,' Victor shouted. 'Do you know where Ulug Beg lives?'

The tune stopped. The man peered up at them. 'No,' he said in broken frightened Russian. 'I don't get around much. I'm blind.' He waited motionlessly for them to leave. As they walked towards the crossroads ahead of them, they heard the sad, rhythmical melody resumed.

At the left of the crossroads they saw a group of children bent over something on the ground. The children noticed Marek and Victor and waved excitedly for them to come closer. They had a scorpion, encircled by paper which they had set aflame. The animal ran helplessly back and forth trying to escape. Suddenly it sank its poisonous tail into its own head. The finger-like body jerked and in a second lay dead, unable to acknowledge the cheers and happy shrieks of the children, applauding its brave suicide. Marek stood speechless, looking at the motionless animal, filled with pity for the strange creature he'd never seen before and with anger at the barbaric cruelty of the children. Victor asked in a matter-of-fact tone, 'Where does Ulug Beg live?'

A freckle-faced, ginger-haired boy dismissed the others and appointed himself their guide. He took them back to the crossroads and led them to the end of the street they had been on before. He ran a few yards in front of them, his sockless feet clattering loudly in his father's huge, wooden sandals. Stopping in front of the last hut, he pointed to the entrance, covered by a ragged carpet. Then without a word he ran back quickly to his group, throwing a glance back over his shoulder from the crossroads.

Marek halted, looking at the flat land stretching from the edge of the town to the horizon. 'Cotton fields,' Victor said as he studied the low bush and the ground netted by ditches filled with water. He waited a few seconds, gazing down, planning what he would say. 'Well, let's go. Remember, I do all the talking.' He lifted the dusty carpet, bent down and entered. Marek followed him. They found themselves in the courtyard of the hut belonging to Ulug Beg.

3

THEY STOOD IN THE SQUARE, empty courtyard, looking at the time-worn hut, its white-washed mud walls sagging under the heavy roof, its small entrance veiled by a red linen curtain, a weak drowsy light seeping out through a small oblong opening in the wall. Victor took a few steps forward and stopped near the well, on the edge of which stood an iron can, its chain winding down into the earth. A sudden strangled baby's cry came from the neighbouring courtyard, through the large break in the wall. A woman's face flashed in the hut's opening and in a moment the curtain again slid down over the entrance. Nobody appeared, but they knew they were being watched from inside. 'Come,' Victor said and they entered the hut, bending their heads as they stepped through the low doorway.

Inside the little room, on the top of a pile of quilts and cushions, an old man was seated, leaning against the wall, his bearded, deeply wrinkled face burned to the colour of red earth. His little yellow, red-rimmed eyes were focused on them expectantly. The small flame from the cotton wick floating in an oil-filled earthen dish threw long moving shadows on the low walls.

'You are Ulug Beg?' The old man nodded. 'Your son asked us to see you,' Victor said, studying the man's face attentively.

Something moved in the shadowed corner of the room. Marek turned and saw a female silhouette—a pair of large hands resting on legs, a pair of shining eyes centred on Victor. A slight momentary gleam lit up the Uzbek's eyes. He looked from Victor to Marek and back. 'There must be a mistake,' he said dully. 'I don't have a son. My son died ten years ago.'

'He did not die,' Victor said, his firm voice emphasizing every word. 'He was arrested ten years ago on the border and is now in a forced labour camp in Siberia.'

A shuddering sigh came from the corner of the room.

Ulug lifted his head, his pale thin lips quivered. Then his forehead puckered and his elongated eyes squinted with suspicion. 'What do you want?' His heavily accented Russian grew instantly harsh and accusing. 'I don't believe it! You wouldn't come here after ten years to tell me that my son is alive! When he had been missing for a month, I went to the police. I went there several times during the first few years. They always said they knew nothing.'

Without a word, Victor unbuttoned his quilted jacket and took out a piece of paper from his pocket. He unfolded it and put it on Ulug's knees. 'It's a mistake,' the old man mumbled, his voice trembling, his chin quivering slightly. He stared for a long while at the note filled with pencilled Latin letters, forming Uzbek words. The sagging skin of his throat pulled taut. He drew the burning oil-dish closer, lifting it to eye level. In the full light, Marek saw his wizened face with bony cheeks, framed by a short, pointed, upward-curling white beard. His forefinger moved slowly along the lines, halting again and again as his yellow lips pronounced the words with almost physical effort. In the dark corner of the room, the woman's unwinking eyes fastened themselves on Ulug's face.

'Isn't that Addin's handwriting?' Victor asked. 'Do you believe me now?'

Ulug Beg nodded, his head still bent, gazing down at the letter. Then he straightened up slowly and Marek saw the old man's eyes turn to the unseen face in the corner with a wordless expression of painful joy. A while passed before he mumbled a few excited sentences in Uzbek. The woman stood up, took the note from Ulug's unprotesting hand, sat down on the floor near him, and fixed her black eyes on the paper, her blotched mouth open and dry. She was an old woman, with heavy hips and large legs out of proportion to the slim-waisted and narrow-shouldered upper part of her body. She was clad in a black paranja, a black kerchief falling from the top of her iron-grey hair. A dark veil covered her chin and cheeks, framing the olive-skinned face wrinkled by sun and wind. Suddenly a short spasm shook her body. She hid her face in her hands and began sobbing, her weeping hollow and gasping. 'She can't read,' Ulug Beg said, looking at her warmly, 'but she recognizes her son's writing.' He put his hand on her head and kept it there, not speaking, until she quieted and wiped her eyes with the corners of her paranja. She went back to the letter, engrossed and absent, completely unaware of the others in the room. A slow soft smile broke on her lips.

'Addin asked us to tell you that he might be released in five years,' Victor said.

'Five years,' Ulug repeated dully.

Marek looked around the room. It was almost empty except for a pile of quilts, blankets and cushions. Some brass pots stood in one corner and a case of skull-caps in another. Three colourful rugs hung on three walls, one of them only partly finished. On the fourth wall hung a collection of old pistols, curved sabres, blow-pipes, daggers and clubs. The Uzbek looked at the two men, studying their faces. Suspicion again clouded his eyes and his voice. 'Who are you?'

'We were in camp with Addin. We slept in the same barrack —for two years.'

Ulug's eyes slanted. 'You—escaped?'

'No. We were released.'

'Why were you released and Addin was not?'

'We are Poles. After an agreement between the Polish and Russian governments, the Russians released all the Poles from the labour camps.' The old man shook his head, bewildered. 'We are not Russians. We are from Poland.'

'What is Poland?'

'It is a country. It is not in the Soviet Union. The Russians took over the part of Poland we lived in.'

'Why did they arrest you?'

Now it was Victor who studied the old man before replying. 'We tried to escape abroad. They caught us at the border.'

Ulug Beg looked at Victor, then at Marek, then again at Victor. He stood up slowly. 'Addin's Mother,' he said to his wife, 'prepare some pilaff for our guests. Can't you see they are hungry?'

The woman made a semi-circle of bricks in the courtyard and put a big, black iron pot on them. She opened a little pantry and pulled out dry juniper chips, put them under the pot, and made a fire. The three men sat on the ground around the fire and watched the chips blaze in the dark of the evening, spreading a pleasant scent of resin. Soft patches of light and shadow played on their faces. The woman waited until the pot had warmed and then threw mutton fat inside. It began to hiss, then melted and started to boil.

Ulug twisted the tip of his beard. 'Maybe they will release him earlier,' he said and looked up at Victor and Marek. In his red-rimmed yellow eyes, Marek read the naïve hope that if the Russians had released the Poles from the camps, maybe the Uzbeks would be the next. The brothers were silent. Ulug sighed and bowed his head.

Marek watched the black-robed, silent woman in front of the open pantry, splitting mutton flesh on a chopping board, cutting the onions, dicing carrots into thin strips and slicing tomatoes. He grinned and winked contentedly at his brother. Ulug's wife carried the food to the pot in a fold of her paranja. She split juniper wood and piled it under the cooking vessel. The flames flared up, sizzling, and lit up the faces of the men. 'Five years,' Ulug said absently, staring into the fire, his voice small and forlorn. 'In five years I might not be alive any more.' He clenched his fists in sudden anger and turned to Victor. 'Why didn't they tell me that Addin was alive? They surely knew, those bastards!' His wife looked up at him and spoke for the first time. Ulug's face softened. He turned back to Victor. 'Addin's Mother asks how he looks? Like you,' he motioned towards Marek with his chin, 'or like your brother?' Marek and Victor exchanged quick glances. 'Addin is a strong man,' Victor said. 'He looks fine.'

Ulug's mouth curved in a little reminiscent smile. 'Yes, he was always strong. He could lift a bale of cotton by himself.' He turned to his wife and pointed at Victor. Her eyes lit up. She went to the well, grasped the chain and lowered the can. There was a dull splash of iron against water. Addin's Mother leaned forward, peeped inside, nodded to herself and effort-lessly raised the can. She walked back to the fire, her bare feet making a thudding sound, the water from the brimming can spattering over the earth.

Marek clasped his knees boyishly and looked up. A faint star of the evening flickered hesitantly on the darkening sky. The pale wash of the young moon reflected on the flat roof of the hut and the courtyard walls. He turned back to watch the old woman bent over the pot, her hand holding the cover, her face glowing from the reflection of the fire. She poured the water from the can into the cauldron, covered it, and stood by, keeping watch over the cooking meal. From behind the wall came the high, female tones of a monotonous lullaby. A wave of wind puffed through the courtyard, blowing the hot smell of food to the crickets, moths and mosquitoes that gathered swiftly around the cauldron, humming and buzzing and flying into their faces.

The old woman went to the pantry, brought a bucket of washed rice, a handful of berberries, and a stick, which she handed to Ulug. He moved closer to the cauldron, removed the cover, and raked the fire. Marek watched the profile of his face grow religiously solemn, the skin tightening over his forehead, as the crooked arch of his nose sniffed the meal.

His eyes, tense and unwinking, watched the pieces of meat boil in the fat until they had completely browned. Then he looked up at his wife and nodded. She poured in the bucket of rice and the handful of berberries. Immediately Ulug began stirring the concoction, removing the stick from time to time, then pausing like a conductor before the introduction of a new movement. Marek's nostrils twitched hungrily as the smell of mutton and rice sweetened the courtyard.

When the water had been absorbed by the rice, Ulug covered the pot again, smoothed his moustache and turned to them. 'It will be ready in ten minutes,' he announced in an elaborate whisper.

'Good,' Marek said, rubbing his hands and moving closer to the pot. Victor waited, his hands on his knees, tranquil and composed, as though he was accustomed to having meat in camp every day instead of just four times a year on the important Communist holidays.

The woman approached with a huge white bowl and a few saucers. She put them on the ground near her husband. The bowl was empty but the saucers were filled with onions soaked in vinegar, red pepper, pickled garlic and grated white radish. 'Eat,' Ulug urged them. 'It's good.' He took a pepper and passed the saucer to Marek. 'Try it. It will make you very hungry so you can eat plenty.'

Marek wondered if anything could increase his ravenous appetite, but he took a pepper and bit it cautiously. He felt his throat burning, coughed and beat his chest. Ulug chuckled. 'It's good, huh?' He grabbed some grated radish from the saucer, filled his mouth and passed the saucer to Victor. Then he lifted the cover of the pot, bent his head into the vapour, and sniffed loudly. He plunged his stick into the stew and tasted the mixture. His eyes rolled in delight and his lips made a pursing complacent sound. He raised the pot and with the aid of his stick emptied the contents into the dish. His wife handed him a fan and sat opposite him on the ground, reverently watching him blow on the pilaff to cool it off. The Uzbek pointed the dish at his guests and, dipping his palm into the stew, he began to eat from his hand, smacking his lips and waving them to start. He chewed happily, rubbing his chin between bites to clear off the fat that dribbled down.

Marek glanced at Victor. Victor looked back at him, raised his eyebrows and plunged his hand into the stew with the expression of an untutored peasant who has just been introduced to table manners and is quick to grasp them. Marek grinned, shrugged good humouredly, cupped his hand, and followed his brother's example. First he picked up the meat with his left hand, chewing it slowly, then he leaned over his hand and sucked in the rice, glancing sideways at the Uzbek, imitating him. He inhaled the heavy, mixed odours of the pilaff, contentedly sensing a pleasant warmth filling his stomach.

The woman now approached the dish, squatted and began to eat. She never raised her head, never glanced at the men or said a word. No one spoke, only Ulug from time to time grunted and nodded in deep satisfaction. 'So, what are you going to do here?' he finally said, rubbing the fat from his face with a greasy hand. 'Work?' He picked up a fresh portion of pilaff.

Marek fixed his eyes on Victor. His hand stopped in mid-air. He let it drop slowly, his greasy fingers half-closing in tense expectation. 'No,' Victor said slowly. 'We didn't come to Kermine to work.'

The Uzbek stopped eating. He looked searchingly at Victor, rubbing his hand on his trousers. 'Why did you come to Kermine?'

Victor looked up at the mountains to the south. He stared at them, then slowly turned his face to the old man, the hint of a smile on his face.

Ulug's eyes narrowed. 'You want to go there?'

'Yes,' Victor said evenly. 'We want to try again.'

The Uzbek gave Victor a quick look and went back to his food. Marek lifted his hand to his mouth, his jaw moved twice then stopped as his eyes darted expectantly from one man to the other. Ulug smiled at him. 'Eat,' he said. 'There is still plenty. Is it good?'

'Very good.' Marek nodded approvingly, looking at the woman. She turned to him, her dark heavy brows arched questioningly, unable to grasp his worldly acknowledgment of her culinary skill. 'We Uzbeks eat once a day,' the old man said, 'but then we eat plenty.'

When the bowl was finally empty, Ulug drew it to him, plunged his palm inside and licked the fat from his fingers. Victor rubbed his hands on his handkerchief and passed it to Marek. 'Addin told us,' he began again, peering at the Uzbek, 'that your son-in-law, Hamlat, could take us across the border.'

Marek watched the crooked figure of the old man, only his chin and lips visible now, the upper part of his face in shadow. His eyes focused intently on Ulug as he listened to the rustle of the crickets, the lonely sound of footsteps outside, the muffled laughter of a woman. The wind blew stronger, lifting the rug in the entrance to the courtyard. Ulug let a few seconds pass in silence, just staring at the dimly glowing chips. Addin's Mother stood up, collected the saucers into the bowl, and left. The old man's face turned to the wall with a passage to the neighbouring courtyard. 'Hamlat went across the border,' he said almost whispering. 'This,' he pointed to the empty pot, 'was my last sheep. There is no food in Uzbekistan, the stores are empty, the rations are small and you cannot get them. We don't get any meat. Uzbeks can't live without pilaff. You can't cook pilaff without meat. Hamlat went across the border to get some sheep.'

'Will he take us across the border when he comes back?' Victor asked.

Ulug shouted something to his wife. In a moment she brought him a leather pouch. He opened it, took out a pinch of green tobacco, and rubbed it for a while in his opened palm. He offered it to Victor and Marek. They shook their heads, waiting for his answer, watching him put the tobacco under his tongue and hold it there, moving his jaw rhythmically, moistening it with his saliva. Then he nodded. 'Why not? If you could pay him.'

Victor felt Marek's eyes on his face. He flashed his brother a reassuring look that told him not to worry and to leave everything to him. 'How much?'

'It has become very difficult,' Ulug went on in an intimate, low voice. 'The frontiers are now well guarded and the guards have hunting dogs.' Marek moved his feet nervously. He felt the muscles of his face twitch. 'But Hamlat will know his way. He has done it many times.' The old man leaned towards Victor, propping his fist on the earth. 'Addin and Hamlat used to smuggle Bokharian Jews across the border—years ago.' Victor nodded knowingly. 'Then when Addin did not come back, Hamlat became more cautious. But he made a few trips now and then. He hasn't gone in the last few years until this time. Don't worry. He knows his way around.'

'How much would he charge?'

Ulug's eyes squinted with the effort to recall Hamlat's fee. 'The last time,' he said, 'he got two thousand roubles for a family.' Marek swallowed. Nervously he ran his hand across his face and looked at Victor hopelessly.

'Do you have two thousand roubles?' Ulug asked.

'No,' Victor said calmly. 'But we could pay half. There are just two of us—both men. We are not a whole family. Perhaps he had children to worry about.'

'Perhaps,' Ulug said, spreading his hands. 'I don't remember.' He pursed his lips thoughtfully and rubbed his nose, looking into the hut where his wife was bent over a skull-cap, weaving in the dim light of the oil-dish lamp. He straightened up and nodded. 'I think I could persuade him to do it for a thousand roubles. After all, you brought me the news that my son is alive and that is worth a thousand roubles.'

'Thank you,' Victor said gratefully.

Ulug Beg raised his forefinger and leaned back, his eyes slanting shrewdly. 'He will do it. He will take you there and come back—with sheep.' He smoothed his beard cheerfully and chuckled.

Victor threw a triumphant look at his brother. Marek moistened his dry lips and leaned towards the Uzbek. 'May I try your tobacco now?' he said with cheerful relief. Ulug passed him the pouch, and Marek took a pinch. It was very bitter, worse than the pepper, but heroically he forced a smile and nodded approvingly. Victor, hiding a grin, rolled a cigarette, lit it from a charcoal and blew the smoke in front of him.

In the opening of the courtyard wall Marek unexpectedly saw the face of a young girl staring in at them. Ulug followed his eyes. 'Aka,' he said. 'Hamlat's daughter.' The girl made her way inside the courtyard sat on the ground at a respectful distance, crossing her legs, her eyes following the strangers with adolescent curiosity. She was about thirteen years old, barefoot and wearing a grey paranja. Her hair was plaited in a dozen braids and on it she wore a skull-cap embroidered with four blue half-moons. 'She looks very much like her mother,'

Ulug whispered, so that the girl would not hear. 'She died. A year ago.' He stifled the beginning of a sigh. 'Addin doesn't know she died . . . '

The men looked at the girl, watching her rub her plump, rosy cheek against her shoulder, her elongated, blue eyes fixed in a silent gaze upon the men. Suddenly she became aware that their attention was focused on her, then, as a deep plum colour tinted her cheeks, she sprang up and strode swiftly in to Addin's Mother.

'I had a son and a daughter,' said Ulug, shaking his head in memories. 'Addin, I thought, was killed. My daughter killed herself. She ran into the desert and set fire to her paranja.'

'Set fire to her own clothes?' Marek repeated in horror.

'That's what Uzbek women do when they are disgraced. A Russian soldier raped her when she was returning from work in the cotton field.' He spoke with unaccustomed passion and angrily spat a dark blob of tobacco juice on the ground.

There was a long, uncomfortable silence. Victor propped himself up and rubbed his hands on his knees. 'When do you expect Hamlat?' he asked, bringing the Uzbek back to their problem.

'I don't know. He left a week ago. He might be back in a week, or two, or maybe longer. Pity you didn't come here a week ago. You might have been across the border already.'

'Yes,' Marek said, looking accusingly at Victor as if it were his fault that they hadn't arrived in Kermine a week earlier. He felt he had held his tongue long enough.

'You'll have to wait for Hamlat, but you'd better not be seen in my house. People know you are strangers. They shouldn't know that you've been here.' The old man scratched his face and then went on to his back.

'Of course,' said Victor. 'We'll take a room and get work. We'll behave in such a way that no one could possibly suspect our intentions.'

'We'll say,' Marek added eagerly, 'that we moved south because of my health. I had scurvy and need sun and vitamins.'

'He has to eat vegetables and fruit,' Victor explained. 'You can't get them at all in the north.'

'That's good,' the Uzbek said. 'You have a room?'

'No, we came here straight from the station.'

'I know of a room,' Ulug said, and stopped to slap his cheek and kill a mosquito, ' . . . not far from here. On Achum Babayeffa Street. It's in the house of a Bokharian Jew, Ibram Shukunov. If he doesn't rent it, it will be requisitioned for an army officer or a Party man and he will get nothing for it.' He flicked the dead mosquito off his palm.

'That sounds good,' said Victor. 'Can we go there now?'

'It's dark,' Marek broke in. 'We might not find our way if it's far.'

Ulug looked up at the sky. 'It is late. Here people go to sleep early and get up early. You can stay with us tonight, but tomorrow you must leave and not come back. I'll let you know when Hamlat comes.' He propped his hands behind him, helping himself to his feet. 'I'll tell Addin's Mother to prepare quilts for you. It's very cold here at night.'

Marek watched his tall, slightly stooped figure melt into the darkness. He prodded the last piece of glowing charcoal with a stick. 'I wish I had some chocolate—for dessert.'

Behind the wall they heard a baby wail again. Marek saw the old man in the hut nudging Aka. She listened for a second, then walked out quickly, flashed a friendly smile at the men and ran across the passage in the wall. Ulug walked a few steps from the house and waved to Marek and Victor.

The baby's cry was hushed and the familiar, dull lullaby took its place. 'Aka's brother,' Ulug explained, pointing at the wall. 'Two years old. Doesn't remember his mother.'

The stirred charcoal flamed up, lighting Victor's face. When a moment later it died down, the darkness again swallowed Victor, the contours of the hut and the surrounding walls.

'Ulug is calling us inside.' Marek stood up slowly, not moving from his place until he felt Victor's hand taking his arm. 'What's the matter with him?' he heard Ulug's inquiring voice.

33

'Night-blindness. With better food he'll soon be all right.'

'Does—Addin have it?'

Marek felt Victor's hand press his arm. 'No,' he heard him say quickly. 'He is fine.'

Suddenly a small glimmering flame emerged from the darkness. 'It's all right now,' Marek said. 'I can see the light.' They entered the room.

Inside the hut, two rugs were taken down from the wall, stretched on the floor and covered with quilts and blankets. A brass bowl stood in the middle of the room filled with burning charcoal. The woman sat in her corner, on her bedding, watching to see if the visitors were comfortable. Ulug began to unroll the lined strips he wore over his shoes and over the edges of his trousers. He pointed to the rugs. 'You'll feel fine on these. Addin's Mother wove them.'

'That one is nice,' Marek said, taking off his shoes and pointing to an unfinished rug hanging on the wall, a cotton flower motif adorning its centre. 'It will be beautiful when it's finished.'

Ulug smiled. 'That's a susaneh. It will never be finished. If it were finished it would bring death to the weaver. There is a susaneh in every Uzbek's house.' Marek rolled up his ragged socks and put them carefully inside his shoes. He looked at the collection of old arms on the wall over Ulug's head. The Uzbek followed his wondering look. 'Mine,' he said proudly. 'I served in the army of the Emir of Bokhara, Commander of the Faithful and Shadow of God on Earth.' His eyes shone, his voice reverential and nostalgic for the old times, happy, carefree youth, glorious battles, abundance of meat, worship of God and his ruler. 'I fought against the Czar and then when the Communists came I joined the Basmachis and fought again. Always against the Russians. Now they have my son in their prison!' He blew out the burning wick angrily. 'Be sure to look into your shoes in the morning. You may find a scorpion there. Good night.' Marek heard him lie down heavily, mumbling under his breath.

'Good night,' the woman echoed from her corner in broken,

34

unaccustomed Russian. Marek and Victor answered and lay down on the carpets, covering themselves with the quilts.

The air was thick, sultry, filled with fumes, mingled with dust and sweat. Marek shifted back and forth, listening restlessly to the whine of the wind blowing between the courtyard walls. He was too tired to sleep. After a while he propped his arm under his head and lay still, staring at the blue column of smoke rising from the charcoal bowl, flowing out through the opening in the ceiling. He thought about the armed guards and hunting dogs on the frontier, the boiling water fountains on every Soviet station, the Ukrainian boys playing cards in the train. He thought about the faraway mornings when he had had to quicken his pace constantly to keep up with the brisk big steps of his elder brother, as they both rushed to school. And then he thought about the bony figure of a young Uzbek, bent double over a sheet of paper, on the upper bunk of the shack, with his back curved against the ceiling. A spasm of pain and nostalgia was wrinkling the brown worn face, as dry lips were silently re-reading over and over the words of his first message to his parents in ten years. Marek heard Victor's breathing, laboured and uneven, and the loud, wheezy snoring of the Uzbek. Something rustled in the corner. In the intense light of the midnight moon that streaked into the room, he saw the black staring eyes of Addin's silent mother, who had lost her name with the birth of her son, only to lose her son twenty years later.

4

VICTOR KNOCKED AT THE WOODEN door. There was no answer, so he knocked again, louder. 'Nobody's in,' Marek said, his eyes travelling around the courtyard. There was a well in the centre, shadowed by a cactus, an outhouse in one corner and a bench under a palm tree in the other. In the windless, sultry noon air the leaves on the palm hung quiet and immobile. The stony pavement glowed with a lead-coloured reflex under the parching sunbeams. Suddenly Marek's eyes caught a fleeting glimpse of a black-curled head in the entrance. 'Hey!' he shouted. 'Wait!' A nose, a few curls and a black scrutinizing eye slipped from behind the wall, but immediately disappeared at the sight of the man walking quickly across the courtyard. When Marek reached the road, the boy was already several steps away. 'We're looking for Ibram Shukunov. Do you know where he is?' The boy didn't answer, stepping backwards and staring at Marek vacantly, as if his words were directed to someone else. Then, as he noticed the man making a step forwards, he turned instantly and vanished behind the curve of the road. Marek returned to the courtyard, shrugging his shoulders. 'He ran away,' he said. 'Let's go.'

Victor knocked once again, very loudly, and then decided to try the door. It yielded easily, making a drawn-out squeaking sound. Victor eyed the room curiously. 'There's no one in,' he said, lowering his voice. Marek went to the door and peeped inside. In the centre of the room was a very low oblong table covered by an ornamented carpet dropping to the floor on all sides. Marek's eyes passed over a flimsy settee standing against the wall, a large, low, blanketed bedstead, a chest of drawers inlaid with metals and mother of pearl. 'Is there anybody in?' Victor asked, raising his voice, noticing a small narrow door opposite in the shadowed part of the room. Presently, they became aware of the sizzle of a kerosene stove from behind the door. There was a click of pots, wooden sandals clattered, and from the door emerged a girlish figure in a long low-necklined grey robe, sashed about her waist. She held her hand on the knob and stood in the entrance, viewing the two men across the room, an unfriendly look in her dark eyes, as if she were shocked by their unceremonious intrusion into her quarters. 'What do you want?' she asked brusquely.

'Anyone could steal all your things without your noticing it,' Victor said, striking an amicable, protective tone to counteract her cold welcome. 'We are looking for Comrade Shukunov.'

She gave them a quick, measuring glance. 'He isn't here now.'

'When will he be back?"

'In half an hour.' She moved away to the kitchen, but as she turned to close the door behind her, she noticed the two men standing immobile on the doorstep. 'I told you my husband will be back in half an hour.' Harsh impatience sounded in her low, throaty voice.

'We were told,' Victor said, 'that you have a room to rent.'

'I don't know anything. Who told you?'

'Some people in a tea-house.'

'I don't know. It's a man's business. Come back later.'

'Could we wait?'

She shrugged, flung a 'Wait!' at them, and went back into the kitchen, dismissing any further inquiry, cautiously leaving the door open. After a moment they again heard the click of kitchen utensils and the sound of a stream of water flowing with the accompaniment of the monotonous sizzle of the oil stove. A whiff of the aroma of beans cooking blew across the room.

With elaborate cordiality, Victor waved Marek to the bedstead. 'Make yourself comfortable.' He stepped inside the room and sat down. He saw his brother craning his neck to peep inside the kitchen, fiddling with his skull-cap, bought from Ulug's wife. 'Sit down, will you?' Marek grinned roguishly and sat beside Victor.

The sun was shining in through the lonely small square window, past the cream hand-woven curtains, throwing a bright splash into the middle of the dusky room. Somewhere a fly circled and hummed around the ceiling. Victor looked into the courtyard at the palm throwing a lazy shadow over the stony surface. 'I hope we'll settle down today somewhere, so we'll be able to look for work tomorrow.'

'How do you expect to raise a thousand roubles?' Marek asked, glancing at the small watch on Victor's arm, assuming the tone of practicality that he knew would please his brother.

Pointedly, Victor arched his wrist. 'We'll get almost seven hundred roubles for this watch. That's what the station-master offered us in Czkalow, remember? And we'll have to make up the rest by working.' He glanced at Marek, examining his brother's meagre, bloodless face, and rubbed his chin, reflectively.

'I would like to stay in this house,' Marek said, his eyes on a chest of drawers, homely-looking in the dim light, with a gleaming brass samovar and a collection of snow white tea-bowls. 'It's clean here. I'm tired of lice and fleas.'

'As soon as we move here, we'll take a bath. I hope there is a public bath in this town.'

Marek's lips parted. 'A bath,' he repeated, savouring the word, shaking his head as if he could hardly believe it. He turned to Victor. 'It would be good to get clean shirts, underwear and shoes.' He glanced at his wadded jerkin, wadded pants and ragged boots. 'How much money do we have?'

'Sixty-five roubles and fifty kopecks. Don't forget, we'll have to pay for the room and keep some money to live on.' Then, after a time Victor added, 'Maybe we'll get an advance when we start working. We'll have to get used things. You saw that all the shop windows were empty.'

'I don't mind. This jacket makes me sick! I just can't . . .' Marek broke in the middle of the phrase, for the kitchen door creaked and the girl reappeared. She approached the chest, without paying any attention to the men, opened a drawer, pulled out a white cloth and walked to the table in the middle of the room. She noticed Victor's skull-cap lying there, took it and ostentatiously placed it near him on the bed, without lifting her eyes. Marek watched the quick movements of her graceful slight figure, accompanied by the clatter of her sandals against the brick flooring. In the full light, centred around the table, Marek saw her small face covered by thin, tawny skin, fresh and delicate, without a single wrinkle on her low forehead. Her brown hair, braided in two thick plaits, was caught in the gleam of the sun-rays. She was spreading the cloth over the table, her lowered eyelashes throwing a long shadow on her high cheek bones. Her whole face seemed to be concentrated on the things she was doing, bringing plates from the kitchen, spacing them over the table-cloth, carrying in the earthenware water jug and putting it in the room's corner, laying three white cushions on the floor around the table and flattening them. She never looked at the men, and only her stiffened body, the tightened skin of her face and the tenseness of her movements betrayed that she was conscious of their presence. Marek listened to the crazy, irritated buzz of the fly striking against a window pane. His eyes travelled up the girl's feet and legs, darting hungrily to her haunches, long narrow waist and slender spine. She turned towards him, inspecting the table, and his eyes jumped to her full cherry lips, slid down and caressed the olive sheet of her skin in her low neckline, then settled on the pair of small, up-tilted adolescent breasts, stretching stiffly against the light cotton material. He felt a sudden pleasurable twinge in the pit of his stomach and a curious pain ran down the veins of his arms. A long forgotten pressure was rising in his chest and closing his throat. The heat clung to his neck and he knew a blush was rising out of his collar. Then he heard Victor's annoyed whisper. 'Will you stop it? We'll never get a room if you behave like this!'

Marek rubbed his face, trying to shake away all the hungry desires piled up during two years' isolation. He turned to his brother, his mouth curving in a little smile that clamoured for tolerance. Victor shook his head reproachfully, and with restless expectation began to watch the entrance into the courtyard. And as if he'd correctly anticipated it, after a while, a short man's figure emerged from the road and crossed the courtyard. The girl noticed it pass the window, she went quickly to the door, her lids raised now, unveiling a pair of deep-sunk almond-shaped eyes, smiling in a soft welcome. She ushered her husband in and said something in a language Marek could not understand, pointing at the men. They stood up and nodded. Ibram threw them an appraising look and slowly bowed his head. The husband and wife talked for a while, then the girl retreated to the kitchen. Ibram closed the door behind himself and stepped inside the room into the streak of light coming through the window. He was at least twice the age of his wife and of the same height. He had a long face with pink lips and a little nose between flat sun-burnt cheeks. A thin, carelessly trimmed moustache covered his upper lip. He was clad in grey, too-short trousers and a brown, too-short jacket, like a schoolboy who has outgrown his suit. A khaki shirt, open at the neck, lay over his jacket collar. 'Shukunov,' he said formally and shook hands with Victor and Marek. 'You have just come to town, I imagine?'

'Yes. How did you know?'

'I have never seen you before. It's a small town. Transferred?' He lowered his eyes, studying Victor through his eyelashes.

'No. We moved south, because my brother had scurvy. The doctor said he needs sun and vitamins and advised us to move south.'

The bright close-set eyes mellowed and a genuine amiable smile appeared on Ibram's lips. 'I wasn't sure that you hadn't come to find out whether we have a room and to get it re-quisitioned for some Party official. Ajmi!' he shouted into the kitchen. 'Give me the key!'

His wife brought him a heavy iron key and he went out, beckoning cheerfully to the men to follow him. They walked around the hut and stopped in front of a side-door. Ibram turned the key in the big lock and invited Victor and Marek to step inside.

They entered a small room, wanly lit by a small, round window. There was a low, large, unmade bedstead, inside a wooden frame lashed from side to side and end to end with ropes of cords and horsehair. 'The bed,' Ibram pointed proudly. 'There is no wardrobe, but there are hooks on the walls. Do you have many suits?'

Victor smiled. 'Not too many.'

'Where are your belongings?'

'We left them in a barber's shop.'

Ibram looked around the room, reflectively. He moistened his lips. 'I'll get a table and a chair or two for you.' He bent down and rolled a rug and blanket lying on the brick floor and put them in a corner. 'A small boy slept here—a relative of my wife. We'll take him to sleep with us. He will clean your room and bring you water.'

The clatter of sandals resounded from the courtyard and there in the doorway, behind her husband, stood Ajmi, arms crossed on her chest, leaning against the doorway frame. There was a momentary silence, as Ibram smiled at his wife and Victor glanced anxiously at Marek and saw him gazing, as if hypnotized, at the olive sweep of the girl's lifted bosom. The girl turned to her husband with a wordless inquiry as to whether she was needed. Victor cleared his throat. 'How about the mattress and bedding?' His voice sounded louder than he'd expected.

'Oh, we've a mattress in the pantry. I'll get it. Don't you have any blankets and sheets?'

Marek's eyes flicked from the girl to Ibram and lit up at the prospect of unanticipated comfort. 'No,' he heard Victor saying. 'We don't have any.'

Ibram glanced at his wife and she nodded. 'I'll get you some blankets and a couple of sheets, and a big pillow. The point is —could you sleep together?'

'Certainly,' Marek said with eager generosity, his eyes again darting to the cross-armed figure in the door. 'It's a large bed.'

'We can make it,' Victor said. 'What's the rent?'

Again Ibram looked at his wife. They spoke for a moment in their language, then Ibram waved his hands in the air, embarrassed. 'I don't know. I never rented a room before, but the housing commission came here a few days ago and looked around, and I heard them say that we don't need this room. I don't want to have it requisitioned.' He raised his eyes shyly. 'Twenty roubles per month, would that be all right?'

'And if we stay a shorter time?' Marek asked cautiously, showing off to his brother that he was very much concentrated on the subject of the room. He got a scolding look in response, and a quick, flat 'It's all right' followed.

'Why should you stay a shorter time? You'll be comfortable here.'

'It's all right,' Victor repeated. 'The room is very nice. . . . Oh, there is the boy. We saw him before.'

In the courtyard stood the black-curled boy, glaring at them from a distance. Ajmi dropped her hands and glanced back over her shoulder. 'Come in, Raim,' she said softly in Russian. The boy approached them slowly, hesitantly dragging his bare feet. He stopped at the door, opening his mouth, his coal-black slanted eyes gazing at the strangers. 'These two citizens are renting this room. You'll clean it every day.' Ibram accentuated every word, as if he knew that this was the only way to get the idea across to the boy. 'You understand?' The boy nodded, his eyes fixed on the pavement. Then they crept slowly to the room's corner. He entered the room, picked up his rug and blanket and carried them away, resignation in his lowered eyes.

'You must speak slowly to him,' Ibram said. 'He's a bit under-developed. An orphan—we took him from my wife's relatives in Bokhara.'

Marek nodded sympathetically and he himself wasn't sure whether he felt pity or wanted to appear good-hearted to the girl. When he glanced again at her, she responded with a quick, brown flash of her eye and it gave his chest a new wrench. He glanced nervously at his brother and his voice was slightly hoarse when he said to Ibram, 'Will you give us a lamp?'

'Certainly.'

'Well, we'd better get our things, eh?'

'Right,' Victor said. He took the paper money from his pocket and counted it, passing it on to Ibram. Involuntarily, Marek looked again at Ajmi. He knew that, though watching Ibram and Victor, she was conscious of his stare. Her fingers picked at her robe and an uneasy wrinkle crossed her smooth forehead. Her eyes swept over Marek's face, she compressed her lips, and suddenly she was gone. He listened to her loud wooden steps receding in the courtyard. 'We'll be back shortly,' he heard Victor say, as he turned to see Ibram pocketing the money.

'Raim will help you.' Ibram said a few words to the boy, but Raim shrugged his shoulders defiantly and remained motionless.

'Oh, we don't have much. Just two knapsacks.'

Ibram took the bedding from the boy's hands and put them

on the floor. 'Never mind, we'll help you.' He pushed the boy ahead, angrily. Raim went out and stopped, waiting with bent head. Ibram led them across the courtyard to the entrance. 'My wife will prepare the room in the meantime,' he said.

'Maybe you could manage to get two chairs?' Victor said, smiling. 'It would be more comfortable.'

'I'll try.' Ibram waved a salute. Marek turned to him with a farewell nod and glanced past his head at the window. For a second he saw Ajmi's face under a raised curtain, but immediately the curtain fell and she walked away.

'It's damned hot,' Marek said wiping his neck. They were walking among sedate Uzbeks slowly strolling in their flowing cloaks and grey turbans or colourful skull-caps; among barefoot, red-legged children, preoccupied with their street games; among many-braided girls, scurrying into the courtyards and staring at them from the safe distance of the raised blankets of their entrances. The boy followed them, trotting a few steps behind, his grudge for dispossessing him of his room still showing in his bitter looks and in his pouting, offended mouth.

Victor regarded his brother, sidelong. 'Don't get any ideas about that girl,' he said, his high voice sounding a warning. Marek murmured something in his throat. 'What did you say?'

'I said, don't worry.'

'You behaved impossibly. It's high time that you learned how to control yourself.'

'I can't stand it any longer.' Marek looked at his brother and his face wore an expression of such misery, that Victor couldn't help smiling. He shook his head and waved indulgently. 'Okay, okay, as soon as we settle down, we'll get ourselves some girls. But just to get it off our chests. No involvements, no attachments.'

Marek nodded, but Victor noticed that his brother's nod was absent and feeble, and that his chest heaved in a noiseless sigh. Victor's eyes rested a moment on his brother's face, then travelled slowly to the horizon, where the mountain peaks carved sharply into the unclouded blue sky.

5

THEY SAT UNCOMFORTABLY ON A dusty carpet in the czai-khana, holding their bowls in both hands, blowing on boiling green tea. Marek, with delight, sucked a small piece of sugar but after taking a sip, his face twisted in a wry grimace. 'It tastes like camomile.'

'You can't get sugar without it,' Victor chanted and bravely swallowed a big noisy gulp of the hot liquid. 'It's pretty bad, but we'll get used to it.'

'Do you think we'll get ration coupons the very first day we start working?' Marek asked in eager anticipation of the monthly portion of half a pound of sugar and sweets.

'I hope so.'

'So let's take these railway jobs and finish with it. I don't care!'

Victor leaned forward, rolling cigarettes. As the two lit them, Marek's eyes roamed curiously around the wide oblong hall with the low arched reed ceiling. On one of the walls, in the midst of the owner's family photographs, hung a dramatic poster warning against the evils of alcohol. The tea-house was filled with old bearded Uzbeks who, sitting cross-legged on their carpets, fuming pots of tea besides them, towels hung over their necks, watched the street traffic with the blessed calmness of people who don't expect anything exciting to happen any more in their lives. 'About this job . . . ' Marek heard Victor saying hushedly in Polish and he turned to his brother. 'I don't think you should take it.'

'Why?'

'You know what it means to carry rails and stones and heavy wooden bales all day in the heat? It's worse than felling trees. You can't do it, Marek.'

'But there is no other work available.'

'I was thinking that you might wait a few days. Something else will turn up for sure. Meanwhile you'll rest well and eat well, so you can get over this damn nightblindness. It will be a lot easier for us, when you can see.'

'You mean we'll have to walk at night?'

'Possibly.'

Marek stifled the beginning of a sigh. 'I didn't think about that.' He glanced helplessly at Victor and his voice broke. 'How did you expect me to go?'

'If you rest and take it easy, you will be all right by the time Hamlat is back.'

'And if I'm not?'

'Then we'll have to wait till you get all right.'

A shadow of guilt crossed Marek's face. 'You should wait a few days and rest, too.'

'No, Marek, I can't! We have to save three hundred roubles, remember?" He stretched his back with decision and glanced at his watch. 'I'll go to the labour office before they break for lunch and tell them that I'll report to work tomorrow. Okay?'

Through the clouds of smoke Marek looked at the pot-bellied bald-headed tea-room manager, sitting besides a fuming brass samovar, reigning over rows of pots, pyramids of bowls, piles of towels and a few boxes of sugar cubes. 'And when we go,' he heard Victor going on in subdued, persuasive tone, 'you can't fail. We'll need all your strength.'

Through the entrance Marek could see the sharp outlines of the distant mountains under the clear sky. Above a house a bird reached the clear sunshine and appeared dazzlingly bright in the air. 'If I rest,' Marek asked, 'do you think I'll be able to see things at night the way I used to?'

'Of course,' Victor said and patted Marek's knee. 'Rest and good food, that's all you need to get back on your feet.' He smiled and put his hand against the floor to stand up. But his eyes suddenly grew attentive and he did not move.

Marek swung his head around and saw the familiar figure of the Konsomol's secretary that they had seen two days ago in the barber's shop. He walked through the central passage, the perennial friendly smile and cigarette glued to his lips, returning salutations with his paper. As he saw Victor and Marek, he nodded and said jovially, 'I met you the other day, remember?' and then stopped to exchange a few words with a group of men sitting in a semi-circle. A moment later he was cross-legged on the carpet, watching the wild-haired boy pour the green fuming liquid into his bowl. His face under the upturned peak-cap wore the idle happy expression of a man who has plenty of time at his disposal.

'I'll go to the labour office now,' Victor said.

'Should I wait for you here?'

'No.' Victor pulled out a five rouble banknote and handed it to his brother. 'You go and buy some vegetables and fruit. Buy whatever you like. We'll meet at home.'

'All right.'

'Come.' They walked out, their figures in the central passage arousing momentary curious, measuring looks from the town-folk.

'Do you know where the market is?' Victor asked, as Marek strode with him towards the labour office.

'Yes, Shukunov explained to me this morning how to get there. . . . Here we part.'

'See you at home,' Victor said, raised his hand, humorously imitating Kisielev's salute, and walked away.

Marek rambled past the bakery and the shop that had sold scissors two days ago and was now selling children's toys, past a street corner where a venerable Uzbek was weighing green tobacco on miniature scales, past a wine store, and a narrow shop, where a Tojik craftsman, clad in white tunic and square skull-cap, beckoned to him to buy some of his glass work. On the road, the carts drawn by Uzbek peasants added a constant undertone of squeaking wheels to the market day's noise. The radio loudspeakers, set up on the corner, stopped transmitting the local folk music and a Moscow radio announcer began to report the Supreme Commander's Order of the Day, reporting further German advances. In front of the closed news stand, Marek stopped to read a poster trumpeting that while twenty-five years ago 99% of the Uzbek population was illiterate, every family in Uzbekistan now read a newspaper. Before

46

reaching the Kermine Tractor Repair Base No. 2, Marek turned left and soon heard the loud murmur of the throng, accentuated by the cries of vendors, the drawn-out bray of donkeys and horses' sharp neighs. Through a large gate he entered a huge walled square, filled with people and animals, carts and hucksters' stands.

He made his way between a row of arbas, displaying home-made carpets, fly-swatters, whips and fans, and a row of unharnessed camels, resting on their bellies, their heads immobile and pensive. He crossed the pottery section, where the many-braided Uzbek girls sat cross-legged and taciturn on the ground behind their earthenware. He passed the stands with muslin and felt articles and multi-coloured skull-caps, and entered an area crowded with people standing behind their ragged valises with old clothing, shoes and all kinds of used home utensils. After wandering among men and women selling their own belongings, he stopped in front of a small, weary-faced man, who had a few shirts, old ties and pieces of underwear placed on a bed-sheet stretched out on the ground. Marek lifted a striped shirt and measured it to his size. 'How much is it?' he asked.

'Fifteen roubles.' There was a suggestion of harsh, Byellorussian accent on the man's speech. 'Do you want it?'

'I was just wondering how much you wanted for it. I might come back later.'

'Later it will be gone.' The Byellorussian turned to a plump Russian woman, who was inspecting a man's night-shirt, holding it out in front of her, her head tilted, perhaps wondering how her husband would look in it as he lay in bed with her. 'Do you want the shirt for twelve roubles?' the man asked. Marek shook his head and walked away.

He strolled among the Russian women in their loose flannelette blouses worn over voluminous gathered skirts, their white neckerchiefs tied beneath their chins, sitting on stools near their cans of pickles and sauerkraut. Then he passed a crowd of weathered and cheek-veiled Uzbek matrons ducking behind glasses of mare's milk, sheep cheese and boiled sour-milk, and finally he entered the fruit and vegetable section of the bazaar.

From the hucksters' stands the goat-bearded Uzbek peasants beckoned to him, urging him to buy their products, offering samples of watermelon or toying with a bunch of grapes, held high for inspection. Marek scrutinized each basket of fruit and vegetables before reaching a decision and then bargained vehemently to get the best buy for his five roubles. Suddenly, when he had wrapped the tomatoes, plums and grapes into a newspaper that he had prudently brought with him, and was about to walk home, he heard the rhythm of a beaten drum. Curiously, he made his way through the crowd encircling a man sitting on the ground with a shovel-like instrument and a pale-eyed little girl summoning the spectators with the vibrant strokes of her fingers against a small leather drum. When enough people had gathered, the girl jostled the man, and the concert began. The musician's face looked familiar, and Marek wondered for a second where he had seen him. Then he remembered. It was the same blind Uzbek, whose courtyard they had entered, inquiring for Ulug Beg. He played now, strumming his instrument, plucking the strings, and in a dragging chanting voice narrating an Uzbek tale of by-gone days.

As Marek listened to the tune, his eyes in idle curiosity roamed over the faces of the onlookers. Suddenly he saw Ajmi. She stood a few steps away from him, a shopping net with vegetables on the ground before her. For a long while he gazed at the young serious features of her face and the pleasant curve of her bowed neck rising out of a grey sashed robe. As if drawn by his stare, she turned her head to him. Something passed through her dark eyes and a tremor shot across her face. She picked up her net and quickly approached the nearest huckster's stand, lifting a green-white watermelon to her ear and knocking it, listening for the thudding sound of ripeness. Her back tensed at the sound of Marek's approaching steps, she put the melon down, took her net and trotted away. Marek quickened his pace and reached her as she neared a cart with

camel and horse meat that was besieged by a swarm of flies.
'Good day,' he said. 'May I help you carry your things?'

'Thank you,' she answered flatly, without looking at him.
'I've Raim to carry them for me.' She walked away towards
the boy, who stood nearby, watching, open-mouthed, an
Uzbek vigorously fanning away the smoke from long iron
spits, pierced with pieces of lamb-meat, tomatoes and peppers,
suspended over a basin of glowing charcoal. Ajmi's call
aroused him; he took the net from her hands, and following
her quick glance over her shoulder, his eyes travelled to Marek
with studious, slow wonder. As Marek watched the two making
their way to the gate, a policeman passed by; the crowd
around the musician dispersed at once, and the tune changed
abruptly into a popular Communist song. Marek waited a
moment, then slowly walked to the street, thinking about the
girl's tightly stretched skin over the neck-bones. A confused
tumult of voices trailed behind him.

When, ten minutes later, he was crossing the courtyard of
the house, through the window he saw Ajmi, Ibram and the
boy, sitting on pillows placed on the floor, eating their lunch.
Marek entered his room, put his package on the chair and sat
down on the bed. He rolled himself a cigarette and lit it. Then
he lay down, watching the cigarette smoke rising up, recollect-
ing in spontaneous pictures the images of all the girls he had
ever known. He thought about the dark girl in his class, a
bench ahead, turning to him with questions and impulsively
touching his hand in thanks. The girl whom he had met in the
public park at sunset and made love to when darkness fell,
and never met again. The scrubbed grocer's wife, who used
to receive him when her husband was busy and who giggled
constantly because she was very ticklish. He recalled the bare
tanned legs of a girl called Zosia, he caressed the smooth
shoulders of another whose name he didn't remember, and
tasted the kiss of his brother's girl friend whom he had never
kissed. Suddenly from behind the wall came a nostalgic,
oriental melody. He listened for a while until Ajmi's voice
was lost in the noise of running water.

Through the half-opened door, voices floated into the room. Marek propped himself on his elbows and saw Victor and Ibram. He got up and walked outside. 'I got you a second chair,' Ibram was saying, pointing to an old wooden chair.

'Have you got a basin yet?' Victor asked.

'Oh, basin? . . . I forgot all about it, I'm sorry. The boy used to come to wash at our place. I'll borrow one for you in the evening. Right now both my wife and I must rush back to work.'

'Where do you work?' Marek asked.

'I work in the Uzbek Cotton Mill No. 17, my wife helps in the field, temporarily, as long as the kolkhoz needs seasonal help. I'll get you the basin this evening.'

Marek watched him walk away, and covertly managed to glance at the window. Ajmi, looking irritated, was peering out, apparently angry with her husband for breaking into his lunch. 'Well, let's go.' Marek grabbed the chair and walked towards the door. He didn't hear Victor following him, and stopped, 'What are you waiting for?'

He saw a broad happy smile on Victor's face, his brows raised in essayed grandeur. 'You just put the chair inside,' Victor said, 'and come with me. We're going to buy shoes and shirts. I got an advance of a hundred roubles. And before changing, we'll take a bath. There is a nice Turkish bath in town, brother!'

6

THE LITTLE DARK ROOM WAS filled with heavy breathing and whistling—Victor sleeping with his mouth open. It wasn't his brother's snoring that kept Marek awake, but the fresh white sheets and soft pillow that were so pleasantly uncomfortable. The cool linen of the deloused Russian nightshirt felt good on his dry body, thoroughly cleansed by the steam of the Turkish bath. The memory of sweet raisins and plums still clung to his lips. Crossing his arms under his head,

Marek tried nostalgically to recall his own beechnut bed in Brest Litovsk with a round night-table beside it on which stood a saucer filled by his mother with sweets for the night. The painting of a little flaxen-haired girl hung over his bed, her cheeks flushed with excitement, as she read a book under the light of a lamp. He knew there was another picture hung over Victor's twin bed, but he could not recollect what it was. His mind, warmed now to memories, plunged into pictures of the narrow river winding across the town, the colourful well-kept flower-beds of the park and the silent cobblestone streets, drowsily lit by yellow gaslamps, smelling of dust, horses' dung and acacia trees. Victor turned on his back, murmured some-thing through his sleep, and suddenly became quiet. Marek felt the warm breath of his brother on his cheek and glanced at him sideways, but only a deep black abyss stretched before his eyes. If it hadn't been for the war, Marek thought, Victor would have completed his work at Warsaw University by now and have become a civil engineer. How happy their father would have been to witness finally the fulfilment of his own unrealized ambitions in his son. When Victor came home for summer vacations, the whole family would sit around the table, sip tea and listen till the small hours of the night to his tales of life and studies in the unseen, distant, hundred-miles away Polish capital. And as Marek, clad in Victor's outgrown clothes, attentively propping his chin on his palms, watched his brother with admiration and respect, he felt proud that the Sobel family would finally produce a University graduate. And because he knew how hard his father struggled, working over-time at night, in order to pay for Victor's tuition and board, and because Victor was older and as such his father's natural first choice, he felt no grudge that for his brother's sake he had to stop attending the expensive Polish high-school and start leaning bookkeeping, so that inevitably the two brothers would become, respectively, the living symbols of their father's dream and his reality.

From all the past, the vision of the night of their departure stood out most vividly in his memory, returning back and back and back to his mind every day since they had left home for the Rumanian border the night before the German tanks had rolled over the peaceful streets of their city. It was late in the afternoon and the guns were shelling the suburbs, when Victor rushed home with the news that every young man could board the last military train leaving the town in the evening.

'I'm going,' he announced. 'How about you?'

'Me?' Marek looked at Victor, taken completely by surprise. Suddenly he was afraid of leaving the town he had never left, of going out into a world he had never seen, of losing his parents now and perhaps losing Victor later somewhere on their way. 'I don't know . . .' he mumbled.

'All right, you're going with me. Get ready.' Their mother filled two rucksacks with underwear and Cracow sausage and chocolate purchased in the black market, and their father gave them his silver cigarette case and golden cufflinks that later on, in the camp, had helped Victor to have Marek shifted from his forest work to the softer job of clearing the paths of snow.

Across the window passed a fleeting gleam of light and thudding steps sounded in the quiet night. Marek sat up in bed and listened, but heard only the hammering of the pulses in his own temples. Apparently the steps belonged to late passers-by lighting up the way before them. Reassured, he lay down again, plugged his cheek and ear into the pillow, eager to resume the interrupted picture that was unrolling itself, enlivening the dull blackness of the room. In the evening, as they walked to the station, accompanied by their parents, they saw army staff-cars with dimmed lights sweeping through the streets and columns of exhausted soldiers returning from the front in irregular groups. The gaslamps' yellow light glistened from the polished bayonets of their rifles and swept small light-blades over the shadowy figures of young men moving from all parts of town towards the station. In the strange, suddenly unfamiliar city, the windows of the empty houses gaped at them like blind eyes. They strode through the square on which Marek and Victor had once played hopscotch, passed the church where they used to pray, the Town Hall where Mr Sobel worked, and approached the wooden bridge that Marek, as a child, was told would break under him if he ever lied. Behind the bridge the sky glowed with an odd crimson brilliance and as they came closer they saw the station building was burning. The huge roaring flames, throwing hot light at the distant rails, illuminated the train already ladened with uniformed and un-uniformed young men. As Victor and Marek embraced their parents and kissed them goodbye, Marek noticed his mother's little wrinkled face suddenly turning into a grimace, her pale dry mouth trembling with a silent sob.

'I'm not going,' he said, 'I'm staying here.'

Victor looked at him and at the same time they heard the shrill whistle. 'Come on,' Victor said. 'The train is leaving in a moment.'

He boarded the car. Marek obediently followed him. Their mother called them back and kissed them again, their father patted their backs and rushed them into the train. Hanging together they elbowed their way to the window. From the platform, their mother cried 'Keep always together, boys! You take care of him, Victor! Remember, he has never been alone. . . . Take care of him!'

As the train moved slowly away from the burning walls of the station and the lit-up platform, Marek strained his eyes through the distance to watch and fix in his mind the receding image of his mother's little plump figure, and her tear-stained face with wisps of greying hair ruffled by the wind.

Suddenly Marek became aware of knocking at the door and realized that it had been going on for some time. As he held his breath, a flashlight beamed across the window and splashed a bright circle on the bed. 'Victor,' Marek whispered tremulously, jostling his brother. 'Get up, get up!'

Victor mumbled, rubbed his eyes, and sat up in bed abruptly. The beam projected itself on their faces frozen to a point of light. 'Open the door,' the harsh voice behind the window said.

Victor leaped from the bed. 'Who is there?'

'NKVD,' the voice answered. 'Open up!'

'God!' Marek muttered. 'God!'

Victor turned the key. The door swung open and two blurred silhouettes pushed into the room. The piercing beam travelled around the walls and stopped on a kerosene lamp. A hand lighted it and Marek and Victor saw before them two uniformed NKVD men with pistols fastened to their belts. 'Get dressed,' a short, ogre-eyed man ordered.

Obediently Marek began to put on his clothes, darting fearful glances at his brother. 'Where do you want us to go?' Victor asked.

'You'll see. Come on.'

When they were dressed, the man blew out the light. 'Go,' he said, waiting for them to walk out first. He noticed Marek warding off the black curtain with fumbling fingers. 'What are you doing? You blind or something?'

'He's all right,' Victor said. 'It is only in the dark he doesn't see.' He took Marek's hand.

They went out of the courtyard into the mud-walled streets, Marek walking with faltering steps beside his brother, the creaking steps of their guards behind them. 'What could it be?' Marek whispered in Polish, his throat tightened with fear.

'Don't talk,' the bluff voice behind them commanded.

Nervously, Marek gripped his brother's palm and looked up to him, his unseeing eyes searching for reassurance. 'Be calm,' Victor said. 'Leave everything to me.'

'Don't talk!'

They walked silently among the quiet, watchful houses of Shadiva Street. Above their crooked, frightened silhouettes hung the moon, pale and cold.

'Turn left,' the man behind them said, and quickened his pace to precede them and stop in a narrow alley in front of a wooden house. Through the shuttered windows slipped streaks of light and the tune of a whining Ukrainian romance, that broke abruptly at the sound of the iron knocker. The door opened and they entered a corridor. A half-dimmed lamp threw light on the figure of a red-cheeked, thin-mouthed uniformed man with an accordion in his hands. Wordlessly he pointed to a narrow door. 'Go inside,' the ogre-eyed guard ordered and opened the door. The piercing light of strong electric bulbs dazzled them for an instant but when they had accustomed themselves to it, they saw behind a desk under Beria's portrait on the wall, the relaxed, pleasantly smiling face of Comrade Kisielev.

'Good evening,' Kisielev said, waving them to chairs in front of his desk, and pushing forwards a box of 'Moskowskihe' cigarettes. They shook their heads, mumbling a simultaneous 'Thank you' under their breath.

Kisielev took a cigarette, lighting it with elaborate slowness. 'I thought we should get acquainted,' he said, blowing out the match and throwing it on the floor. Marek looked at his clean-shaven face with determined chin and high-bridged nose. In the corners of his mouth played a light, quizzical smile. 'I hope I didn't wake you up,' he said. 'I've just a few routine questions and you'll go back to your room. You're new in town and it's one of my duties to know anyone new in town.' He put the cigarette on a glass ashtray and folded his hands before his chin, talking with ingratiating softness as if he were a college professor delivering a lecture on national security. 'Why did you come to Kermine?'

Victor repeated the chant of Marek's illness. Kisielev nodded and brushed back his fine mane of oily, golden brown hair. 'What do you intend to do here?'

'Work,' Victor answered. 'I already have a job at the depot.'

Kisielev laid his folded hands on the table, rolling his thumbs. A smell of soap and eau de cologne floated into Marek's nostrils. 'What kind of work did you do in Chkalov?'

'Chkalov?' Victor asked, surprised, then went on hastily, 'We worked on the construction of a house.'

'What house?' Marek noticed the purse of his lips and the melodical emphasis he gave to his words.

'On one of the main streets,' Victor answered.

'What street?'

'I don't remember the name. We weren't there long.'

'And where did you come to Chkalov from?'

'Molotov.'

'And you—too?' Kisielev swung his head and aimed it at Marek.

'Yes—we both came from Molotov,' Victor said.

'I'm asking *him*.' Kisielev's voice arched with a surprising sudden tone of authority.

'Me, too,' Marek said. He could feel the thickness coming into his throat. 'We're brothers.'

'How long were you in Molotov?' Kisielev's eyes continued to hold him with an insistent stare.

'Oh, just a few days,' Victor said.

'He can talk for himself, can't he? He is not deaf or mute or dumb! And where did you come to Molotov from, may I know?'

Marek crossed and uncrossed his legs staring back blankly, tongue-tied, into Kisielev's small, insistent eyes. 'From a camp,' after a while Marek heard his brother's voice, low and hoarse. 'We were released from a labour camp.'

Kisielev's thumbs stopped rolling instantly and he held out his hand. 'Your papers,' he said with sharp abruptness. Victor reached into his pocket and pulled out a ragged leather billfold, but before he could open it, Kisielev took it from his hand. He unfolded each slip of paper on the desk, studying it attentively and asking for the meaning of the drawing of a poplar tree Victor had doodled in an idle hour, and the Polish address of the family of one of the inmates of the camp, and the addition of the previous day's expenses for food and clothing. He finally opened two official documents from a Pechora camp announcing that Victor and Marek had been released from the camp on the basis of a general amnesty granted to Polish prisoners.

'So you are Poles,' Kisielev said slowly, curling his long deeply channelled lips at the corners and reaching thoughtfully for his cigarette.

'Yes.'

'Why did you come all the way here?'

'I told you, my brother . . . '

'But why here and not to Tashkent or Alma Ata? You could find plenty of fruits and vegetables there.'

'Oh, we just took the train going south and got off without much thinking, trying our luck here. And we were lucky, for I got a job at the depot the very first day.'

Marek watched Kisielev pick up the phone. A second later he put the receiver down with decision, threw the butt of his cigarette on the floor and rubbed it with his foot. He copied parts of the camp documents on a sheet of paper and handed the papers with the billfold back to Victor. 'Do you know why I called you here?' he said, the tone of his voice again assuming the previous sing-song intonation.

'No.'

'Because war regulations require any newcomer to a Soviet city to register within twenty-four hours with the NKVD. You failed to do so.'

'We didn't know that. I'm sorry.'

'Now you *are* registered,' Kisielev said and stood up. 'And we *got* acquainted.' His face again wore a gallant, white-toothed smile.

Victor looked at him for a second, then his eyes wandered to the portrait on the wall. He stood up and said softly to Marek, 'Come.'

'Goodbye, Comrade Kisielev,' Marek said courteously and they walked out of the room. As they stepped out of the building, the plaintive accordion tune resumed behind the wall.

As Marek, holding his brother's hand, was led back home, he kept silent, but any time they passed the street lamp, his eyes darted to Victor's face. 'Well,' he finally said, 'it was just a routine check, wasn't it?'

'I guess so . . . '

'He was rather polite and quite pleasant, wasn't he?'

'Yes,' Victor said absently. They crossed Shadiva Street and entered a narrow side road. Marek somewhere heard a door open and shut and a bucket splash against water. Then Victor became audible again. 'Remember Alexandrov?' he said. 'He was polite and pleasant too, wasn't he?'

Marek fell silent and as he walked slowly on, his feet sinking into the sand of the road, the unwanted memory of the Carpathian mountains came back to him. Again he thought he heard the frightening howls and shrill whistles, and among the pine trees he saw the approaching shadows of wolf-dogs and armed green-uniformed frontier guards. And, as the picture dissolved softly, he saw the gentle face of their prison investigator, Alexandrov, lecturing them suavely that the Red Army liberated the people suffering under the yoke of Polish landlords and at the same time took them under its protective wings before the Germans could advance further. Because Victor and Marek had ungratefully tried to escape abroad, he informed them, the Soviet court, in absentia, sentenced them to ten years of rehabilitation in a corrective labour camp.

7

ALL THE NEXT DAY MAREK slept. The fatigue of the two-weeks-long journey on the wooden floors of freight trains, the endless hours waiting on station benches and the restless nights in Kermine had piled up and now overwhelmed him in a day's deep sleep. At times he would unglue his eyes, glaring dazedly around and again sink into lethargic oblivion or into a dream which seemed more real than the reality surrounding him. Once he thought he saw the hazy silhouette of his brother shaving in a piece of mirror propped on the window's edge. Later, he danced with white-clad Anushka in a Warsaw night club, to the tune of 'When the Lilacs Bloom Again'. Then the orchestra stopped playing and when it struck up 'White Roses', Marek found himself holding Ajmi but he was not at all surprised by the miraculous change of his dancing partners. A moment later Raim was near him, sweeping the floor with a broomstick, and then he saw comrades Kisielev and Alexandrov cross-legged on the carpet of a tea-room, scrutinizing the people as they entered. When Marek finally awoke, he sat up in bed, his whole body sweating. Breathing heavily, he swung his legs over the bed's edge, his eyes wavering around the room until its walls came into focus. Yawning and stretching himself, he shuffled to the door and opened it. The mid-afternoon sun flickered bright stains on the palm leaves waving lightly in the breeze. Above the white court-yard walls the small grey clouds curled on the horizon. Marek looked around the room for the basin that Ibram had promised to bring, but it wasn't there, so he dressed and went to knock at the Shukunov's door. There was no answer and he remembered that they were both working. He drew a bucket of water from the well and washed his face, neck and ears over the ground. As he was drying himself with a towel, merry girlish laughter sounded on the road. Curiously, Marek walked to the gate and noticed Victor and a blond girl approaching the house.

'This is my brother,' he heard Victor introducing him from the distance, and saw the girl's face adopting a small social smile. She was a pretty, short girl, with hair tumbled at her neck, a roguish snub nose and delicately rouged lips.

As she approached the gate, her gay blue eyes squinted in playful menace, mimicking Marek's grave, studious stare at her. 'Why are you looking at me like this? I haven't done anything wrong, honestly.'

'I must have seen you somewhere.'

The girl laughed. 'Sure. In the station dining hall. I serve there.'

'No. . . . Oh, I know, I saw you in the street.' He turned to Victor. 'She passed by when you were shaving the other day.'

'Possibly,' the girl said, grinning. 'I often pass in the street.'

'Shall we go inside?' Victor suggested, staring invitingly towards the entrance.

'One second.' Marek rushed into the room and began making the bed.

'Oh, you don't know how to do it.' The girl was standing

in the door, shaking her head disapprovingly. 'Here, let me do that. You men! . . . ' As she neatly patted the pillow into place, Victor clasped his hands over his belly twiddling his thumbs triumphantly with princely grandeur. When the cover was spread over the bed, the girl sat on it. 'My name is Marusia,' she said. 'What's yours?'

'Marek.'

'Nice to meet you, Marek.' She shook his hand with both of hers. 'I hear you're from Chkalov. I'm from a big town myself —Vladivostok. A year ago they transferred my father to this remote, boring, uncultured hole. You know, they don't even have dances here. Listen, why don't we make up a private party? I know a few boys here—Russians.'

'How about girls?' Marek asked.

'Oh, I'm afraid I don't know any girls. All the girls that work with me are Uzbeks. They don't go out with boys at all, silly. Don't you know any girls?'

'No,' Victor said, sitting down beside the girl, telegraphing over her head the message that Marek knew would be coming.

'Oh,' the girl murmured, disappointed. She turned to Marek. 'Your brother is very nice. He is not like the others here that immediately talk to you and try to get a date. He is cultured.'

'Yes,' Marek affirmed, gloomily, getting up.

'In Vladivostok the men are very cultured and very well brought up. They give up their places to ladies in the bus and always escort them home after a date. Have you read Tolstoy?' Marusia's busy voice was again directed to Victor. 'He writes marvellously, doesn't he?'

'Oh, yes. I read "War and Peace" and I saw "Anna Karenina" on the screen.'

'Oh *that* Tolstoy? No, I mean our Tolstoy—Alexij. He writes wonderfully, doesn't he? You can get all his books in the Konsomol's library here. Do you belong to the Konsomol?'

'No,' Victor said.

'Neither do I.' She stopped, noticing Marek picking up his skull-cap. 'Where are you going?' A slight suspicion crept into her high, melodious voice.

'I have to go somewhere.' Marek waved importantly in the air.

Marusia glanced judiciously at Victor. 'I hope you didn't make any arrangements, boys. Remember, I'm not a girl you can just pick up and bring home to make love to.'

'I know,' Victor said gravely.

'I won't be gone long,' Marek said.

'I must leave shortly anyway, to rehearse in the railwaymen's chorus. It was nice meeting you, Marek.'

'All the pleasure was mine, Marusia,' Marek said with good-humoured gallantry. As he walked out, he heard the girl laughing again, as she described to Victor how uncivilized Uzbeks used to sell their daughters for fifteen donkeys in the old pre-revolutionary times.

Aimlessly he strolled through the main street, looking at store windows decorated with empty cans, bottles and cartons. A banner had been posted on huge poles across the road, its red letters shrieking that the cotton growing programme must be more than met. Near the mail box a little pig-tailed girl was licking a stamp, then posting a letter and flashing Marek a smile of hidden pride. The Armenian barber stood in the door of his shop, unshaved, saluting Marek with a curt, uncertain bow. At the bus stop, people were waiting for the truck to take them to the station. Marek saw a big headline spread across the paper protruding out of the pocket of a tall Uzbek dressed in European clothes. He stopped beside him, but even with bent head was unable to read it. A discouragingly long queue stood in front of the news-stand. After a while, pretending to be waiting for the truck, he turned to the man. 'May I ask you for the paper?'

The man took his newspaper from his pocket, cut a square from one page and handed it to Marek. Dumbfounded, Marek looked up at him. 'Oh,' the man said after a while, raising his brows. 'You want to *read*? I'm sorry. Here it is, but don't take it away. I need it to make cigarettes with.' As Marek looked at the Russian page of the Uzbek paper, telling about the steady German advance and great successes of Soviet partisans, he thought about the sign on the news-stand boasting of the elimination of illiteracy in once backward Uzbekistan. The bus came and the man reached for his paper.

Marek left the main street and entered a narrow road. Ambling idly along, he tried to imagine how Victor and Marusia would be behaving now in the room. Victor had always been lucky with girls, he thought grudgingly. He had a healthy, cynical approach that the girls claimed they resented but fell for. 'It's useless to analyse a girl,' Victor would tell Marek in his rare lectures on women. 'Men are born to be consistent, but women, thank God, are not. So never wonder why they tell you no today. They might say yes tomorrow. Be patient and sure of yourself and you'll never lose.' Victor never lost with a girl. He was always the first to break off an affair. 'Always sense when the end is approaching,' he would say, 'and break a day before the girl does. She will then discover that she is madly in love with you and will beg you doggedly not to leave her.' Yes, Victor was quite an authority on women, for he had met and loved and left plenty of girls during his three years of studies in the big city. It wasn't fair somehow, Marek thought, that Marusia had become Victor's girl, for he, Marek, had noticed her first. For a moment he was angry with his brother, but then he shrugged, humorously dismissing his jealousy, and began to think about Ajmi, imagining that her husband was called to the army and then as the days passed, her looks at him softened and that finally an encouraging smile crossed her face. A familiar oriental tune struck up behind the wall and Marek realized that he was near the hut of the blind musician who performed at the market, and not too far from the house of Ulug Beg, and he remembered that he wouldn't have much time left to wait for the Army to draft Shukunov and for Ajmi to start longing for a man's attention. Then it occurred to him that he should see the old Uzbek and tell him that they had taken the room at Shukunov's house, so he'd know where to find them when Hamlat came back.

Before reaching the entrance, he slackened his pace and

cautiously waited for a couple of thick-legged boys to disappear behind the curve of the street. Far ahead of him he saw workers toiling in the flat cotton fields. He glanced back and forth, and when reassured that he was alone on the road and that the workers were too far off in the field to notice who he was, he lifted the rug and scurried into the courtyard.

In front of the hut, Aka was rocking a sheepskin sack filled with mare's milk to make it sour and buttery. As she noticed Marek, the sack fell from her hand, and she called Addin's Mother. In the corner of the courtyard, Marek saw the squatting woman collecting flat round unleavened bread from the ground into her folded paranja. 'Is Ulug Beg in?' he inquired.

The woman shook her head and stood up. Aka left her sack on the ground and made a few steps forwards. 'He went to town,' she said in pleasantly lisping, lilting Russian.

'Do you know when he'll be home?'

'No.' Her bright eyes regarded him with open candour.

'Did your father come back?'

She pouted and shook her head. 'No.' The old woman, holding the corners of her paranja piled with bread, approached slowly and stopped quietly besides the girl. Marek smelled the fresh bread, baked by the sun's heat and the glowing earth.

'Could you tell him that we took this room at Shukunov's house?'

'All right,' Aka said.

'Thank you.' He smiled politely at Addin's Mother and turned back. 'Oh, also tell him that my brother got a job on the railway. He worked there today for the first time.'

Aka nodded her head a few times in friendly agreement. 'Goodbye,' she chanted as Marek lifted the rug. He grinned back and waved a salute, then listened for a second, and when he heard no sounds of steps outside, he briskly left the courtyard.

On the road he stopped; his eyes travelled to the workers in the field, their curved figures sharply outlined against the clear pre-twilight sky. He stood, motionless, for a long while, then started to walk slowly towards the field. Very soon he found himself ambling along a narrow path among young men and women with turned up trousers, their bare legs wading in ditches filled with brown water, as they shovelled out the mire and clapped it firmly on the embankment. He passed an empty donkey-cart, its driver dozing on the ground in the shadow of a big wheel. A few steps past the cart, a square-headed Russian foreman in leather jacket, waving a fly swatter, was shouting orders to the workers. Marek looked around scrutinizing the bent heads of the women. Finally he saw Ajmi. She stood in the main canal, water coming up to her knees. With rake in hand, she was removing the weeds from the canal-bed, letting the water carry them away. Mud was splashed over her chin and her thick canvas blouse with its turned-up sleeves. On her cheeks flickered sunbeams that had forced their way through the leaves of the cotton plants. Marek saw her stretching herself after a while, wiping the mud and sweat from her face with her bare forearm. Suddenly her eyes focused on him and her hand froze by her forehead. With an alerted gaze, immobile, she watched him wave to her a salute, then stroll further on. As Marek walked away observing the working people with assumed studious curiosity, he preferred not to look back, but knew that Ajmi's suspicious eyes were on his neck.

When he reached the last ditch, the suddenly sloping ground opened a view on several little yellow huts. A caravan of three dromedaries, led by an Uzbek riding a donkey, was leaving the village. Marek heard two short dramatic blasts and as he turned, saw the jacketed foreman blowing a metal trumpet. Men and women began leaving their ditches, walking towards a cart on the path to lay down their tools. Marek strode back towards the workers receiving from the foreman slips attesting their day's work. In the queue, he recognized the slight figure of Ajmi, as she bent to roll down her trouser legs.

When, strolling slowly along, Marek reached the hut of Ulug Beg he stopped and turned, watched the small group of workers walking on the path towards the town. The three dromedaries, their heads swaying rhythmically, were near the queue of workers, and Marek heard the warning tinkle of the bell hung on the neck of the leading donkey. He resumed his walk, slackening his pace, hoping that Ajmi would soon pass him on her way home. He tramped along on the road, listening to the squeaking of his newly bought second-hand shoes, watching a small girl making a hole in the ground, a group of women gossiping in front of their house, an old man scolding his wife for purchasing unripe sunflower seeds on the market. The first groups of workers overtook him on the road. A couple of girls giggled and jostled their elbows when his eyes swept over their faces, searchingly. Finally he saw Ajmi's short slim figure between two rotund loudly chatting women. As she passed him by, with eyes focused on the winding trail of cart wheels on the road, her body tensed under the clumsy masculine workdress and a slight flush spread from her bare neck.

Again, as on the day when he had met her at the bazaar, he followed her from a distance, his eyes lingering absently on her indolently swaying figure. Street lights went on in the early twilight hours and Marek quickened his pace, frightened to meet the evening alone. Ajmi said goodbye to the girls, glanced over her shoulder at the approaching Marek, and scuttled through Achum Babayeffa Street to her home. As Marek crossed the courtyard, he watched the curtains on her window drop. Through the open door he saw Victor lighting the oil lamp. Marek knocked on the door.

'Come in, I'm alone.'

'Didn't work out?' He sat on the bed, watching Victor turn up the lamp wick. Soft shadows were flung on the bare walls of their room and on Victor's face.

'She ran to her rehearsal, but will be back after it.'

'So what shall I do then? Get out again and wait in the courtyard? You know I can't move away from home in the night.'

'Don't get excited. I don't want you to go anywhere. Where have you been?'

'Oh, I just walked around. I stopped at Ulug's house, but he wasn't in.'

Victor looked up at him, a flash of anger crossing his face. 'Are you crazy?'

A worried frown wrinkled Marek's forehead. 'I thought it would be wise to tell him that we have taken this room, so he will know where to find us when Hamlat comes back.'

He watched his brother take a few steps and stop in front of him. 'Marek, will you do me a favour? Me and yourself. Leave all these arrangements to me! Didn't it occur to you that we might be under observation?'

Marek spread his hands apologetically, as he faced Victor's irritated eyes. 'I was very careful, I looked around before entering his house.'

'You musn't ever do it again, understand?'

Marek rubbed his face, worrying whether Kisielev had not ordered his men to follow their movements in the town. 'I won't do it again,' he said meekly, and after a while asked, changing the subject, 'How was the work?'

'Oh, you know, physical work. No brains required. Hard, but I'm used to hard work. Have you eaten?'

'No.' Only now Marek realized that he hadn't eaten all day and that he was very hungry.

'My God, is that the way you're going to regain your strength? What did you do all day?'

'I slept, I was so damn tired. Did you get your rations?'

'I'll get them tomorrow. They took my name down. But we've tomatoes, bread and herring from yesterday, haven't we?'

'I've eaten the tomatoes, but we still have herring and bread. Shall I make some sandwiches for you, too?'

Victor looked around the room, as if to decide whether the bare walls and the clothes hanging on the nails looked nice enough for Marusia's visit. 'I ate in the station's dining hall. In a few days I'll try to take you there.'

'Is that why you became friendly with Marusia?'

Smiling, Victor folded himself on the bed near Marek. 'Not only that. I think she is a nice girl. And not so stupid.'

'No doubt—she is from Vladivostok, not Kermine.'

'Any objections?'

'Oh, no!'

'Listen. Ibram hasn't brought that basin yet, eh?'

'The basin? Oh!' Marek got up eagerly from the bed and bolted for the door. 'I'll get it for you. You'll need it tomorrow morning.'

Through the darkness he groped his way to Shukunovs' home. 'Who is there?' he heard Ajmi's high, inquiring voice.

'Me, Marek Sobel.'

'What do you want?'

'May I enter?' He pressed against the door, but it was locked. For a moment he heard nothing, then the approaching sound of wooden sandals, then the click of the turning key. In the half-open door appeared Ajmi's face, washed and clean, framed by carefully plaited braids. 'Yes?' Her voice sounded flat and high, no welcome in it.

'Is your husband back from work?' He was very careful to keep his face serious and voice matter-of-fact.

'No. Why?'

'Yesterday he promised us a basin for washing.'

'He said he would get it on his way home tonight. I'm sure he will be here any moment.'

'May I wait?'

She shrugged, walked into the room, and pulled the curtains. She had on her usual grey robe, but this time it was sashed by a red belt. Marek stepped into the room and sat on the sofa. 'I never before saw a cotton field,' he said. 'And I was very curious.' She threw him a dubious, side-long glance from slanted eyes. He watched her walk to the settee, take a skein of wool and knitting needles and start to work on a blue sweater, her half-shut eyes focused on her work. 'You don't mind me talking to you, do you?' Her knitting hands began to move swiftly and she said nothing. 'Can I talk to you?' Marek repeated.

She bit her lips and snapped. 'Why should you?'

Marek folded his hands over his knees. 'I don't know anyone in town. I've no one to talk to.'

'So what do I care?' Her slim shoulders again rose in abrupt defiance, her long fingers now moved the needles with such speed that Marek was sure she would hurt herself any moment.

'Don't you have any friends?' he asked.

'No.'

'Why? People can't lead a solitary life. They need company, other people to talk to.'

'I've my husband. And I don't need anybody else to talk to.' She flashed him a brief look, daring him to object.

Modestly hunching his shoulders, Marek sat for a while, silent. His eyes roamed moodily over the shining samovar, the kitchen door and the carpet on the wall. 'Why don't you have a susaneh?' he asked, determined to get Ajmi to talk to him somehow.

'My husband is a Bokharian Jew,' she said.

'Oh, is he? What are you?'

'Uzbek,' she said with an impatient gasp.

'How long have you been married?'

'Why?'

'I just asked. Can't I ask?'

'Three years.'

'Have you ever been out of this town—in some big cities?'

'No.'

He caught her glance at the window, followed by a sudden frown, that darkened her low forehead. Turning he saw Raim's flattened face behind the window pane, his elongated black eyes peeping into the room. When Marek stumped to his feet and crossed to the window, the boy's face broke away from the pane and he darted out of the courtyard. Slowly, Marek returned to his place, and sat down again. 'I've been to many places,' he resumed after a while. 'Molotov, Chkalov, Tashkent.' He waved his hand in a broad gesture to indicate that he had travelled widely. She remained silent, so he continued; 'Some of the places are very nice—Chkalov for instance. And some are not—Kuibyshev for instance.' He heard his own voice sinking into uncertainty, as he noticed her drawn face and tight lips. Ajmi studied her sweater for a second, then her hands began to move again, the steel needles glistening in the light of the oil lamp hanging from the ceiling in the middle of the room. Time and again she raised her head and glanced uncomfortably out of the window at the white edges of the courtyard's gate. 'I don't think I will wait any longer,' Marek said, getting up. She swung her head to him and for the first time he noticed a sign of relief on her face. 'Maybe you can ask your husband to bring the basin to our room.'

'I will,' she said, her eyes ready to accompany him to the door. Slowly, he walked to the entrance, but as his hand reached the knob, he heard steps outside, and opened the door to let Ibram in. Ajmi threw her knitting on the settee, stood up, and said something rapidly in Uzbek.

'I gave the basin to your brother just now,' Ibram said. 'I'm sorry I didn't have time to get it yesterday.'

'That's all right, Thank you.' Marek curled his lips in a polite smile of farewell and left.

'Oh, Citizen Sobel,' he heard Ibram's voice behind him, followed by his steps.

'Yes?' he turned, though he could not see him in the blackened courtyard.

'Would you like to come to the stadium with us on Friday? There will be music, songs and playlets.'

'Very gladly. What's the occasion?'

'It's the 7th of November, you forgot? The anniversary of the Great Revolution.'

'Oh my, how could I forget? We'll come gladly. How could we miss it? Thank you very much. Good night.'

As Marek approached the door, he heard a quick trot, so he stopped and waited. In the light of the open door of their room, he saw Marusia's figure emerging from the darkness, holding a package wrapped in newspaper. They entered the room. 'Good evening,' Marusia said gaily from the door to Victor. 'Look what I got from our pantry. I skipped the rehearsal.' She winked gleefully and began to put the things she had brought on the table, naming them proudly—'Kerosene stove

—packet of tea—oil—cutlets, fresh from today's dinner, and sugar. Who is going to make the tea?'

'Oh, God.' Marek clasped his hands, looking at the things on the table, then he started to pick up each one and scrutinized it with the expression of a diamond dealer who has just bought magnificent stones cheaply. Without a word, Victor busied himself with pumping the kerosene stove. He brought water from the well in a little empty can and put it on the stove. Now Marusia took over. She opened the colourful package, let them see and smell the *black* tea, then threw a pinch into the can and lit the stove. As she was helping Marek make sandwiches, suddenly a nostalgic Uzbek song came from behind the wall. Marek raised his head and listened. Marusia sat on the bed near Victor, and, watching the sizzling yellow-blue flame, entwined her arm around his shoulder and put her other hand on his knees. 'You've all the luck in the world,' Marek said in Polish, his voice filled with flattery and envy.

'What did you say?' Marusia raised her head.

Marek waved in the air and grinned. 'Oh, just that you're a lucky girl. You've got yourself a nice, romantic fellow, who you can be sure won't take advantage of you.'

Marusia looked up at Victor. The light of the stove flame was playing on his face, shaping it into delicate patterns of light and shadows. 'I knew it,' she said, her bright eyes gleaming affectionately. 'When he talked to me there in the station dining-hall, I felt immediately that he was different from all the men I had met before.'

8

THE MAIN STREET OF KERMINE was decked out in festive red. Flags hung from the buildings, and shop windows were adorned with pictures of Soviet leaders framed in beige cloth. Even the wheels of passing carts were wound with orange crepe paper. Stretched on poles across Shadiva Street a new banner, glorifying the 24th anniversary of the Great Revolution, replaced the old slogan dedicated to the cotton growing programme. On their way back from the stadium, Ibram and Ajmi in front and behind them Marusia, holding the boys' arms, all mingled with the crowd that was listening on street corners to the broadcast of the holiday-inspired list of ten vows of the Party and the Government to the Soviet peoples. Marek was still deafened by sounds of megaphones in the stadium, blasting speeches, chorus songs, orchestral marches and applause. He looked at Ajmi's long, slim figure in front of him, moulded into a silver-embroidered brocade paranja. She looked beautiful and festive, and the contrast of her age with that of her husband was underlined by her hair, much braided and gaily beribboned. Ibram led her by the hand with pride, pleasantly aware of the appreciative nods and whispering re-marks of the townfolk. Looking at the two in front of him, Marek found himself away from the holiday atmosphere, long-ing for the quiet of the small hospital room and Anushka's solemn look into his face and her cool hand on his hot forehead.

The megaphones on the street corner began to report the Supreme Commander's Order of the Day, announcing that the German armies had been stopped all along the front and that the heroic troops of the Northern Front had recaptured fifteen villages near Leningrad. As the street became loud with vigorous tunes of the army marches, the men in the street jubilantly slapped each other's backs, clasped each other's hands and exchanged confident shouts that from now on the Red Army would drive the German attackers from the last inch of Soviet soil. As the five passed the tea-room filled with old, bearded Uzbeks, who, unmoved by festivities, squatted and drank their daily tea, the crowd in front of them suddenly pulled backwards under the pressure of hand-chained police-men just released from the parade march. In the middle of the police-cleared square stood groups of Uzbek peasants. A small orchestra composed of three men sitting on the bakery's steps struck up a gay oriental tune on the stringed instruments. The girls uttered shouts of joy, snapped their fingers invitingly, and the men went into a wild Lesghinka dance, whipping out their

71

daggers, jumping high and striking their leather boots against the ground with every chord of the music. As the long flapping coats and shining red boots and glittering daggers cut the air more wildly, the women screamed fanatically and the whole street now clapped hands in rhythm. Marek saw Marusia propping her chin on Victor's shoulder, her finger-tips circling over his hand in a delicate caress. Slowly he turned around and cast his eyes on the slender back of Ajmi. He made a step forward and his eyes slid down towards the sheet of olive skin in the V-neck of her dress and then lifted to the heightened colour on her cheeks, her shining eyes and lips parted in a smile revealing small white even teeth. She clasped her small hand under her chin the way delighted children do at a circus. Suddenly Marek heard his brother's whisper, 'Look to your right.' He turned his head away from Ajmi and saw three boys clad in wadded jerkins, their heads uncovered in spite of the hot sun. 'I heard them talking,' Victor went on. 'They speak Polish.'

'Released from the camp?"

'I guess so.'

'What are they doing here?'

'I don't know. Maybe they have the same idea we do.'

After several repeated chords, the tune stopped abruptly. The dancers bowed and waved their skull-caps in the air, happily acknowledging the applause of the audience. Ibram touched Victor's arm. 'Shall we go?' Victor nodded and they left the square. 'You must all come with us now,' Ibram said, rubbing his hands cheerfully, as they walked home on Achum Babayeffa Street, 'and have a glass of good wine. A holiday is a holiday, and what is a holiday without wine?'

'Right,' Victor said, spreading his hands approvingly. 'There is nothing better than good wine,'

In front of their house, they saw Raim sitting on a stone, his eyes, unaware of the approaching people, focused dully on a hairy-legged tarantula, lazily creeping along the road. Ibram touched his shoulder and said something to him, pointing towards the town. The boy slowly turned his head. His eyes wavered over the people, his lips were parched and forehead covered with sweat. 'My God,' Ajmi said, and went to the boy quickly, laying her hand on his forehead. 'He's not well!' She spoke a few Uzbek words to the boy, took his hand, and led him unprotesting to the house.

'As soon as she puts the boy to bed,' Ibram said, 'I'll come for you.'

'Oh, maybe we'd better skip it,' Marusia said.

'No, no, that's all right.' He followed his wife.

'Well, let's go inside,' Victor said.

'I'm working in the evening today, I must leave at six.' They entered the room.

Victor glanced at his watch. 'You've time.'

Marusia sat on the bed and pulled Victor's arm, forcing him to sit near her. With one hand she hugged his neck, with the other she raised his wrist, and looked at his watch. 'You've a beautiful watch. My father planned to make a wrist watch from a pocket one but then we thought it would look too big, wouldn't it? Though some people here do it.'

'If your father wants a wrist watch I could sell this one to him.'

'Oh, no? . . . Really? Why should you do that?' Smiling, she looked into his face with playful suspicion as if convinced that he would do it just to please her father.

'Oh,' Victor said, 'we need money to buy things—clothes and some furniture. We must make this room liveable some-how.'

'Yes,' Marusia said. 'Some furniture would make this room look nicer.' Marek squinted suspiciously, as her eyes in careful scrutiny travelled around the room as if she was about to move in with Victor and evict Marek. 'How much would you ask for the watch?'

'Oh, the same price that I paid. Nine hundred roubles.'

'Really? Oh, my father will be so happy! I wish I could talk to him about it now! Victor, why don't you come to our house so you can meet my father and my mother, and talk to my father about the watch?'

'You find out first if he is interested in buying it,' Victor said soberly. 'Shall we have tea?' He glanced at Marek and saw him getting up from his stool and approaching the window. 'What is it?' He joined Marek and peeked out of the window. In the gate little Aka was standing undecided, gaping expectantly at their house. 'Excuse me,' Victor said and quickly left the room.

'What's the matter?' Marusia asked.

Marek shrugged, for he didn't know what to say. He saw his brother approach the girl and listen to her message, related in quick, excited words. When Aka nodded and disappeared behind the wall of the courtyard, Marek walked out of the room, undisturbed by the questioning stare of Marusia. 'Has he come back?' he breathed in Polish.

He saw a hidden smile wandering on his brother's face. 'Yes, he came back an hour ago and went right to sleep. I'll go to see him tomorrow night.'

Marek noticed a sudden uneasy frown crease Victor's forehead. He followed his brother's sidelong glance. In the threshold of his home stood Ibram, watching them silently.

9

SITTING ON THE BED, VICTOR took off his boots and greasy socks. 'This damn patriotism,' he grumbled, stretching his bare toes, immense relief on his face. 'Two more hours a week of work. For the fatherland—no pay. As if the job wasn't hard enough already.' He mumbled a curse under his breath.

'Who imposed it?' Marek asked, preparing sandwiches for his brother, becoming hungry himself.

'Imposed? We volunteered.' Victor stood up, took off his shirt and began to wipe his sweaty body with a towel. 'Just when I was ready to leave, two of the workers, Konsomol members, called a meeting, and proposed it. Then one of them asked, "Who is against it?" No one was against it, so we stayed on the job. Bastards!'

The water began to boil on the kerosene stove and Marek threw a pinch of tea into the can and turned down the flame. Victor took the stool with the basin and walked out to wash himself near the well. When he re-entered the room, the towel slung around his neck, his tea and sandwiches were ready for him at the table.

'Thin slices of bread the way mother used to make them,' Marek said, waiting for his brother to pick up a sandwich so he could follow suit. Victor took a big bite and, chewing the bread, began to put on a clean shirt that he picked from the nail on the wall. 'Why don't you finish?' Marek asked. 'Aren't you hungry?'

'I'd better go. Hamlat might go to bed early. I'll drop in at the Shukunovs' on my way to ask how the boy feels.' Marek followed him to the door and waited there until Victor emerged again from the house, crossing the courtyard towards the gate. 'Ibram took him to hospital,' he said. 'See you in an hour or so.'

Marek returned to the room and lifted the cup of tea to his lips but immediately put it back on the table. 'Victor!' he shouted and ran out to the road. 'Victor!'

'What's the matter?' He saw his brother turn and come back to him, so he strode to meet him half-way.

'What should I tell Marusia if she comes?' Bewildered, Marek watched his brother, who instead of answering him, proceeded to walk around him in a semi-circle. 'What are you doing?'

'Marek, can you—can you see me?'

'Yes. You know I can see by strong moonlight.'

'But there is no moon, not even stars. And not a street lamp in sight. Marek, I think you are beginning to get over it!' Excitedly, he ran several yards, crossed the road, and stopped. 'Come to me now.'

Marek walked to him, a slow smile spreading across his face, as it dawned on him that he was neither stumbling nor groping, just walking straight ahead towards the silhouette awaiting him in the shadow of the wall.

'It's wonderful!' Victor yelled joyfully. 'You're cured, Marek!'

'I couldn't see you too clearly, but I knew where you were.'

'You did it fine.' Victor patted his brother fondly on the back. 'Do you want to come with me?'

'Sure,' Marek said happily. 'Let's go.

And as they walked along the dark path, he kept on marvelling at his recovered night-sight and the wonderful timing of this recovery. Victor beamed, 'You see, it's because you listened to me. If you'd worked, all the calories would have been used up and left nothing to cure you.'

'Yes, doctor,' Marek said with sympathetic mockery. They didn't go by the main street, but winding their way through narrow ill-lighted side streets, reached the road on which Ulug Beg and Hamlat lived.

Suddenly Marek stopped. 'God,' he said grimly. 'I can't see anything again.'

'You silly,' Victor chuckled. 'Don't worry, I can't see anything either. It's dark as hell here. Come.' He took Marek's hand and they groped their way along till the road widened and brightened.

No sounds of music came from behind the wall where the musician lived and the children were probably at home after their sunset-time street games. Only the freckled ginger boy who had showed them to Ulug's house when they first came to town, stood in the gate, leading to one of the stony courtyards, enjoying a secretly smoked cigarette butt. He greeted them with an earnest 'Good evening, Comrades,' and a flaunting puff on the cigarette. Shortly before reaching the end of the road that linked up with the path winding through the cotton fields, Marek glanced over his shoulder. He couldn't see the boy any more. 'There is no one around,' he whispered as if the mud walls of the lonely street could overhear him.

'Let's go to Ulug's house. It's safer.' Marek nodded. Before entering the familiar rug-covered gate, Victor again looked around. 'Let's go,' he motioned. 'Quickly!' He raised the carpet and they both sneaked swiftly into the courtyard.

76

Outside the hut, around the dying embers of a fire, sat Ulug, his wife, Aka, and a huge broad-shouldered man. 'Good evening,' Aka sang out cheerfully, as Ulug squinted at them through the smoke and darkness. As they approached the fire, the big man stood up politely. The woman motioned to the girl and they immediately started for the house, leaving the men alone.

'Ah, it's you,' Ulug said and stretched out his hand in greeting. 'This is Hamlat.' They all shook hands and sat down around the fire. Ulug yelled a few Uzbek words to his wife and blew at the fire. 'You'll get coffee in a moment. Yes, coffee!' He winked flatteringly at his son-in-law, and Hamlat answered with a modest smile.

As Marek sat on a pillow, he looked at Hamlat, and at the sight of his fierce bristle of hair and muscular body that looked as if it was made from iron bars and riggings, he felt suddenly certain that with this man as their guide, they had nothing to fear.

'So he *is* alive,' Hamlat said, shaking his big head as if he could hardly believe it. 'We used to work together, you know. And then, that time I was sick and he went alone.' His little grey eyes blinked at the remote memories. In the red light of the embers Marek saw that he had a pleasant dimple in his chin.

'He has to serve five more years,' Victor said. 'Then he will come back.' Ulug drew a big sigh, and with a stick prodded the embers to cover his emotion. In the door of the hut Addin's Mother appeared, carrying a brass coffee pot, which she handed to her husband, and then left. The old Uzbek placed the pot on the fire. A long, reverential silence followed as they waited for the coffee to boil.

'When do you want to go?' Hamlat said matter-of-factly.

'Any time you say.'

'How about Friday?'

'All right.' Marek felt his heart stop for a moment, as their plan to cross the border suddenly became a matter of impending reality. Hamlat bowed his head in agreement.

Ulug removed the pot from the fire and with the other side

of his stick stirred the liquid a bit. Then he moved the pot back over the embers. 'The more times you bring it to the boil the better the coffee is,' he said, raising his stick to accentuate the importance of good coffee-making. A wonderful aroma drifted into Marek's nose making him think involuntarily of all the mornings in their house with his mother in the old faded dressing gown, carrying a steaming cup for her husband before he hurried off to his work. Silently, Addin's Mother was again near Ulug Beg, carrying a brass tray with four little empty brass cups and a fifth filled with sugar, a spoon protruding from it. Through the door, Marek observed Aka sitting on the bed, leaning forward curiously to watch the events in the courtyard. Over his head, in the dark globe of the sky twinkled a few faint points of melting stars. Except for the calling of crickets, the surrounding labyrinth of walled deserted streets and silent courtyards seemed to rest in an unstirring and peaceful sleep.

'Here is your cup,' Ulug said, his trembling hand spilling some liquid on the ground.

'Thank you.' Marek modestly took one spoonful of sugar, stirred the coffee, then slipped the wet spoon back into the sugar cup, and passed it on to Hamlat. As he took the first sip, he felt a forgotten pleasant bitter bite on his palate and the warmth of the liquid travelled from his chest to his stomach. For a long time, the avid sucking sounds filled the courtyard and they lasted till the empty cups were replaced on the tray.

'Well,' Ulug said contentedly, rubbing his hands. 'Now, let's talk business. I told you,' he turned to Hamlat, 'they only have a thousand roubles.' Hamlat nodded. 'I told him,' Ulug went on, turning to Victor with the tone of a mediator, 'that he could bring back sheep again, so it would pay him.'

'We don't actually have a thousand roubles,' Victor interrupted, 'but a watch which is worth a thousand roubles.' He showed off his wrist. 'Maybe you'll take this, otherwise we would have to sell it.'

Hamlat glanced vaguely at the watch. 'You'd better sell it. I don't want to bother with it.' He leaned towards Victor. 'I'll take you, though it isn't much money that you're paying me, but I think I'll get a few other people to go along.' His mouth opened in a yellow-toothed smile.

Victor and Marek exchanged fearful glances. 'What do you mean?' Victor asked, his voice sinking.

'There are a few of your people here in town that are trying to do the same thing you are.'

'Oh God, how can you be sure you can trust them?'

'Don't worry. I can smell people. I wouldn't do it for just a thousand roubles, even if I could bring back sheep. And this way it will pay me.'

'It's more suspicious to go in such a large group,' Victor said, still trying to protest.

Hamlat gave a confident chuckle. 'Don't worry. I've made this trip at least twenty-five times and have never been caught.'

'Addin was.'

'If he had been patient and had waited for me, he wouldn't be where he is now. You can trust me. I know every inch of earth around the border.' He looked up at the sky. 'It's getting late and I don't want you to stay here too long. Let's talk details.' He hitched himself a bit closer to Victor and went on in subdued whispering tones. 'We'll meet at the station on Friday at five in the afternoon. Just come into the hall and buy tickets for Bokhara. The train comes from Samarkand fifteen minutes later and leaves at five-thirty. But it will take you about twenty minutes to get tickets. Do not talk to me or even look at me. Just follow me into the same car. During the train's stop in Kagan, get out and buy tickets to Kaakhka. Between Dushak and Kaakhka the train stops in a field. You'll hear the conductor announce, "Red Star Kolkhoz". Remember, we all get down there. People will think we belong to the Kolkhoz. I'll walk towards the huts and you'll follow me, but as soon as the train moves away, we'll leave the track and go up the path leading into the mountains. I've a friend there, who is a state forester. We'll eat in his yurt and then go south. When the dawn breaks, we will be on the other side of the border.'

Hamlat finished speaking, but Marek's thoughts were far

away, in Persia, as following the Uzbek's lyric description, he embarked on a picnic-like crossing of a frontier unprotected by guards and dogs.

'Some more coffee?' Ulug suggested, raising the pot that shook again in his hand.

'Better not,' Hamlat said cautiously. 'I'd rather that you went as soon as possible. If anybody sees you coming out of here, remember you bought a little carpet.' He stood up, walked into the house and came back with a small red rug. 'Keep it,' he said to Victor.

'Fine. So we'll go now.' Victor got up.

'On Thursday evening I'll send my girl to your place. Give her half the money. The rest you'll give me after we've crossed the border.' Victor nodded. Hamlat's face assumed a reassuring smile, as he shook Victor's and Marek's hands. 'Just take it easy. Oh! leave all your belongings here, no valises or knapsacks or anything. When we reach my friend's yurt you'll get felt shoes to wear.'

'What for?' Marek asked, suspicion rising in his voice.

'So that dogs won't get on our tracks.'

A sad smile of dispelled illusion crossed Marek's face, as he approached the old Uzbek to bid him farewell. Ulug Beg stood up heavily. 'Best of luck,' he said heartily and took Marek's hand in both of his, then Victor's. As they were crossing the courtyard, the woman and the girl came into the entrance of the hut. Lifting the rug, Marek threw an all embracing glance at the courtyard—at the female silhouettes, sharpened by the yellow light of the lamp, at the stooping figure of the old Uzbek by the dying embers of the fire, at the tin bucket over the well, and he felt somehow nostalgic about this place that he knew he would return to no more.

The road was empty, but far away near the main street they saw the shadow of a man propped against the corner street lamp.

'Let's go back to the same street we came by,' Victor said. As they strode forward, keeping close to the wall, the man's silhouette separated itself from the street lamp and froze attentively, the unseen eyes apparently scrutinizing their shadows. Marek fearfully looked at his brother. 'Oh,' Victor shrugged, 'he's probably waiting for friends to go somewhere for a glass of vodka.' They turned into the side road, and as they approached its end, Victor looked back, but saw no one.

'Friday,' he said. 'Six more days.'

Marek was silent and deep in thought. But after a while, when they entered Achum Babayeffa Street, he asked slowly: 'When you walk in felt shoes, can't dogs smell your tracks?'

'Of course not, silly, because you won't leave any tracks in this stony mountain.'

Reassured, Marek raised his head and began to walk quicker. 'You know,' he said, 'I really see fine now. I see everything.'

'Wonderful.'

As they approached their house, they heard rushing steps behind them, and a moment later from a side road emerged the shadowy figure of Ibram. His head bowed, he walked quickly and did not see the two until he approached the gate and found himself suddenly facing them. 'I just came from the hospital. The boy is very ill. He is delirious. The doctor doesn't know what it is.' He crossed the courtyard and stopped in front of his house. They saw him standing there for some time before he finally turned the knob and entered the room.

10

THERE WAS A SHY KNOCKING at the door. Marek turned from his bundle spread out on the table and looked at his brother bent over the kerosene stove in the corner. Victor straightened and pointed to the door with a stove cleaner. 'Open it.'

Marek pushed down the handle. 'Come in, Aka.' The girl glanced over her shoulder at the courtyard's gate, then came into the room. Marek closed the door behind her and turned the key. Victor left the kerosene stove and came closer.

'Grandfather said to bring you these two embroidered

handkerchiefs you ordered from his wife.' With the twinkle of a smile in her eyes, she put a little parcel on the table. Victor reached into the back pocket of his trousers and took out his billfold. He counted the money and gave it to the girl. She hid it quickly in the recess of her paranja, but didn't leave; her narrow black eyes turned to Marek and held him for a split second. A gleam of reflected light came from between her long unblinking eyelashes. Her lips parted in a sweet, disarming smile that dimpled her cheeks. 'All the best to you,' she lisped melodiously and scuttled out of the room. Through the window, Marek watched her tiny figure, her girlish narrow hips swaying a little in the anticipation of oncoming femininity.

'Come on,' Victor said. 'Get your things ready before Marusia comes.' He started working again on the stove with his cleaner. Finally, the stove hissed with the gas that had found its way out and Victor lit it. 'I'm not too happy about these three boys,' he said, tending the blue circle of flame. 'But I guess there is nothing we can do. Maybe it's even better; we could help each other in case of trouble. Listen,' he went on after a while. 'I'll have to come to the station directly from work. It's safer that I work till the last minute.'

'All right.'

'You'll buy the tickets. I'll be there a few minutes after five.'

Marek nodded. He picked up a cardboard-framed photograph of their mother and father sitting on chairs with their sons standing respectfully behind them. With a meek smile, he studied the picture. 'It was taken the day before you left for Warsaw.' He handed it to his brother, but Victor busily waved the photo away. 'Put it in your pocket. Take all the pictures and documents out. I'll check them later.' He put the can with water over the stove, then stretched a newspaper on the table. From the corner of the room, which served as their kitchen, he brought cups and plates, a fork and knife, bread and finally a white radish. Then he fumbled among the old newspapers. 'Is that all we have—this radish?'

'I couldn't get anything else today. I got to the market too late.'

'What about my rations? They promised them a week ago.'

'Now they say they'll get them on Saturday.'

'On Saturday we'll buy all the unrationed food we want."

He propped his hands on his hips, scrutinizing the table. 'It's not much for a farewell party, is it?'

Marek piled up the papers and photographs, replaced his belongings in the bundle, and dropped it into the corner. 'You look over these papers,' he said, 'and let me arrange the party.'

'You think you'll be able to transform radish into sashlik?'

'Perhaps.' With a secret smile, as Victor sat at the table and began to sort out the papers, Marek sliced bread, cut thin pieces of radish and made small oblong sandwiches that he arranged on a plate. 'The first course,' he announced.

Victor raised his head. 'Hors d'oeuvres?'

'Yes.' Marek went on slicing chip-like strips of radish and mixed them well with oil on another plate and salted the meal. 'That's the main course—entrée,' he said. Victor, smiling tolerantly, crumpled some paper and threw it into the corner. Marek diced the radish, then bit off the heads of matches and stuck them into the cubes, as if they were toothpicks in cubes of pineapple. 'And that's for the dessert.' With a triumphant smile on his face, he displayed the three full plates to his brother. 'Well?' His voice rose in expectation of a compliment.

'That's great,' Victor said with real admiration. 'Where did you learn that?'

'In the kitchen,' Marek said. 'In the kitchen in Brest Litovsk. Imagine what I would be able to do with radish if I had studied home economics at Warsaw University.'

Victor chuckled. 'You know, Marek,' he said expansively, 'sometimes I'm very fond of you.'

'Thanks,' Marek said, his voice sour-sweet. 'Now you'd better change the object of your fondness. I see your fiancée coming.'

Victor quickly pulled the papers from the table and hid them under the pillow. There was a knocking and almost simultaneously Marusia appeared in the doorway. At once they both noticed an elaborate pyramid of hair on her head. For a while she let them admire her new hair-do, then slanting her head coquettishly, gave Victor her cheek to kiss. 'Do you like it?'

'Yes indeed,' Victor said. 'Did you copy it from an American fashion magazine?'

'I created it,' she said proudly, and only now noticed the plates on the table. 'Oh,' she said, 'what's that? It does look good.'

'*He* created it,' Victor said dryly. 'Oh God, I forgot all about the tea. Sit down.' He took the boiling water can from the kerosene stove and turned off the brass tap. With a final gasp, the flame died.

From her chair Marusia looked up gaily at Victor making her a cup of tea. 'What's the occasion? A birthday or something?'

'No occasion.' Victor shrugged innocently and went on pouring tea into two other cups. 'Sorry, no sugar. Marek finished it up.' He sat on the bed with his cup and a sandwich.

'Father was very pleased with the watch,' Marusia said. 'It was nice of you to sell it to him, Victor. Listen, boys, I've some great news.' She picked up a cube on a stick and raised it to her mouth.

'This is for dessert,' Victor instructed her. 'Start with the sandwiches.'

Marusia obediently put the cube back and took a sandwich. 'Good,' she said appreciatively, chewing bread and radish. With full mouth she went on talking enthusiastically. 'The railwaymen chorus and drama circle is organizing a dance in our dining hall on Sunday. The first dance I ever heard of here. Isn't that great?'

'Marusia——' Victor said, holding his cup, his head bowed, but she didn't hear him.

'They put me in charge of decorating the hall. You want to help me? We'll go, all three of us, nicely dressed, and I'm going to find a girl for Marek.'

84

'Marusia . . . We won't be able to go. We're going to Bokhara for a few days tomorrow. To visit our relatives.'

The girl's rosy cheeks faded rapidly and the smile fled from her lips. 'I didn't know you had relatives in Bokhara.'

'We have a married cousin. Didn't I tell you?'

'No. Couldn't you go a few days later? What's the difference?'

'They've already made all preparations, got a room for us.'

Marusia got up, and flung herself on the bed, beside Victor. Her back arched, her hands slid limply between her parted knees. 'I don't believe you'll ever come back,' she said in a low, sullen voice.

'What nonsense! We'll be back on Tuesday. We're leaving all our clothes, everything.' The girl raised her head and stared into Victor's eyes. Marek turned uncomfortably and looked through the window at the gate, white-washed by the moonshine. 'Don't be a baby, Marusia. If I'm telling you I'm coming back, I am.'

'Do me a favour, just this once.'

'I can't postpone this, Marusia. It's not simple to reserve a room in Bokhara, you know.'

'Let me stay here tonight. All night.'

Marek propped himself on the window-sill groaning inwardly at the dreadful prospect of a night-long walk. 'How about my brother?' he heard Victor say. 'You know that we sleep in one bed.'

'Can't he sleep somewhere else?'

'Where?'

'I've the key of the dining hall. We can put some chairs together. Is that all right with you, Marek?'

Marek turned, but before he could open his mouth, Victor said, 'No, Marusia. I can't do that. He has been very sick and he needs rest, especially before this journey.'

The girl looked at Victor with a wretched little smile, then hitched herself closer to him and rested her head on his shoulder. As Victor put his arm around her back, she closed her eyes and her chest heaved in a little gasp. 'It took

85

me several hours today to make this hair-do,' she pouted.

'I feel like taking a walk,' Marek said.

'What about our party?' Victor asked. 'Let's eat first.'

'I'm not hungry,' the girl said. Marek picked up two sand-wiches and a few cubes of radish and left the room. He walked to the well and sat on its edge. The blue globe of the sky was studded with sharp glimmering stars. From the mountains the cold night breeze blew into his face. He looked to the south, but the dark curtain of the night veiled the horizon and he could only imagine the arid, desolate, yet softly curved chain of mountains that somewhere hid the hut in which they would be spending the next night. Marek turned his head towards Shukunov's lighted window with the delicate white curtains hung across its top. And as he looked at the hazy contours of the distant brass samovar on the chest of drawers, he thought nostalgically about the romance that could have been, but never was. Slowly he got up and, stepping quietly, like a thief in the night, he approached the window. What he saw inside, made him come closer and almost press his face against the glass, for Ajmi was stretched on the carpet, her head hidden in her hands, her body shaken with sobs. On the settee he saw the immobile, arched profile of Ibram, with bent head. Marek thought he could hear his heart's thud against his chest. He knocked at the door and entered. Ajmi raised her face for a second and he saw the tears dripping down her cheeks to the corners of her throbbing lips. At sight of him she burst into a new loud, hollow lament and covered her face with both hands. From the settee, the tear-stained red-rimmed eyes of Ibram looked up at Marek. 'The boy died,' he said dully. 'This afternoon.' For a moment Marek stood in the threshold, tongue-tied. Finally he moved his lips in a few unspoken words of consolation, then bowed his head and withdrew, closing the door quietly behind him.

Outside a gust of wind whined through the open gate of the courtyard and drummed briefly against the bucket that stood on the well's edge, glittering in the light of the moon. The window of his home went suddenly dark and from behind it came quick, subdued whispers, sighs and groans. Then, after a period of silence, the melancholic, grateful voice of Marusia singing a Russian song floated into the night. The wind quieted and between its sporadic gasps, Marek thought he heard Ajmi's dry, tortured sobs.

II

THE BUS DROVE AT WALKING pace to the front of the tea-house, its motor throbbing heavily. Following an enormously fat Russian woman whose breasts swung loosely under a gay-coloured print, Marek climbed the step-ladder that the driver had pulled out of the cab and placed at the back of the truck. He wedged himself between two goat-bearded, tobacco-smelling Uzbeks sitting on an unfastened bench. The driver collected the fares, then lifted the truck's tail-gate, bolted the bars and took the step-ladder with him. A moment later, the starter whined rustily, and with a sudden jolt, the bus slithered along Shadiva Street. Through its back Marek saw the Tajik craftsman in the door of his shop blowing on his water-pipe, a group of children with their satchels on their backs returning from school and a column of recruits with a few sobbing women clinging to their arms. Pyramids of cans and bottles again replaced the pictures of the leaders in the shop windows. The bakery and the news-stand were closed and the square was empty, except for two workers standing on ladders, restoring the pre-holiday banner on cotton production.

The bus stopped outside the tractor repair base where mechanics clad in overalls sat on a street bench, eating thick pieces of bread with whole salted herrings. A few Uzbeks left the bus and a tall Russian boarded it, ploughing his way with his battered cardboard valise.

Creaking and groaning, the bus went on, made a circle around the station square and stopped in front of the entrance. Before the driver could put out his step-ladder, Marek jumped down from the truck and ran up the steps into the crowded station hall. The aged clock over the platform exit showed ten minutes to five.

He looked around and saw the three Polish boys occupying a bench under a wall. One of them glanced up from under a newly acquired peaked cap and gave Marek a long stare. The other bus passengers entered the hall, so Marek swiftly moved to join the queue at the ticket window. Pushing each other impatiently, the people lined up behind him. Against his back Marek felt the pressure of the huge, warm breasts of the Russian woman with whom he had entered the bus on Shadiva Street. At the sight of the undisciplined line, a pudgy, apple-cheeked NKVD guard left his colleague with whom he had been chatting at the platform exit, and came to enforce order. 'Citizens,' he yelled, 'will you kindly behave in a cultured way? This is not a bakery. There are tickets for everyone.' Then his small cold eyes rested on a one-legged soldier on crutches. 'Comrade Private, you don't have to stand in line. Shame on you, people! The man gave one leg for the Fatherland and you force him to stand in line on the other!'

'I took a place in the queue myself,' the invalid protested. 'I'm not in a hurry.'

'Please, come here.' With polite firmness the NKVD guard took the soldier under his arm. 'Where did you lose your leg?' he inquired with loud sympathy, destined to teach the people to respect their fighting men.

'In the Ukraine,' the soldier said, limping on his crutches to the window. 'Near Poltava . . . Ticket to Kagan.' He put a paper on the counter. 'Here is my army ticket for exchange.'

'I've a brother at the Ukrainian front,' the Russian with the ragged valise said. 'In the seventy-first division.'

'They are fighting the best they can—our boys are,' commented the buxom woman behind Marek. 'We shouldn't blame them.'

'Nobody is blaming them.'

'Well, the Germans are advancing.'

'The other day at the Leningrad front our army took fifteen villages back, the radio said.'

'Yah, but that was an anniversary day,' the woman grinned.
'What do you mean?'

The woman shrugged and said nothing. The guard, leading
the soldier to the platform exit, glanced at her over his shoulder.
Marek's eyes travelled back to the Polish boys. They were busy
rolling themselves newspaper cigarettes and idly observing the
people lying on the benches and on the floor. Holding a ticket
in one hand and a bundle in another, Hamlat left the ticket
window, and as he passed near the line, his eyes swept over
Marek's face indifferently. But when he sat on the bundle in
the distant corner, after searching around the hall, his eyes
turned back to the queue and for a split second Marek met the
Uzbek's brow-lifted, inquiring look. Marek blinked reassuringly but his face swung to the door then to the wall clock and
an impatient frown came on his forehead. The clock showed
seven minutes past five.

The NKVD guard returned from the platform and
approached the fat matron in the line. 'Woman—Citizen!' he
said, beckoning gently with his finger. 'One second, please.'

The woman looked up timidly at his calm, round face, a
nervous tic making her lips quiver. 'What is it?'

'Just one second. They will keep your place for you.'

The woman wrapped her shawl closer around her head and
left the line. The people in the queue watched her walking
away beside the guard, her head time and again turning
inquiringly to the man's immobile face, before they both
disappeared behind a small narrow door without a sign.

'She should have kept her mouth shut,' the Russian man
said. The door of the men's toilet swung open as a charwoman
entered it with a can and broom. A sour smell swept into the hall
and mixed sickeningly with the thick odours of sweat and
tobacco. When Marek approached the ticket window, the
charwoman was back, her can full of water that spilled on the
floor. She closed the door behind her and waved an Uzbek
family away from a wall, so she could wash the floor. 'Two
tickets to Bokhara,' Marek said, with sudden fearful anticipation that the woman-cashier would say 'Just a second,' and

call an NKVD guard. He saw her turn to the stamping machine, heard two clicks and the tickets were laid in front of him.

'Sixteen fifty.'

He smiled at himself, paid the fare, but as he turned from the counter, his face grew troubled at the sight of the empty entrance and the clock's hand that moved uninterruptedly towards the time the train was scheduled to arrive.

The door of the dining hall opened and Marusia in a white waitress's apron came out, searching around the room till her eyes found Marek. She smiled and approached him quickly. 'I thought I'd say goodbye to you both. Where is Victor?'

"He should be here any moment now,' Marek said, peering wishfully at the door. 'He was to come here directly after his work."

Marusia glanced anxiously towards the dining hall. 'I've got to get back. I'll come again in ten minutes. Tell Victor to look out of the train's window. I brought my picture for him, so that the bastard won't forget me during these few days in Bokhara.' She winked and darted back into the dining room. Through the glass window, Marek saw a railway official pounding the table and snapping an angry complaint at Marusia for leaving him without service.

With a sudden rustle the loudspeaker hung on one of the walls awoke and a girl's voice announced first in Russian then in Uzbek that the train would be delayed for fifteen minutes. Marek grinned with relief. Beside him, a Russian woman was busy mixing green tea in a can of boiled water. Her blond, pig-tailed little daughter opened an old gramophone and put on a record. Through the trumpet-like rusty megaphone the melody 'Sasha, d'you remember our first rendezvous?' drifted into the hall. At the dining hall's door an Uzbek quarrelled with a guard, unable to understand that the place was reserved for railwaymen.

Again Marek's eyes travelled to the clock, then to the empty door, and again to the clock, with a worried stare that unsuccessfully tried to hold back the moving clock hands. The boys peered at him from the bench. Hamlat's face sent him a short, hardly perceptible message of anxious inquiry. Through the small door the NKVD guard returned without the woman, and with his foot jostling the people that lay on the floor, he ordered them to make room for the expected passengers of the incoming train. One of the Polish boys flashed Marek a smile, that did not draw a response from his aggrieved face. Suddenly a distant rattling was heard, becoming more distinct with every passing second. Nervously, Marek rubbed a hand across his neck. He jumped to his feet and ran to the station's entrance to peer out at the road leading to the depot, but he saw only the back of an old Uzbek swaying on a horse. For a second he thought that if he ran immediately, he could still get to the depot and back in time, before the train's departure. But then he remembered his brother's constant advice never to move from an arranged meeting spot. The sound of the train rolling over the rails into the station grew louder, like dramatic emphasis of the musical background in American films. The rattling stopped with a squeak, followed by wheezy locomotive gasps and the tumult of a human crowd. The people in the hall were pushing towards the door, and several railway guards summoned to help the NKVD men tried to push them back. 'No one will be allowed on the platform before the passengers come out!' an angry man's voice that replaced the girl-announcer's yelled over the loudspeaker. 'Step back or we'll let the train go without you!' Finally the crowd backed and split into rows, giving room to the incoming passengers, who crossed the hall with the usual hurry-home vigour. Helplessly, Marek saw Hamlat getting up and lifting his bundle. The boys got up from their place. Marek's body went limp and he felt a lump closing his throat. The clock showed half past five—the time that the train had originally been scheduled to leave.

Once more in the exit Hamlat looked back at him, and one of the three boys glanced over his shoulder and whispered some remark to his friend, who shrugged and hushed him up. In a moment the station hall was empty, with Marek alone hanging on to the door, his eyes focused on the sandy road with the swaying horse's rump receding in the distance.

Suddenly, he had a notion that his brother might be somewhere on the platform, and he dashed across the hall. 'I want to see if my brother is there,' he said at the door flashing his ticket to the ticket-taker. 'Don't punch it. I'll be right back.'

'Okay, go.'

Marek ran alongside the train, passing one car after another, searching the windows for Victor's face. His eyes swept over the faces of the Polish boys and stopped for a second on Hamlat's in the next window. A muscle on the Uzbek's cheek moved in a gesture calling him to get on the train without his brother. Marek shook his head, and went on running till he reached the locomotive. Then he went back re-checking the same windows. Finally, panting and sweating, he stopped beside a red-peaked station master and looked over the men queueing at the bubbling hot water faucet. 'Where is Victor?' he heard Marusia's voice behind him. Her eyes roamed searchingly over the train.

'I don't know what happened,' Marek said, biting his lips in impotent rage. His legs were all pins and needles and he could not marshal his thoughts to decide what to do.

'Why don't you run and see if he is at the depot?'

'I won't make it in time now.'

The station-master glanced at him. 'The train won't leave for another twenty minutes,' he said calmly. 'They're pouring water into the locomotive.'

'Oh, won't it? All right! Marusia, you stay here and if he comes in the meantime tell him I'll be back immediately.'

'I can't, Marek. I've got to go back to work.'

'Well, never mind then.'

'If he can't make it today, so what? You will go tomorrow or the day after.'

As Marek ran through the station hall, and across the square, and then sprinted into the road leading to the depot, the muscles in his jaw pulled nervously as they always did when he was frightened or enraged. The heat clung to his wet neck, and to his chest. The sun was in his eyes and the distant view of the road showed only in outline. Through the cactus wall, among the leaves, he could see tracks, coming in and separating and joining again to be linked by a railway switch. Finally he heard voices and saw the cactus wall end. The red brick depot building was on the other side of the tracks. Through its three large gates he could see locomotives with mechanics in overalls working on them. He cleared the rails, and reached the first worker, carrying a box with big nails. 'Have you seen Citizen Sobel? Do you know him?' Marek asked, puffing and blowing from the run.

The man put down the heavy box, wiped the sweat from his face and looked around. 'Don't ask me, boy. I never remember names.'

From behind a huge wooden hammer the head of another man lifted at the sound of the name. 'Oh, maybe you know my brother?'

The weasel eyes watched the big drops of sweat rolling over Marek's face. 'He is in the hospital.'

Marek's legs became instantly heavy. He gulped the air. 'God, what happened? An accident?'

'No, he just fell sick. They took him away about two hours ago.'

'What do you mean "They took him"? To what hospital?'

'Ask the supervisor.'

Marek walked down to the side track, where the supervisor sat on a stone in the shadow of a freight car, eating bread with herring. 'I'm Citizen Sobel's brother,' he said. 'What happened to him?'

'Oh,' the Russian said, chewing the bread. He swallowed and wiped his mouth. 'I suppose this intolerable heat knocked him down. He got shivery so I called the hospital and they sent a cart for him. Even here, in the shadow, one can hardly breathe.'

'Where is that hospital?'

'On the other side of the station. Follow the road near the track. About three kilometres behind the station. Or maybe four.'

'Thank you.'

'I'm sure he'll be all right in a day or two. Tell him not to rush back to work till he feels well.'

Marek walked back to the road. But once there, he started to run again as if he could still get his brother to the train in time. The chanting of the Uzbeks unloading cotton bales from a caravan of carts came to his ears, growing louder with his approach to the station. As he crossed the tumultuous square he saw the train still standing. 'Marek!' There was Marusia running towards him down the steps. 'I noticed you through the window. Well, where is he?'

'In the hospital. He fell ill on the job. This heat took hold of him.'

'Are you going there?'

'Yes.'

'I'll be right there. The dining hall closes in fifteen minutes.' She dashed back into the station.

Marek entered a dirt road, pounded by horses' hooves and marked by wheel ruts, with a few bare, truncated, dusty, smelling trees on one side, close to the track. A cart was blocking the road, with an Uzbek pulling his donkey's head and talking to him to persuade the stubborn animal to move forward. Behind him, Marek heard a sudden whistle, a few shuddering gasps and the slow clatter of the trains. He stopped abruptly, and with black misery gnawing at his heart, watched the grey-blue streak of smoke approach, and heard the swelling noise of the wheels. Then over a few curved spines of cactus appeared the locomotive, followed by passenger cars, that one by one reached Marek's level, then passed him by. He saw Hamlat's face in one of the windows and the Polish boys' heads protruding from the next one. His lips throbbed and a quivering blob of pain twinged in his chest. For a long time he stood on the road, motionless, following the iron, smoking serpent that wound across the saturated valley, glittering under the level light, and then disappeared at the horizon, where the rocky mountains rose into the sky.

The donkey cart overtook him now, with the Uzbek smacking his lips to urge his animal not to change his mind. He looked at Marek's red, sweaty face, and waved to him to take a place beside him. Marek jumped on to the cart. 'Going to the hospital?' he asked. The bewhiskered man smiled and said nothing. 'Do you speak Russian?' The man smiled again and nodded, then said something in Uzbek. 'All right,' Marek nodded. As the cart went slowly on, his eyes roamed over the mountains with the weary, sorrowful expression of a man who has suddenly had all his dreams, so close to realization, shattered. The driver pulled a pouch from his pocket and offered Marek a pinch of tobacco. Marek shook his head and nodded thanks. Impatient minutes of travel dragged on with the two men silent and only the donkey's hollow steps and the rattle of the wooden wheels heard in the quiet, deserted road. A few wooden barracks appeared in front of them. When the Uzbek turned his cart into a side road, away from the railway track, Marek pointed out the direction in which he was going, and jumped from the cart waving his thanks for the ride.

Now rested, he began to run again. On his left, under an old mud wall on the slope of the hill, lay an Uzbek cemetery with its barrel-shaped mud tombs. Shortly afterwards Marek found himself in front of a big billboard with painted white letters: 'Kermine Town Hospital No. 1.' Over the short gravelled piece of road, he reached the four wooden barracks. Around the last one, workers were putting up a fence of barbed wire under the supervision of two armed soldiers. A small sign 'Administration' hung over the first door Marek came across.

He entered a small room, and an aproned, motherly-looking nurse raised her kindly fat face from a magazine. 'Yes?' Behind the plywood wall Marek heard the hiss of a gas stove.

'You brought Victor Sobel here about two hours ago. I'm his brother. What's the matter with him?'

'I've been away this afternoon,' the woman said and reached for a book from a drawer. 'Sobel, you say?' she asked, moving her forefinger down the list. 'Oh, yes . . . ' Her lips moved, as she tried to decipher the hardly legible entry of the doctor. Her head suddenly lifted and she gave Marek a long look. 'Just a second. Pavel Stepanovicz! Will you come for a second?'

From behind the plywood wall came a tall, lean, grey-haired, and grey-bearded doctor, holding a steaming cup of tea in his hand. 'Here is your tea, Anna Matviejevna.'

'Thank you. This is Victor Sobel's brother.'

'How is he?' Marek asked.

The nurse put her cup on the table and showed the doctor the open registration book. Pavel Stepanovicz waved the book away. 'I know the case.'

'Where is your cup? Shall I get you one?'

The doctor nodded, as his mild blue eyes examined Marek's face. 'He has typhus,' he said slowly, taking off his pince-nez and rubbing his nose.

Marek thought the earth was opening under him. He felt dazed as if he hadn't quite understood. 'Typhus? . . . ' he murmured with quivering lips, tears coming into his throat.

'An epidemic has broken out,' the doctor said, polishing the pince-nez with a handkerchief. 'A few days ago we couldn't even identify the illness.' The nurse came back with a cup of tea and placed it in front of the doctor on the table. 'Thank you, Anna Matviejevna.' He looked at Marek's clouded, imploring eyes. 'We'll do all we can,' he said.

12

THE NURSE PULLED A TIN box out of the drawer and opened it. 'Sugar, Pavel Stepanovicz.'

'Thank you, Anna Matviejevna.' The doctor got himself a lump of sugar and put it into his mouth, lifted the cup, and after blowing a few times on the hot liquid, took a loud sip.

'May I see my brother?' Marek asked.

'See your brother? You don't want to get typhus too, do you?'

'I can't get it,' Marek said, his voice calm and even. 'I had typhus when I was a kid.'

'You had it? . . . Where?' the doctor asked suspiciously.

'In Poland.'

Small washed-out eyes held Marek's face for a second. 'You come from Poland?'

'Yes,' Marek said after a moment's hesitation.

'What town?'

'Brest Litovsk.'

The doctor moved his cup on the saucer, then again blew on the still steaming tea. 'When did you leave Poland?'

'Two years ago.'

In the door appeared a little plump woman, carrying a basket of piled-up rough blankets. The nurse took the basket from her and placed it in the corner. The doctor twirled the spoon in the cup, forgetting that he held the sugar in his mouth. 'Take this boy to barrack No. 3, Anna Matviejevna,' he said. 'Ten minutes—no more. Do not sit on the bed or touch anything in the barrack. Even if you did have typhus in Poland.'

'Thank you, Doctor.'

'Will you come with me?' The nurse walked out, Marek following her.

There, outside the office, Marusia was waiting, holding the corners of a white shawl wrapped hurriedly around her head. 'What's wrong with him?' She leaned forward, her forehead curling with anxiety.

'He has typhus.' Marek saw her lips tremble and then she burst out crying. He walked on to join the nurse who had already passed through the entrance between the barbed wires.

Marusia trotted quickly behind him. 'Are you going to see him?'

'Yes.'

Heavy tears were coursing down her cheeks. 'Can't I come with you?'

'I'm afraid not.' He entered the enclosure.

'Marek!' Marusia shouted through a smothered cry. 'Tell him to look through the window! I'll be standing outside!'

Marek and the nurse climbed a few steps and crossed the little dim corridor to a door over which hung a red bulb. The woman turned the knob and Marek saw a very large room with several dozen wooden beds. The patients lay on their backs motionless, staring vacantly into space, as if in a stupor. But here and there some of them would awake for a moment, moan with pain and restlessly toss their heads and then again relapse into this strange state of trance. The room was filled with the sourish odours of sweat, medicines, and urine from white pots under the beds. In one of the far corners two orderlies were trying to place a man on a stretcher. Anna Matviejeva stopped at a black board with chalked columns of names, numbers of beds, and their temperatures. 'Sobel, you said?'

'Yes.'

He made a few steps between the beds, searching the sweaty faces, dried like parchment, burned by fever to the colour of brown earth, partially buried in pillows of folded jackets or overalls. The orderlies passed by with the stretcher and Marek noticed that the blanket was covering both the body and the face. His knees suddenly became heavy and his eyes instantly swept over the beds with a prayer that he would find his brother lying there on one of them. The nurse's voice behind him, saying, 'Bed 23, in the fourth row,' calmed him. 'I'll be back in ten minutes.' She left.

Marek approached the iron bed with the number-tag tied to its front. He saw the profile of a face with red spotted cheeks and the corners of parched, throbbing lips, whispering as if in sleep. 'Victor!' There was no answer and he repeated his brother's name. Slowly, the head turned and he saw the swollen, perspiring face of a stranger, whose clouded, red-rimmed eyes looked up at him dully. 'It's me, Marek. How do you feel?' He forced his face into a bright smile of welcome, as he tried hard to fight back his tears. The scorched lips moved in hard, laboured spasms of breath, but no words came through. 'It's me, Marek—your brother!' Heavy drops of sweat appeared on Victor's forehead and rolled down his face. When his head bowed slightly and his mouth curled in what was meant to be a smile but was a momentarily painful twist of the lips. 'I just saw the doctor,' Marek said cheerily. 'He said you will be all right soon. They will take good care of you!'

Victor looked into his brother's face and after a second his lips moved. 'Hamlat?' he gasped. 'Hamlat?' His mouth remained open, as if he were unable to close it, and Marek saw that it was foul and that his tongue was coated with a dense, brown fur.

'He left, but he will soon . . .' Marek did not finish because Victor made a sudden attempt to sit up in bed, and Marek rushed to him, and if in the last moment he had not remembered the doctor's warning, he would have pressed Victor's shoulders down to keep him from getting up. 'Be quiet, Victor!'

'Why didn't you go?' His face was shrivelled with pain and his hands trembled.

'How could I leave you? He will be back. After he takes these three boys over there, he will come back and take us.'

'What boys?'

'Those three Polish boys that had to go with us, don't you remember?' Victor's forehead wrinkled with effort. 'Well, never mind. He'll come back and as soon as you are all right, we'll leave—together.'

Victor's eyes closed wearily as if they could not stand even the dusky light of the barrack. Marek could hear the loud, feverish hiss of his breath resume.

On the left of Victor's bed the low moan of a strained-faced man with suppurating eyes grew into a painful lament, broken only by convulsions of tearless sobbing. 'Do you need anything?' Marek asked his brother. Victor's eyes opened again, then he shook his head absently. Marek looked at the folded jacket under his head, and the dirty undershirt over his chest, exposing a coppery skin rash. 'I'll get you a pillow and linen. And I'll buy you pyjamas in the market. It must be cold here in the night. Are you cold?' Victor nodded. 'I'll get you another blanket. Did they give you a meal?'

'I don't want any.'

'But you must eat. Shall I get food for you?'

'Not now. Later.'

'They only let me in here for ten minutes. I'll see you again tomorrow or the day after. You'll be much better by then.' Victor's head shook in a slow denial. 'Oh, don't start talking nonsense. The doctor said you'll be all right soon.'

'I won't.'

'Oh, God! What's happened to you? You were always so sure of yourself.'

His brother's eyes blinked drowsily. 'I'm not sure any more . . .'

'But Victor, please . . .' That was all Marek could manage. A sore lump in his throat did not allow him to marshal his thoughts, as he tried vainly to talk about something, anything, just to get his brother out of this apathetic, turbid state that came with the sickness. Then through the window, behind the barbed wires, he saw Marusia on her toes. The red brilliance of departing daylight shone on her face peering towards the barrack. 'Marusia is outside,' he said, attempting a light, garden-party tone of voice. 'Why don't you raise your hand and wave to her, eh?' Victor's eyes blinked tiredly and Marek knew his brother did not understand what he was saying. In the first row a stocky, green-shirted man abruptly sat up in bed and, raising his fist, yelled frightfully, 'Fix bayonets! . . . Company ahead to attack! . . . Charge!' His hand swished through the air several times as he summoned the rows of unwilling patients to move against the enemy. 'Come on! . . . Soldiers! . . . Forward!' From the door emerged the plump figure of Anna Matviejevna rushing to the shouting patient, 'Calm down, Sergeant, please. You're in the hospital, not at the front.' She held cold sponges against the patient's forehead. Slowly, the battle shouts died away and the nurse laid the exhausted man down. She attended to a patient, shaken by a sudden fit of coughing accompanied by a severe nosebleed, then directed the orderly to change the blanket of a man who had involuntarily passed urine. 'Time,' she turned to Marek. 'Ten minutes have passed.'

'I'm leaving in a second.' There were a hundred things that Marek wanted to tell his brother at once. About all their work to get out of Russia, the nearness of the border, his need for his brother, and the waiting of their parents for their return. An orderly entered the hospital barrack with a box of dried dung cakes and began to build a fire in the iron stove that had a pipe curving to the upper part of the front walls. 'You'd better go,' the nurse said, walking among the rows of beds, scrutinizing the sick.

'Marek!' Victor whispered, and he bent over him. 'They have my trousers. There are five hundred roubles there. And my fountain pen and the documents.'

'All right.'

'Take them, because they may steal them—you know.'

'Time,' the nurse said, moving Victor's weeping neighbour on to his side and covering him with a blanket.

'Be good, Victor. I'll see you soon.' He saw the heavy, exhausted lids drooping again over the eyes. As he crossed the barrack towards the door, among the pants and groans behind him, he could distinguish the uneven whistling gasps of his brother. Even when he walked outside towards the exit in the barbed wire, this tortured hiss was in his ears, and it took him a whole minute before he noticed that Marusia was beside him, asking him over and over, 'Why didn't you tell him to look out? Why?!'

'I did, but he couldn't make it. He is very ill.'

She made a thwarted gesture in the air and fixed her eyes on the tips of her shoes.

'Going home?' she asked quietly after a while.

'Yes. . . . Wait for me a second. I'll come right back.'

He walked into the office. The doctor was sitting behind the table, a new cup of fuming tea in front of him. His forefinger wandered over a small Russian atlas. 'Yes?' he asked, reacting to the sounds of steps, his eyes focused on his map. Then he groped for his cup and looked up. 'Oh, it's you?'

'My brother told me that his trousers are here and asked me to get them.'

'How will he walk out of the hospital?' the doctor quipped.

'I just want to get some things out of his pockets.'

'You don't trust us, eh?' Humorous lights played in the doctor's amiable little eyes, as his hand left the cup and twirled the top of his beard. 'Misha!' he shouted. After a while a red-cheeked, thin-mouthed orderly emerged from the courtyard.

'Bring the trousers of Comrade Sobel,' he said. 'But be sure they have been disinfected. Otherwise leave them where they are. Sit down, young man. It will take him a while.' As Marek sat on a stool, the doctor turned the atlas around, pointing to a name with his finger. 'Here is your town,' he smiled. 'Right?'

'Yes.'

'I like to play with maps. I can do a lot of travelling this way.' He turned the map to himself and examined it again. 'There is no Poland on it. Just the German-Russian border. But don't worry. It will be on there again after this war.' His eyes squinted thoughtfully and his lips rehearsed some silent words. Then he said in broken Polish: ' "Poland is not yet lost while we live." Right?'

Startled, Marek looked into the doctor's face. 'You . . . Polish?'

'Was—was,' the doctor said. 'I came to Russia right after the 1905 revolution. Almost forgot the language. But I still remember the words of the anthem. We used to live in Lublin. Do you know the town, it's not far from yours?'

'I do,' Marek said, 'but I've never been there.'

The orderly entered the room with Victor's trousers. 'They were boiled only two hours ago. Aren't quite dry yet.' Anxiously, Marek plunged his hand into a back pocket and came out with Victor's wallet. He opened it, saw money and documents in order, pulled out the pen from another pocket, then returned the trousers to the orderly. 'Thank you,' he said, getting up. The orderly left, passing in the exit a small chubby Uzbek woman, holding a barefooted boy by the hand, both peering shyly inside. 'Wait,' the doctor told Marek. 'I'll be right with you.'

'What's the matter, Grandma?'

'The boy has headaches and he vomits. I don't know what's wrong with him. So I came to ask for medicine. They told me I wouldn't have to pay.' Marek looked at the boy and recognized the tea-house helper.

As the doctor approached the youngster, he stepped back,

frightened. 'Don't worry, I'm not going to eat you. Well, come on!'

'Go,' the woman said, pushing the boy forward. 'Citizen Doctor will stop your pains.'

'Show me where it hurts.' The boy pointed to the top of his head and groaned, more from fear than actual pain. Humming an old tune, the doctor divided the hard, bristly hair to get to the skin. Then the tune broke and Marek saw something unbelievable. It looked like a nest in the head, with hundreds of busy insects running back and forth. But they weren't ants—they were lice.

'God!' Marek turned his eyes away.

The doctor unbuttoned the shirt over the boy's protruding belly and exposed a mulberry rash on the dark skin. 'Show me your tongue.' The boy opened his mouth and kept it open, unable to stick out his tongue. Pavel Stepanovicz nodded to himself, then walked out, and came back with the nurse. He gave her orders to take the boy to the bathroom, shave his hair and wash him, and give him a bed in the Barrack 3. 'We'll have to put him in the hospital,' he informed the old woman.

'Why? Can't you give him something for his headache right here?'

'I'm afraid not.' As the nurse was taking the boy out, he turned in the door, his eyes as frightened as if he were being led to his execution.

'When will he be back from the hospital?' the woman asked dully.

'I don't know.'

'I'm too old to work. The boy earns our living. Does he get his pay while he is in the hospital?'

'I don't know, Grandma, I'm just a doctor. You ask the labour office.'

The woman nodded, wrapped her head in the shawl and, with a heavy sigh, left.

'I'm sorry you had to see it. I didn't expect it to be another case of typhus.'

'Well, I must go. Someone is waiting for me outside. I do

hope you'll take good care of my brother. He is the only person I have. My parents remained over there.'

'And so did mine,' the doctor said slowly, smoothing the puffiness under his eyes.

'Please, tell me, Doctor,' Marek said, 'how bad is it? I lied to him, I told him that he would soon be all right, but please tell me, how is he really?'

The doctor opened a book with the data on patients. 'He is in the third or fourth day of the disease. It's hard to say. Maybe even the fifth.'

'You mean he didn't know he was ill?'

'When I contracted typhus twenty years ago, I didn't know I had it for a week.' He glanced at Marek. 'How was it with you?'

'How long does it take?'

'The crisis usually comes on the twelfth or thirteenth day. The temperature, which stays very high all the time, suddenly drops below normal in a few hours. Then it is all a matter of heart. If you've a strong heart, if it can stand this sudden change of temperature, you live; if your heart is weak—well, then it depends on camphor and caffein and glucose, and adrenalin if it's very bad, so that these medicines can boost your heart.'

Marek smiled with relief as he leaned forward across the table. It was the first time he had smiled that day. 'Thank you, Doctor,' he said gratefully. 'Now I won't worry so much. My brother is strong as an ox. He's one of the healthiest men you can imagine.'

The doctor's eyes remained fixed on the cup of cold tea. He moved it back and forth on the saucer before he said, 'Unfortunately, your brother's heart is weak.'

Marek gulped the air as he stared miserably at the doctor. 'You must have made a mistake. He never complained of heart trouble, never was ill in his life. He always did all my jobs for me, because he was the strong one.'

'I've examined him very carefully. I could not have made a mistake.'

Sweat broke out on Marek's forehead and he rubbed his face.

There was a pressure behind his throat that he could hardly control. 'What about those medicines you mentioned? Please don't spare them!'

'I'm afraid we don't have any of those medicines. We were not prepared for epidemics. I cabled Moscow, though, and hope to get them in a few days. Meantime,' and the doctor spread his arms, 'we use—aspirin.' He looked up at Marek, who stood immobile, speechless, his eyes fixed absently at the cup of tea on the table. 'I'll let you come here every day for a short while. If the heart can't help, nor the medicines, because we lack them, maybe you can.'

'Thank you, Doctor.'

'You're welcome.'

In the door Marek turned. 'May I bring my brother a pillow and linen tonight? So he will be more comfortable.'

'Yes. Give them to the nurse. If you can, get some port wine for him. It's a good stimulant. And maybe some rice. He has diarrhoea and his stomach won't hold any other food.'

'I'll get them. Thank you, Doctor.'

When he walked out of the room, he had to stop for a second till his dazed eyes could see through the black curtain of the night that had fallen a short while ago. Marusia's silhouette rose from a bench to join him. 'What did the doctor say?' Marek explained his brother's condition to her, as they walked along the hospital road, its fresh gravel crunching under their feet. When they reached the dirt road that led to town, they both turned and for a moment gazed at the distant barrack behind the barbed wire. The windows were lit up and in their light they could see a blue streak of smoke rising from a hole in the front wall and the silhouettes of immobile soldiers with their bayonets on their rifles, hung over their shoulders. Marusia took Marek's hand and led him away. They resumed their walk over the quiet, dark road, parallel to the railway track Marek had watched so frequently the last few days. A sudden gust of wind whisked the sand from desert dunes on to the road and brought the sound of bells from a distant caravan. The sky was dark and starless; only in front of them the lights of the town glimmered reddishly like sparks hanging in the air.

13

THE OIL LAMP STANDING ON the stool in the room's corner cast a faint glow over the low ceiling, over the stripped bed, over Marek's figure at the table, his head buried in his hands. There was a gentle knocking, and Marek raised his head, and listened absently, as if the knocking was at the neighbour's door. 'Is there anyone in?' he heard Ibram's inquiring voice.

'Come in.'

The door opened and the short-sleeved figure of Ibram appeared in the threshold. 'Good evening.'

'Good evening.'

'There was a man from NKVD here, asking for you and your brother.'

Marek stared dully at Ibram's face. 'What did he want?' he asked after a while in a low, tired voice.

'He wondered if you were still in town. I didn't know you wanted to go away.' He looked at Marek and his voice quivered a little when he asked, 'Where are you going to?'

Marek shrugged. 'We're not going anywhere.'

Ibram's eyes fell on the stripped bedstead. 'What happened to the bed?'

'My brother is in the hospital. They didn't have any linen there. Not even a pillow. I should have asked you——'

'What's the matter with him?'

'He has typhus. They promised to disinfect the bedding . . .'

'Typhus? . . . We haven't had a case of typhus in Uzbekistan since the epidemics shortly after the revolution.'

'It has broken out again. The hospital was packed with cases.'

Ibram shook his head with consternation. His eyes travelled again to the bed. 'If there is anything I can do,' he said after a pause with comradely compassion.

'Thank you.'

'I have to go now. I hope your brother will be all right.' He turned to the door.

'Did this man say I should come to the NKVD office?'

'No. He said they were just making a routine check of all newcomers.'

'I'm sorry about the linen and pillow.'

Ibram waved his hand, dismissing Marek's concern for the bedding, and grunted sympathetically on his way out. In the door he turned, however, as if wanting to ask something, but then apparently he changed his mind, for he walked out without saying a word. Marek heard Shukunov's door open and shut and after a few minutes open again and shut again; then footsteps receding, until they died away down the road.

A whimper of wind, blowing across the courtyard, drummed against the window and rattled the open door. The flame of the lamp flickered, arousing the shadows on the walls. Marek stared at the courtyard darkness, seeing the image of the hospital barrack, with the lead-coloured light of the sunset falling through the window on his brother's unfamiliar, sweaty face. Marek's lips moved, rehearsing words of consolation and courage to give his brother on his next visit. He suddenly wished that his mother were here to take care of Victor as she had always done when he, himself, had been ill. As if it had happened yesterday, he saw himself in bed in a long night-shirt tied at his neck, having mumps, with a row of medicine bottles at his bed-table, the doctor visiting him daily, and his mother spending most of her time by his side. He recollected his anxious inquiry whether he was gravely ill, and with the mother's nod, the sudden feeling of fear and pride that swelled his little chest. He was at a period of endless questions, and he asked several in rapid succession: 'How serious is mumps?' and 'Can a person die of mumps?' and 'What are the worst illnesses in the world?'

'Cholera,' his mother had answered, he remembered, 'leprosy and typhus.'

'And mumps?' he heard his own high-pitched, disappointed voice of fifteen years ago.

'It's very grave but not as grave as typhus.'

Again he saw the hospital barrack and Victor's dishevelled hair, parched lips, and the red spots on his restless face, and he heard his brother's gasp, 'I'm not so sure any more.' And suddenly Marek broke down. His head fell over his crossed arms on the table and a fit of uncontrollable sobbing shook his body. A fresh gust of wind ruffled his hair and chilled his face. Slowly he regained control of himself and wiped the tears from his eyes. When he opened them, by the fitful glow of the lamp, he saw Ajmi, standing immobile, watching him silently from the door, a bundle of fresh bedding in her arms.

He blinked, and uncomfortably turned his face away from her. He heard the door close and saw her felt shoes passing him by, then he raised his eyes and regarded her agile, supple back, bent over the bed. Absently he listened to the rustle of fresh stiff linen in her hands. 'Thank you,' he said, when she patted a pillow over the spread blanket.

She turned her head to him. 'Have you eaten?'

'I don't want to.'

'I'll bring you some soup left from dinner.' Ajmi walked out, paying no attention to his protests, and a few minutes later came back with a bowl of hot barley soup, and a chunk of bread. As she stopped behind the table to make certain that he was eating, Marek took a few spoons of the thick liquid. 'You mustn't cry,' she said. 'A man shouldn't cry.'

He looked up at her face filled with candour and sympathy, framed by a black head-shawl kept close to her chin. Under his gaze, her heavy lids fell, screening her eyes. She walked to the lamp and turned up its wick. Then she sat opposite Marek on a stool, waiting for him to finish his meal.

Marek put the bowl aside. 'I can't eat, I just can't.'

'You must eat. One can't live without eating.' She pushed the bowl back towards Marek. He again, reluctantly, took the spoon. Her slanted dark eyes stayed for a moment on the untouched slice of bread. 'My parents died of typhus,' she said slowly, 'when I was a child.' Marek's eyes darted to her face, but he said nothing. 'Your brother, I'm afraid,' Ajmi went on, her eyes pensively fastened on the table's edge, 'got it from Raim. Now I know it was typhus that killed him.' She lifted her head, an expression of utmost guilt crossing her face. Then she got up and walked to the window. Behind it the white laundry hung out on a line fluttered up and down in the wind. She looked at the dark clouds gathering in the sky. 'A Buran is coming in from the desert.' She turned to Marek. 'Does your brother get enough food over there?' In her voice Marek read the association of memories of post-revolutionary years of starvation when the epidemics that killed her parents had broken out.

'The doctor said some rice and wine may help. I don't know where to get them. The wine in the wine-shop on Shadiva Street is sour, and the grocer never has rice in his store.'

'I'll get them for you.' She threw him a quick measuring look. 'Don't tell my husband. He doesn't let me buy things on the black market. He's afraid I'll get caught. There's quite a severe penalty for it, higher than for stealing.'

'I wouldn't want you to take the risk. Why don't you tell me where to go?'

'They wouldn't sell it to you, they don't know you. Don't worry, I have my ways.'

Marek got up and pulled money out of his pocket. 'Here, will fifty roubles be enough?'

'When I bring the things, you give me the money then.'

'Thank you, Ajmi.'

'Now finish your soup and bread.' Obediently Marek sat down and ate. When he finished, he smiled faintly as he pushed the empty bowl and spoon aside.

She went to the table and took the bowl. 'Where is Poland?'

'Poland?'

'This NKVD man said you were from Poland.'

'Oh, it's far away. About ten thousand kilometres, or more.'

'What's the country like?'

'Oh, it's full of forests and meadows.'

A wistful smile appeared on the girl's lips. 'I have never seen a forest or meadow in my life. It's nice when all around you is green, isn't it?'

'Oh yes, very nice.'

She sat on a stool and propped her chin on her palms. 'Your parents are there?'

'Yes.'

'You don't get letters from them?'

'How could I? The Germans are there.'

'Oh. . . .' She nodded thoughtfully, stood up, then picked up the spoon from the table. 'You want some tea?'

'No, thank you very much.'

Ajmi drew her head-shawl around her chin. 'Good night.'

'Good night, Ajmi.'

He caught her throwing a fleeting glance into the room, as she passed by the window. He crossed the room and watched her figure among the clothes-lines in the courtyard, struggling with the fierce wind that billowed up the white linen and her own robe. She finally piled up all the laundry and carried the bundle into her house.

Marek remained at the window, staring out at the white chimney of a hut across the street, shining hazily under the misty pale moon. In the distance dogs howled and from the desert jackals whined in response. Marek turned down the wick of the lamp and blew out the flame. The room merged into darkness, relieved only by a moonbeam that made its way slowly over the table and part of the wall.

He undressed and lay down in bed, covering himself with the camel-hair blanket. Closing his eyes, he focused all his senses on his own body, wondering whether a fever was rising in him, alert to any itch on his skin or a sign of a wandering infected louse. The doctor's pale blue eyes peered at him from behind the pince-nez and his lips were saying, 'If the heart and medicine can't help, maybe you can.' Marek shook his head and opened his eyes, wishing that he had just awakened and that it was all a bad dream and that Victor was snoring peacefully at his side. But he was alone in bed. The dark room looked odd and alien without the outlines of Victor's clothes hanging on the wall, without his shoes on the floor and without his wrist-watch shining on the table. After a while Marek cupped his hands behind his head and stared into space. Sometime during the night he heard Ibram's returning steps, then the shutting of the door behind him. Twice he listened as the sound of a cudgel banging on the gates of the courtyards approached and receded—the night watchman's message that he was earning his pay.

When the low mist began to creep up, erasing the inky surface of the sky, the dawn's pearly violet drifted into the room and lit up Marek's face, and his untired eyes that had kept a night-long watch. It was the first time in his whole life that he had been in a house without his parents or his brother.

14

MAREK AWOKE WITH THE FEELING that he was being observed. Ajmi was sitting on a stool. But she did not look at him, she was looking out of the window. The sun was coming into the room, throwing bright splashes of colour on to the table, lighting up a bottle of red wine and an improvised cone of newspaper. She gave a start, looked at him, and stood up. 'I brought you rice and wine.'

Marek sat up in bed and rubbed his face. 'Thank you, Ajmi. What do I owe you?' He reached for his trousers lying on a stool.

'Ten roubles.'

'Ten roubles?'

'Yes, I got the stuff from a friend,' she answered, her eyes fixed on the small rug hung on the wall that Marek and Victor had got from Ulug Beg.

He put the money on the table. 'Thank you. What time is it now?'

She peeped out of the window. 'Around noon.'

'Aren't you working today?'

'We cleaned up the canals. There won't be work for us until the second harvest—in December.' Ajmi made a step towards the door. 'I brought you water.' She pointed to the full bucket in the corner. 'I'll clean up your room when you go out.' She took the money from the table and left.

Marek leaped from the bed, poured water into the basin and rinsed his face vigorously. As he was drying himself, he heard a knock at the door. 'Who is there?'

'Citizen Sobel?'

'Yes?' Marek glanced through the window and saw a man in front of his room. He went to the door and pushed it open. A long-jawed face, blue-black with beard, looked at him.

'Men are coming here to disinfect the room. When you go out, leave it open.' The man pulled a notebook out of his pocket and presented it to Marek, pointing to Victor's name at the bottom of a long column of names and addresses. 'Please sign on the same line.'

Marek signed. 'When do you think the men will come here? I would like to disinfect my clothes as well.'

'It will take them several hours before they reach your street.' The man chalked a big white circle over the door, then left.

Marek dressed hastily. He wrapped the bottle and the bag together in a newspaper and scuttled out of the room. Hurriedly he strided down Achum Babayeffa Street, his shoes whipping dust into the thick sultry air. A few Uzbek women stood in front of a house, exchanging the day's gossip in discreet whispers that died for a moment as he passed them. From around the street corner a girl appeared barefoot, bent under the weight of a wooden yoke with a pair of water-filled buckets. The shadows clung to the mud walls, too low to give protection from the blistering heat. When Marek reached the main street, the sweat rolled from his face and he constantly had to moisten his lips, dried out by the torrid, desert wind. The street was almost empty, and only a few people were gathered around the loudspeaker to listen to the news bulletin announcing the fall of Kharkov. The barber-shop was closed. Opposite, in the entrance of the czaikhana, Marek could see the pot-bellied manager, sweating from the sun and the samovar, despatching a new helper with fuming pots and towels to his only customers, a group of three goat-bearded Uzbeks crosslegged on a carpet.

A cart went lazily along the street, its huge wooden wheels squealing on the uneven road, carrying a fur-hatted Kirghiz with two unsold, caged hunting eagles from the bazaar. Marek crossed the street and entered the grocery store.

Behind the counter an auburn-bearded manager was reading a paper that had been published in Moscow a few months ago. The shelves of the store were nicely decorated with empty cans and crêpe paper. Across a great dustless square on the wall, where a picture had once been, hung a red-lettered poster, 'Everything for the front.'

'Did you finally get our rations.'

The grocer folded his paper aside and said with a glittering smile, 'No, but I've got chocolate. Last bar—especially kept for you.' He looked at Marek, while his hand fumbled in some secret place under the counter, and then swiftly came out, with a magician's emphasis, displaying the chocolate bar in the air.

'Is that all?'

'You'll get the rest in a day or two.'

'You're always telling me the same story.'

'What can I do?' the grocer said, spreading his hands. 'Everything for the front!' He made a broad gesture towards the sign on the wall.

Marek took the chocolate and paid. And as he walked to the door, holding it in his hand, a wry smile crossed his lips at the thought of the curiously remote day-dreams about the hard brown tablet that would crunch and melt sweetly in his mouth. The empty bus creaked and moaned past the street, its driver not bothering to halt at the stop where no one waited nor anyone descended. In Makul Ol Square three people queued up outside the unopened news-stand, rolling cigarettes in the paper that one of them courteously shared with the two others. From a side-road two white-aproned, rubber-gloved men walked out, dragging heavy spraying equipment. Marek stopped and waited, wondering if they would go towards his house to disinfect his room. But the men crossed Shadiva Street and entered the road leading to the bazaar. He watched them stop at a house and knock at the door marked with a white circle

'Citizen,' Marek heard behind him. 'Will you come with me for a moment?'

He turned quickly and recognized the fat uniformed NKVD man who had awakened him and Victor on their second night in town. 'What is it?' he asked, gulping, clasping the package tightly to his chest. The muscle in his cheek twitched in its usual uncontrollable manner.

'Someone wants to ask you a few questions, that's all.'

As they walked past Shadiva Street, the prying eyes of the passers-by would linger on them for a second, then cautiously turn away. On the door-steps of the wine store sat its manager, nibbling on sunflower seeds with grim concentration. He glanced curiously at Marek and the NKVD man, then turned to a railwayman knocking on the closed door of the glass craftsman's shop. 'The Tajik is in the hospital.'

'I gave him my glass lampshade to repair. I'm leaving today.' Marek heard the railwayman's angry words, punctuated by a distant curse, as they turned into a side street.

'Are we going to Comrade Kisielev?'

'You'll see.'

All the questions Kisielev might possibly ask him skimmed the surface of his mind as he absently watched an Uzbek on a hill behind a low courtyard wall, spreading grapes on the earth to dry for raisins. A barefoot woman stopped washing her clothes in the dirty street canal to look at them across the street.

They stopped in front of the NKVD building. The NKVD man rapped with the iron knocker. In a moment Marek saw the Ukrainian's face. He nodded to Marek's escort. 'Go in,' the NKVD guard said.

As Marek was passing along the narrow corridor, he mustered his composure and it was with a calm, serene face that he entered the room and faced Kisielev. But no familiar smile was fixed on the Russian's lips, nor did the friendly wave of a newspaper welcome Marek. Kisielev sat grimly in his straw-bottomed chair, in a waiting pose, impatiently twirling a lighted cigarette in his hand. 'Sit down,' he said in a let's-get-down-to-business tone. Marek lowered himself slowly into a chair, putting the package at his feet.

Kisielev got up. His new leather boots creaked at every step as he crossed the room to the window to pull down the blinds. The alternate streaks of light and shadow that striped the wall were washed out by the piercing beam of the standing lamp that Kisielev turned on Marek. He became dazed and blinked his eyes when the first question was flung at him: 'Why didn't you cross the border?'

'What do you mean?' Marek's throat was dry and his voice sounded hoarse. His whole body went limp because this was one question he hadn't rehearsed an answer to.

'I mean,' Kisielev said with an icy smile, sitting down at the table and moving the lamp left and right, so its light played over Marek's face, 'that you and your brother came to Kermine to contact a smuggler, who would take you to Persia. You got in touch with a man and arranged everything in detail. Right?'

'I don't know what you are talking about,' Marek said, trying to keep his face away from the piercing beam of light that was sweeping on and off across his face. He heard an edge creeping into his voice, accompanied by a trifle of accent which he could not hide. 'We did not contact any man nor did we intend to cross the border. Why, we're happy in the Soviet Union.'

Kisielev smiled indulgently and suddenly switched to his nonchalent, detached way of talking. 'Does the name Hamlat mean anything to you?' He paused before the name. 'Do you know him, or don't you?' Marek's shoulders dropped and he clasped his hand between his knees, conflicting thoughts confusedly hammering at his mind. 'You don't have your brother with you, so don't wait for him to prompt you now. Answer!'

The sharp abruptness of the last word started Marek. 'Yes, I know him. But I didn't know he was a smuggler.'

'Didn't you? Why did you go to his house, eh?'

Past the sharp ray of light, Marek looked slowly at Kisielev. For the first time he saw something he hadn't noticed before—

under the small, alert eyes tiny crowsfeet were forming. 'I've never been to Hamlat's house,' Marek said, surprised at the even, smooth tones of his voice. 'My brother and I met him at the house of Ulug Beg.'

'What did you do there?'

Now the accent disappeared completely from Marek's speech. 'We've been there twice. The first time we bought skull-caps and the second time a rug. We have it hanging in our room, if you want to see it.'

'Don't try to be too clever with me.' Kisielev leaned forward to Marek. 'What were you doing on Friday at five o'clock at the station?'

'I had to meet my brother after his work.'

'And to meet Hamlat as well?'

'I didn't see Hamlat.'

'Didn't you?' Kisielev pounded his fist on the table. 'You knew him and you did not notice him there?'

'No.'

'And you didn't notice three other Polish boys?'

'No. I was preoccupied, worried at my brother not being there.'

'What did you and your brother intend to do?'

Marek looked into Kisielev's red face. He smelled of toilet soap and standard perfume. His little eyes narrowed, as he peered at Marek, waiting for his answer. 'We wanted to go to Bokhara. I bought two tickets.'

'And so did Hamlat, and so did the three Polish boys. They all bought tickets to Bokhara.'

'I don't know what they did.'

Kisielev crossed his legs and his upper foot swung in little jerks. 'And may I know why you wanted to go to Bokhara?'

'To visit our cousins. We have two cousins there.'

'Where do they live?'

Only for a moment did Marek hesitate. 'We came from camp together.' He listened to Kisielev's questions and his own answers as if he were an observer witnessing his brother's verbal duel with the NKVD official. He was suddenly filled with admiration for the self-restraint, rapid process of thought, and clear-headed, ingenious answers of Kisielev's adversary. 'We got out here, they went on to Bokhara. We agreed that we'd visit them to see where conditions were better. They were to leave their address at the station's news-stand.'

'How long had you intended to stay there?'

'Oh, just a few days.'

Kisielev sat down in his chair and leaned back, grinning victoriously. 'You're lying,' he said softly. 'You're lying like a dog. How could your brother go away without getting permission to leave work?'

Marek moistened his lips. 'Could you take this light away?' he said. 'Please.'

'After you've answered my question.'

'I can't stand it.'

'After you have answered my question.'

'My brother intended to ask for permission, but he didn't have time. At two o'clock they took him away to the hospital.'

'I know—he has typhus, and that's why you didn't leave with the others. But what would you have done, if he couldn't get permission, eh? The cashier would not have returned you the money, you knew that, and still you bought tickets immediately after coming to the station, without even waiting for your brother. How come you were so sure he would get permission?'

'In the worst case, we thought, we would go to Bokhara, spend the evening with our cousins and return on the night train, so my brother would still get to Kermine before his work.'

'Night train, did you say?'

'Yes. . . . ' Marek's voice wavered uncertainly.

Kisielev moved the light away from Marek's face and calmly lifted the telephone receiver. 'Railway station,' he said. An old familiar quivering blob of pain hit Marek's stomach. The idea that he had made a mistake, that there was no night train from Bokhara cried out in his mind, and he could not marshal the dozens of possible answers that piled up in disorder, one after another, all senseless and unconvincing. He was again himself, a helpless small boy, who could not think or decide for himself. A trace of sweat broke upon his brow when he heard Kisielev asking, 'Comrade Supervisor? Do you have any night train leaving Bokhara for Kermine?' He adopted an intimate tone of speech that was directed to Marek and not to his party at the other end of the line. A self-assured smile played on his lips. Marek folded his hands limply over his knees, his feet burning with returning blood. 'Oh, do you? Since when?' The smile left Kisielev's face. 'I didn't know about the change in the timetable. A week ago? . . . What time does the train arrive here? . . . Thank you.' He put the receiver down and let a few seconds pass. He took a pencil and drew figures on the green blotting paper covering his table.

Marek grinned inwardly at his luck and said, as if he were exonerating Kisielev for an unjust suspicion, 'I was going to visit my brother. He's very ill. May I go now?'

Kisielev looked up at him, put his pencil aside, and clasped his hands before his chin. 'Sobel,' he said evenly. 'There is no need for us to play hare and hounds. I wanted to see if you would confess and tell me all you know. If you'd admitted the accusations, confessed, and supplied us with a little information, you might have secured some leniency from the Soviet justice. But your stubbornness in denying everything only increases your guilt and stiffens the court's verdict. As to you and your brother's participation in the plan to escape abroad, we don't need any further evidence against you. We have a witness.'

'Witness?'

'Yes—Hamlat himself. He was caught last night at the border and promptly confessed. From him we learned all about you and your brother.'

Marek looked blankly across the table into Kisielev's face. From behind the door came the rhythmical pacing of studded boots on the stone floor. Marek's legs were heavy and he felt the nervous twitch in his jaw again resume its work. 'It's not true,' he retreated behind a mumbled denial. 'I'm not responsible for what he has said. We did not intend to escape. Why should we? We're both happy here.'

He broke off at the sight of the NKVD official rising abruptly from his chair. Kisielev gripped the shirt on his chest, pulling him forward. 'You louse!' he growled. 'We put the likes of you against a wall and shoot them. Just shoot them! Come on, we're going!' His fingers left Marek's shirt. He opened a drawer, pulled out a cigarette and lit it up. 'Or would you rather confess, eh?'

Marek glanced at the hand, twirling the cigarette between two fingers. 'I've nothing to confess.'

'Come on then!' Kisielev jammed his visor cap on his head at his own peculiar angle and walked out first.

'Follow us,' he told the NKVD guard who brought Marek.

The man moved behind them. They passed down the corridor and entered the courtyard surrounded by tall walls with barbed wire. Across the empty square they walked towards a row of tin barracks, guarded by armed sentries. At the corner of the courtyard was a tower and Marek could see another sentry standing at the top of it by a mounted machine-gun. From behind iron bars on the windows, unshaven faces peered at them curiously. One of the guards ran ahead with the keys and opened a door. Kisielev pushed Marek inside, into a dark corridor where an electric lamp threw a dim, red light. The fat NKVD man slipped in behind them. The door closed and Marek heard the loud click of the lock. 'Go left.' Kisielev ordered and they went into a narrow passage between the prison cells. The mingled odours of bad breath, sweat and dust reached Marek's nose. Behind the bars he saw unwashed, ragged prisoners, their heads shaven except for a small tuft of hair in front. They lay on the floor, passing a single cigarette around a circle for a puff, or obligingly picking the lice off each other's backs. In front of one of the cells Kisielev stopped. 'Do you recognize them?' he asked, indicating the group with a slight lift of the chin.

Marek saw the three Polish boys sitting on the floor, staring back at him. He shook his head. 'I never saw them before.'

With sincere wonder he looked straight into Kisielev's face. 'Come on.'

They came to an empty cell and Kisielev pushed Marek inside to a wooden bench. 'Sit down.' Obediently Marek took a place on the bench. The bare walls smelled of desertion, damp and sourness. 'I'm giving you the last chance,' Kisielev said in a subdued hoarse whisper. 'If you're willing to testify at the trial that you were one of the people that Hamlat offered to smuggle across the border, I'll let you go. I'll even let you say that you turned his offer down. If you don't accept this deal, you'll be foolish, very foolish, because you'll never see your brother again!'

Marek ran a sorrowful hand across his face, wiping from it a few drops of sweat that came on to his forehead. 'I don't know anything,' he murmured.

Kisielev looked at him menacingly for a second, then left. A long time passed. Marek was alone in the cell, listening absently to the boot-steps of the guard in the corridor, advancing and receding, advancing and receding again. The heavy lump was in his throat and he fought hard to keep his tears back. Somewhere a high-pitched voice rose above the tumult of the crowd, striking up a song:

> 'Spring will pass, summer will come,
> all trees and flowers will be in full-bloom
> —but I, the unfortunate one,
> will be chained and sent to Siberia.'

A few raucous voices joined in and now the whole chorus of prisoners was singing:

> 'I'm not afraid of Siberia,
> Siberia is also Russian land.'

'Shut up!' Marek heard the guard's voice. The hasty scuffling of sentries' boots followed and then Kisielev's yell came, ordering the prisoners out for an hour-long punitive march. The song broke, the cell locks clicked open one after another, several doors creaked, and the shuffling sounds of the prisoners' shoes tramping out of the barrack was heard. After a while, through the small window, Marek could see the sentries with rifle butts shoving the men into an orderly line. And as Marek watched the living circle of stooping prisoners moving aimlessly around the courtyard, he prayed silently for just a few more days of liberty to help his brother. Finally, he heard approaching footsteps and into the cell came Kisielev and a moment later the huge body of Hamlat appeared, his big hands chained together. Marek's heart stopped beating as he threw the Uzbek a piteous glance which escaped Kisielev's attention, for his eyes were focused on Hamlat. The Uzbek looked back at Marek and did not flick an eyelash. 'One of your people,' Kisielev said. 'How much did he pay you?'

'I don't know this boy,' Hamlat said calmly. 'I told you I don't know him.'

'Ah, don't you? That's interesting. Because he said he knows you very well.'

Marek gulped. 'We bought a rug from Ulug Beg——'

'Shut up!' Kisielev shouted.

'Did you? Oh, yes, I remember now. He did buy a rug from my father-in-law. I was there that evening. A small, red one, I think, isn't it?'

'That's right.'

'You came with another man. Wasn't it your brother?'

'Yes, it was.'

'Listen, Hamlat!' Kisielev's angry face was now blotched with red marks. 'Don't try to cover up for anyone. If you co-operate, we will take that into consideration. But you can't save anyone. We have watched you long enough to get anyone involved arrested. You saw today all the black-marketeers that you supplied with smuggled sheep, joining you here in prison. You won't succeed in covering up for this Pole.'

Little grey eyes swept quickly over Marek's face and it seemed to him that the dimple in Hamlat's chin became more prominent.

'I'm not covering up for anyone. Just telling the truth.'

'Don't be tough, it won't help you a bit. And if you get tough, you know what's waiting for you?'

'I know—death. If I confess or don't confess, co-operate or don't co-operate, you'll shoot me just the same. But this boy had nothing to do with it. I could hardly even remember him.'

'Get him out of here!' Kisielev yelled. Hamlat didn't throw a glance at Marek as he bent down in the low doorway, trailed by the guard. When the clanging of chains died out in the distance, Kisielev looked at Marek thoughtfully. 'Come,' he finally said and strode out through the corridor. The door of the barrack was open and they walked into the courtyard. The prisoners were shuffling around in a circle under the watchful eyes of armed guards. At the tower a new sentry took up his station, pacing back and forth on the small platform. They entered the office building, where in the semi-darkness the Ukrainian sat on a stool, pressing the keys of the accordion, munching raisins and humming a tune. 'Stop it, you bastard!' Kisielev shrieked. The music broke down and the Ukrainian quickly put his instrument under the stool and stood up. Kisielev entered his office, Marek following him. Standing uneasily in the door, he watched the blinds go up and the daylight pour into the room. With a heavy heart, he listened to the distant steady tread of prisoners, accompanied by short rasping orders of the guards. Kisielev sprawled himself into his chair and took a cigarette. From under his cap his small eyes looked up at Marek. 'What are you waiting for?' he asked. 'If we need you, we'll know where to find you.'

Marek opened his mouth, gaping at Kisielev. A whole second passed before he understood that he could go. 'I told you,' he said weakly, 'we had nothing to do with it.'

'All right, all right.' Marek moved to the door, slowly, for he still was not sure that Kisielev was not playing a trick on him. 'Just a second!' Marek turned. He knew this was coming, and glanced tiredly at Kisielev's figure leaning forward across the table, his forefinger beckoning to Marek to come back. 'What do you have there?'

Marek drew the package close to himself. 'Rations—for my brother.'

'You can't draw his rations while he is in the hospital, don't you know that?'

'These are the rations due to him which he did not collect before.'

'I see. I want to give you one bit of advice though, for your own sake. Keep your mouth shut. No one is to know that Hamlat is here. No one, you understand? If you tell someone in his family or anyone else about it, you'll be right back here and this time for good.'

'I won't tell.'

'All right you may leave.'

Marek was surprised that he crossed the corridor, opened the door, closed it behind him, without Kisielev calling him back or the ogre-eyed guard who had returned from the cell halting him. He walked ahead quickly until he reached Shadiva Street. Then he stopped and sighed with relief. Life in the main street was following the same routine events, undisturbed by a different world secluded a hundred yards away beyond the high walls topped by barbed wire. The line in front of the news-stand had grown to some dozens of people. A few women with their brown net-bags rushed to the bakery that was about to open. Serious-faced neckerchieved Pioneers scurried in and out of shops collecting scraps for the war factories. And a goat-bearded Uzbek sat on the ground in the shadow of his cart, lazily eating rusks that he soaked in a cup of boiled water. Small white clouds began to gather on the horizon, tossed restlessly by the sultry squalls of desert wind. A far-distant train whistle was carried to Marek across the low hills, the sand dunes and the mud huts. Marek turned towards the hospital, quickening his pace, hugging the package of wine and rice proudly to his chest.

15

MAREK WAITED NEAR THE CZAIKHANA for the bus. He held a new portion of rice wrapped in a newspaper that Ajmi had bought for him in the black market. The hot wind was blowing into his face and time and again he had to wipe the sand from his eyes and lips. A few steps from him in the czaikhana's entrance sat the bulky owner beside his ever-boiling samovar, his slanted eyes roaming slowly over the dense white clouds that loomed in the distance. 'Buran is coming,' he said, pouting thoughtfully. 'It won't be long now.' Behind him a group of high-booted, bearded Uzbeks in flapping coats, like colourful dressing gowns, discussed in quiet undertones the epidemic that had again hit the town after twenty years. Marek's eyes travelled to the opposite side of the street, where a white circle was charcoaled on the closed door of the barber-shop. A slow caravan of high piled carts with bales of pressed fibres, drawn by heavily laden camels, trundled through the street towards the station. A woman's sudden outcries floated from the side-street, arousing the Uzbeks in the teahouse and a few women who bartered bread for tobacco outside the closed bakery.

Out of the dust whipped up by the caravan loomed the bus and skidded to a stop in front of the czaikhana. As Marek was climbing the step-ladder, he saw a donkey cart reaching the main road, with a little sobbing boy holding the reins, and behind him a dishevelled Uzbek woman clasping her hands in anguish, lamenting and praying over the blanketed body of a man. In the bus were only two Uzbek matrons carrying their bundles made from knotted kerchiefs and table-cloths. Marek felt the driver climb up into his cab, felt the engine start and the clutch go in, and then the bus move in jerks, accompanied by a groaning noise that engulfed the wailing of the woman.

At the station Marek got out and walked past the alleyway of naked trees towards the hospital, struggling with the wind that lashed his face. He turned for a moment, put up his collar and then, stooping and shielding his face with his palms, he thrust on over the rutted road that wound emptily into the distance.

At last he saw the cemetery and then the barracks darkening the barren yellow hills. On the road a Khirgiz woman in camel-hair stockings and pantaloons busily collected dung into a carton for fuel. Her shepherd husband herded his two sheep towards the felt yurt, where he, his wife and his sheep lived. As Marek approached the hospital area, he saw soldiers putting up barbed wire around the two remaining barracks. The office door was shut and his knocking was drowned out by the wind's wail. With an effort he pulled the door open. As it slammed back behind him, Pavel Stepanovicz, dozing at the table, awoke with a start.

'I'm sorry, I brought rice for my brother. The nurse told me he'd eaten all the first lot.'

'I'll give it to her.'

'Can I see my brother today?'

The doctor took off his pince-nez and rubbed his hazy, red-rimmed eyes. 'By all means, after coming in such weather.' He wore a tired smile on his wrinkled face. On the table stood a cold untouched cup of tea.

'Thank you, Doctor. Did you get medicine?'

'No.' Pavel Stepanovicz looked through the window at the soldiers putting the barbed wire around the barracks, then turned his head and fixed his eyes on the cup.

The door opened and with the help of the wind's pressure, Anna Matviejevna blew into the room. 'Are you ready, Pavel Stepanovicz? Good afternoon.'

'Good afternoon,' Marek said. 'I brought rice for my brother. Thank you, nurse, for taking care of him.'

'I wish I could have forced some port into him today, but he wouldn't touch it.'

'When you've seen him, come back here,' Pavel Stepanovicz said.

Marek walked back to the table. 'What is it?' he asked. The gravity of the doctor's voice arose in him a fearful premonition. 'Please tell me.'

Pavel Stepanovicz waved. 'I must see my patients now. Come on, Anna Matviejevna.' The doctor surrendered the comfort of the tiny coal stove behind the plywood partition and walked out of the room, with the plump nurse tripping behind him. Marek followed them to the barbed wire enclosure. The soldier that guarded the entrance, glanced into his face, recognized him, and let him pass.

He entered the room and walked among the rows of beds with the sick moaning and muttering incoherently, their hands covered with rash and bulging veins, tremulous over their blankets. He stopped in front of his brother's bed, the only one in the barrack that had fresh linen and a pillow. The rash had spread over Victor's chest and arms and had darkened to a reddish-purple. His lips were covered with sores, the pupils of his eyes were contracted pinpoints. He breathed rapidly and unevenly and his body was shaken as if he were having a chill. Marek sighed painfully and whispered his brother's name. Slowly Victor's unshaven face turned to him, wincing, as if the move caused him terrible pain. 'I brought rice for you.' A few incoherent words came out among the whistling gasps. His forehead was sweating and his hair was wet and plastered together. 'Don't talk. You should lie quiet and rest.'

The clouded eyes looked up at him and Marek knew that for the first time Victor did not recognize him. With an aggrieved heart he came nearer to the bed's head. 'Victor,' he said. 'The doctor told me you're getting better.' The parched lips trembled briefly, but no words came through them. Marek repeated what he had said, painstakingly enunciating every word as if he thought it was the only way for his brother to understand his message. But Victor's face did not change, and Marek looked helplessly at the entrance, hoping for the doctor or the nurse to come into the barrack. But in the door was only an orderly, helping a new patient, who was fainting on his feet, to a bed. As the two passed by, Marek recognized in the sick man the young, apple-cheeked NKVD guard that had a few days earlier been assigned to duty at the railway station. From the bed near Victor came the hardly audible whisper of a little boy. He had replaced the old man with suppurating eyes who had died at sunrise. Beyond the boy an old Uzbek was vomiting and in the corner of the room a patient was yelling at the nurse, who wasn't there, to get out. Marek noticed the wine bottle and a glass with a spoon in a carton under his brother's bed and poured some of the liquid into the spoon. 'Victor, please take it.' His brother's open-mouthed face stared at him vacantly. Marek forced the spoon between Victor's teeth and tipped it slowly when he saw the muscles on his brother's throat reacting laboriously. He was about to pour another spoonful of wine, when he saw the nurse entering the barrack and he hastily deposited the bottle and the spoon in the carton and moved away from the bed's head. The doctor came in and stopped at the chart. He glanced at Marek across the room, then started his routine inspection, commanding the orderly to shift the patients who were lying on their backs to their sides, to avoid dangerous bedsores that would threaten them with gangrene. He directed the nurse to open the windows for fresh air, to bandage the hemorrhagic rash of the patient in bed No. 28, disinfect the foul mouth of his neighbour, and to repeat the lumbar puncture of the delirious patient who was cursing her.

Marek saw Victor's swollen hand moving over the blanket and he leaned to him. Victor's voice was slow and he had to think a long time before he whispered: 'Hamlat?'

'What?'

'Ham-lat . . . Ham-lat . . .?'

Marek watched the throbbing lips, before he managed the answer. 'He is back. As soon as you get out of here, we will go.'

Victor closed his eyes with a painful expression that could have been a smile. The nurse passed by and opened the window. A gust of hot, brisk air blew into the room. The doctor came close and leaned over Victor. 'Did he talk to you?'

'Not much.' Marek peered miserably at the doctor's face as he was examining Victor's pulse. 'He is in very bad shape, isn't he?' The doctor said nothing, but pulled up Victor's undershirt and put his ear against his heart.

The boy on the neighbouring bed whispered again. The nurse came over to him. 'I can't understand what he says.'

'How is my brother?' Marek asked.

'Come to my office in a few minutes and we will talk.'

'Pavel Stepanovicz, will you look at this boy? They brought him this morning, you remember?'

The doctor approached the boy and in that moment Marek distinctly overheard the boy's call for water in Polish. 'He is a Pole!' he said to the doctor. 'He wants water. How did he get here?'

'I don't know. He was among several sick that were brought from the station this morning. I think his younger brother was with him, wasn't he?'

'Yes,' the nurse said. 'I did not see him afterwards though.'

The doctor leaned over the boy. 'I examined him this morning,' he said to the nurse. 'In addition to typhus he has pneumonia as a complication. Don't give him anything cold to drink.'

'What did you prescribe for him, Pavel Stepanovicz?'

The docter threw her a quick, slightly annoyed glance. 'Aspirin, what else? Come with me,' he said to Marek.

Marek leaned over his brother's bed. 'I'll come back tomorrow,' he said slowly and loudly.

'I'm afraid he doesn't hear you. Come! Will you look after the others, Anna Matviejevna?'

'Yes, Pavel Stepanovicz.'

'Don't give the boy anything cold.'

In the office the doctor indicated a chair to Marek and sat behind the table. 'I expect the crisis now in two or three days. I am not going to wrap up in cotton wool what I tell you. He is getting weaker every day. I can hardly detect his heart now. I dug out a bit of camphor yesterday and gave him an injection but it didn't help. If you want to save your brother, you must get adrenalin. If you can manage it any way at all, get adrenalin before the crisis.'

'Where can I get it?'

The doctor looked at the table and said quietly, 'They might have it on the black market in Samarkand or Bokhara.'

The door opened and the nurse walked in. 'The patient in bed No. 28 passed away when I was bandaging him.'

'Call the orderlies and check him out from the chart.'

'Yes. I'll make your tea, Pavel Stepanowicz, when I come back.'

'Thank you, Anna Matviejevna. I don't want it now.'

'You must have some tea with rusks. You just can't carry on like this.'

'Maybe later, Anna Matviejevna.'

The nurse left. Wearily the doctor rubbed his face. 'I don't know how we carry on. We were promised another doctor from Tashkent. Today I got a letter advising me that the one they had in mind was called by the army. I was offered a medical student instead. I bet all he knows is how to apply cupping-glasses to the back.'

There was a slight knocking at the door and Marek opened it. A little boy of about seven stood behind it, wearing a big wadded jacket and a huge shawl wrapped around his neck and lips. Crude coarse socks fell over his shabby shoes. He peered bashfully inside, holding a visored cap respectfully in his hand, a wisp of blond hair falling over his eyes. The nurse was returning from the hospital barracks. 'Come in,' she said and nudged the boy inside. 'This is the brother of that boy in Barrack 3.'

'Oh, where have you been all this time?' the doctor asked.

'At the station.'

'Where are your parents?'

'We lost them during our journey a few months ago. So my brother and I travel and search for them.'

'What did you do at the station?'

'Watched the trains. Maybe they would pass by in one of them. How is my brother, is he still sick?'

Marek saw the doctor's Adam's apple twitch in his throat, as he took off his pince-nez and rubbed it vigorously. 'Make him a cup of tea, Anna Matviejevna.' He pulled his tin box out of his drawer. 'You want a piece of sugar to suck, eh?' The boy nodded, approached the table, and for a long while he eyed the rows of white slabs before finally taking one.

'I'll make a cup for you too, Pavel Stepanowicz. You need it,' the nurse said from behind the partition.

'All right, I'll have it with the boy.'

'I'll go now,' Marek said. 'Good-bye Doctor.'

'You'd better wait a bit. The wind's dropping, I think.'

'Never mind, I'll go. Thank you, Doctor.' He left.

The wind tossed gravel over the road as he walked out of the hospital area. From the direction of the town the squealing cart wheeled, slowly carrying the lamenting family group that Marek had seen when boarding the bus. Up on the hill, among the tombs, he saw two Uzbek orderlies shaping a mud vault over a white-blanketed form. The third man held slices of fried bread and an oil-cruse so the dead would have food and light on his two-week long celestial journey. Marek turned on the dirt road that ran beside the track and walked quickly to town, away from the sick and dying, away from the boy that, as if typhus was not enough, also had pneumonia, away from his brother whose heart grew weaker and weaker, away from the hospital and the nearby cemetery and the old-fashioned world of 'Anna Matviejevna' and 'Pavel Stepanovicz' that had somehow survived the revolution and the roughening of human gentility.

16

FROM BEHIND THE SAND-HILLS that stretched away to the far horizon a streak of smoke advanced towards the station. The stormy wind had subsided and only occasionally would a sudden gust blow dust into Marek's face or whirl over the road the refuse that had earlier been blown from the station garbage dump. On the yellow desert surface appeared a black locomotive that grew louder and bigger until it became clearly visible with its hammer and sickle, and Kaganovich portrait, and a charcoaled slogan on the importance of cotton for the front. As Marek reached the bare trees, the empty flat cars rolled by, slowing at the approach to the station, bringing into Marek's mind pictures of the many freight trains he and his brother had travelled on before reaching Kermine, and then with a sudden start evoking a vision of the passenger train that was to be their last in the long journey across Russia. On the spur of the moment he began to run towards the brick station that stood out, red among the white mud huts. He looked at the sun showing its edge behind a flock of lumpish, heavy clouds gathered over the town, reproaching himself for never asking the Polish peasants how to tell time by the sun.

In front of the station building, around the square, waited carts and patient laden camels of the caravan that had passed Marek on the street some two hours earlier. As he sprinted up the steps, dozens of barefoot Uzbek workers dashed towards the carts to start carrying the cotton bales to the freight train that had just arrived. In the hall Marek looked up at the clock and calmed down. He had a whole hour in front of him.

Surprisingly, the station hall was almost empty and there was no line in front of the ticket-window. The two Uzbek women with whom he had ridden in the bus squatted on the floor next to the exit, waiting patiently for the train with the habitual canniness of early queue-makers. On a bench a turbaned Sart lay face down, an empty bottle of eau de cologne on the floor, snoring loudly in his sleep. From the exit an old, skinny ticket-taker watched the chess game being played by two Russian railwaymen, their board on a valise placed across the bench between them. Marek approached the ticket-window. 'Ticket to Bokhara,' he said.

The woman looked at him through her steel-rimmed glasses. 'Do you have a permit?'

'What permit?'

'Permit from the Health Department.' She pointed to a small bi-lingual poster outside the window. From it Marek read, all his hopes falling low, that in view of the epidemic of typhus, in order not to spread the disease, a special permit from the Health Department was required for anyone wanting to leave the town. 'If no one was sick in your home, you'll have no problem,' the woman informed him. 'You can easily get to the Department and come back in time.'

Marek gazed at her for a long moment before he opened his mouth. 'Where is it?'

'On Khidirialeff Lane. Right after the Tractor Repair Base No. 2, but on the opposite side of the street.'

Gloomily, Marek turned away. As he walked through the hall, past the glass door he saw Marusia at a table in the empty dining hall, hurriedly eating a bowl of soup. In the exit he passed a blond Russian woman, holding her little pig-tailed daughter by the hand. The girl looked at him over her shoulder with the slight grin of secret acquaintance. It was the same girl that he had once seen posting a letter and a few days later reciting at the stadium.

The street was loud with the rhythmical cries of skull-capped Uzbek workers unloading arbas and camels. The empty bus circled around the square, then slowly drove away into the empty street. Workers carried on their repair job in the ancient mosque from which the coloured mosaic façades were chipped off in fragments, exposing the yellow mud walls they used to clothe. Marek crossed the street and turned into Khidirialeff Lane. The smell of cabbage and boiled mutton pursued him as he walked by the street canals, the dragon-flies buzzing among the tall clover that grew in the dirty water. A girl holding a brass jug on a wooden headcircle passed the road and entered a courtyard where a bare-legged Uzbek led his horse by the reins around in a circle, both dipped in a white liquid-filled pit, their legs whipping up slaked lime. A woman darning socks at a window looked at Marek curiously as he stopped before the building where a crimson flag hung over the sign 'Kermine Health Department'. He knocked at the door.

'Come in.' From the room's corner looked at him the square, red face of a big man with broad buttocks, clad in a severe jacket with stamped metal buttons. His hands stopped expectantly in the air before reaching a kettle steaming away over an iron stove.

'I wanted to get a permit to go to Bokhara,' Marek said from the door.

'Sit down, Citizen.' As with nervous humbleness Marek sat on the edge of a chair, clasping limp hands between his knees, the Russian crossed the brick floor to his table. 'Was anyone ill in your home?'

'No.'

'May I see your passport, Citizen?' The health official sat down.

'I don't have it on me.'

'Then bring it.' He looked at the empty glass at his table, then glanced impatiently at the steaming kettle on his stove, and got up.

'The train leaves shortly. I won't make it in time to get home and back.'

'So you'll go tomorrow then, Citizen.'

'I've a document indicating my name.' Marek heard his own voice slightly faltering. He opened his pocket-book and handed his camp release certificate to the Russian.

From under the bushy brows sprouted at the low overhanging forehead came a quick, sharp look of protuberant eyes. 'I see,' the health official drawled, 'that you don't have any passport.' He slowly folded himself into his chair and pulled a notebook out of a drawer. Marek watched his thick forefinger moved down the columns of names, hoping for a miracle that didn't come. The man's finger stopped and in the colourless, barren voice of a person who learns the alphabet at a late date, he read: 'Victor Sobel, Achum Babayeffa Street No. 7. Documents: Release from corrective labour camp in Pechora No. 26, 247. Admitted to the hospital on November 14, 1941.' With a conclusive gesture he put Marek's certificate back on the table and without a word walked to his stove, picked up his kettle, returned to his table and poured the boiling water into his glass. From a drawer he pulled out three newspaper bags, pinched a few leaves of tea from the smallest one and stirred them in the hot water.

'I must go to Bokhara,' Marek said, imploring the man. 'Please give me the permit.'

'You're subject to a two-weeks' quarantine from November fourteenth.' The Russian watched the liquid getting slightly green, then he added some salt from the second bag and a piece of fat from the third.

'My brother's very sick. I've got to get medicine for him immediately. Otherwise he will die!'

'He is in the hospital under the care of the Soviet doctors.'

'But they don't have the necessary medicine.'

'They have everything they need and if they don't they will get it upon request.' The Russian gripped a lump of sugar with his front teeth, and sucked his tea through it.

'But then it will be too late. My brother's crisis may come tomorrow or even in a few hours!'

The man looked at him coldly. 'We issued our orders to prevent the spreading of epidemics. We cannot consider individual cases that conflict with the measures taken for the benefit of society.'

For a second Marek watched the tight swelling of flesh below the man's lips, then with a sigh he took his document, put it back in his pocket-book, got up and walked out.

The woman with a sock in her hand was bending out of the window, anxiously watching the man on the opposite side of the street charcoaling a white circle on a shut door. A Russian soldier approaching, noticed the mark on the door and skirted around the house. Marek ambled to the main street, but once there, he began to walk quickly, a new determination settling in his mind. A cart plastered with a row of Stalin's pictures slowly wheeled by the station, marking its way by splashes of green saliva, spit by the tobacco-chewing driver. In the old mosque the workers stood in line, checking in their tools with their overseer before leaving their job. As Marek approached the station, the now unloaded camels, sensing the homeward journey, were grumbling restlessly. The loudspeaker went on in the station hall, reporting the five o'clock news. The chess players raised their heads from their board and listened gloomily to the bulletin that the Germans had crossed the Don river and occupied Rostov. Shaking their heads, both cursed under their breath and returned to their game. Marek sat on the bench beside the Russian woman and her child, his back turned to the ticket-window. The little girl winked at him. Immediately her observant mother drew her closer to herself, whispered a few words of rebuke in her ear and handed her a piece of framed embroidery out of her net shopping bag.

Marek looked around the hall. The only new person, an old Uzbek, sat at the floor in the corner, drinking water from a sheepskin sack in long draughts. The woman cashier was reading a book. The ticket-taker, after advising the Uzbek women not to go out to the platform, approached the chess-board and began to argue with one of the players of the inadvisability of his knight's attack. On the radio a news commentator reminded the listeners of the lesson the foreign invaders had taken at Borodino one hundred and thirty years ago, then Moscow University's two hundred student chorus began its quarter hour of army songs, but in the middle of 'Victory Will be with Us' it went off and a girl's voice came on, announcing the train's arrival. Marek heard the distant clatter of wheels and the remote warning whistles of the locomotive. The ticket-taker reluctantly left the chess-game and dashed to take up his post at the door. 'Citizens, please form a line,' he called. The Uzbek women quickly got up and started a queue, which a moment later the old Uzbek joined with slow, senile dignity. The chess players unwillingly got up, their eyes glued to the board, which one of them held propped against his chest, while the other carried the valise. 'Your move,' the humid-eyed man with the valise said.

'Push my pawn ahead.'

The railwayman made the move, then examined the board, looked at the face of his adversary, frowned, and began to chew his nails. The ticket-taker watching the board shook his head, grinning vindictively.

From behind the narrow unmarked door came a squat Uzbek NKVD guard and looked around the hall. He bowed his head to the Russian woman, then walked to the Sart sleeping on the bench and nudged him with his knee. 'Get up, the train is coming!' The Sart murmured a curse and turned on the other side. 'Your train is here!' the guard yelled and shook the man.

The drunk sat up for a second, his eyes half-closed and blurred from sleep, and pushed the guard away in annoyance. 'I'm not going anywhere! Get going and leave me alone!' His body fell back on the bench and in a moment he dozed again with loud snores that mingled discordantly with the whistles of the approaching train. The guard glanced at the Russian woman, then his bulky hands grabbed the drunk, pulled him up to his feet and with the help of a knee shoved the dazed and startled man out into the street.

The wheels of the train cars rattled and squealed, changing tracks. Holding his out-dated ticket to Bokhara, Marek joined the line behind the board-carrying chess player, who was impatiently needling his adversary. 'Come on, make a move.'

'Let's finish the game in the car. I've got to think.'

'I wish you'd make a move.'

The NKVD guard came back to the platform entrance. 'Do you all have permits from the Health Department, Citizens?'

Both Uzbek women fumbled in their thick camel hair stockings that were knotted like carpets and got out their tickets and health certificates. The old Uzbek nodded to the guard and began to comb his tuft of beard. The railwayman with the valise cautiously moved a step away from him, then turned to his friend. 'Listen, if you are tired of holding the board, let me carry it and you take my valise.'

'No, thanks, you might drop the men and then we won't be able to reconstruct the game.'

Morosely Marek gazed at the guard's cheek with a hollow scar of tropical sore brought about by a night-biting sandfly. With a sudden decision he left the queue and approached the door of the dining hall. The ticket-taker shouted after him, 'You don't have much time, Citizen! The train is late. It will leave immediately.'

With a gesture Marek acknowledged the remark, his ears catching the outside sounds of slowing down wheels and the loud heavy gasps of the locomotive. He knocked at the glass door. Marusia looked up at him from a table she was cleaning. He saw her, open-mouthed, throwing a quick measuring look at the white-aproned Russian matron who was scanning pages of a magazine behind the counter, and then coming towards the door hesitantly, carrying a wet rag with her. She unlocked the door. 'What is it?'

'Victor is in very bad shape,' Marek said hurriedly. 'I must go to Bokhara to get medicine for him, and you must help me.'

'What do you want me to do?' He could not help noticing a frown on her forehead and reserve in her tone. He heard the noise of opening of iron doors, the station-master's orders, quick steps of the conductor and the approaching voices of passengers. 'They wouldn't let me in without a permit.' Let me through the dining hall.'

'They check the train before it leaves.' She glanced again at the counter, but the woman was now preoccupied with a story.

'I will hide myself in a toilet.'

'They check the toilets. They would arrest you! And me, too!'

'All right, if you're scared. Just go away, I'll manage the rest myself.'

'The woman will see you and raise hell. Please go away.' Her eyes roamed anxiously over the incoming passengers crossing the station hall.

'I thought you cared about Victor,' Marek said bitterly. 'But you won't risk your skin a bit! I must get medicines, if he is to live!' He spoke in a hoarse loud voice that was swelling with almost hysterical malice.

'Go away. I can't talk to you! Please go!'

Marek looked at her with disbelief, then as he saw the frown deepening on her forehead, her eyes fearfully peering at the hall, a sudden suspicion brushed the edges of his mind and a question whether she had been interrogated by NKVD sprang to his lips. But he did not have time to ask it, for a sudden tremor shot across Marusia's eyes, she jammed the door against him and ran quickly away back to her work. Marek turned and saw in the middle of the station the tall figure of Kisielev, a leather brief-case in his hand. The Russian woman kissed him and the little girl threw her arms around his neck. 'I'll come back to you in a minute,' Marek heard Kisielev say. Then he saw him walk through the unmarked door of the NKVD office, the squat Uzbek guard following him. The woman sat back on the bench and her daughter complacently resumed her handwork. The drunk Sart suddenly appeared again in the hall and lay down on the bench. Marek turned his head and saw the woman behind the counter watching him attentively. He left the door of the dining room and as he was crossing the station hall, he heard the station-master's whistle, the sounds of slamming doors, and the squeak of starting wheels. From the exit he looked at the woman cashier peeking out from under the half-closed shutter at the snoring Sart, and at Kisielev's wife and her little girl embroidering a little girl playing ball.

17

THE SUN HAD DIMINISHED INTO an uneven spot, dully red, behind the bluish mist of dusty air and the darkening clouds, when Marek descended the steps of the station. The caravan was receding down the street, leaving behind it in the square pools of foamy camel urine that lured swarms of buzzing flies. The workers, their shirts soaking in sweat, queued to get slips attesting their day's work from their overseer. From the near distance a sound of drum-rolls was heard. As Marek reached the poster addressed to the proletarians of all countries, he saw a funeral procession. Shoeless men and women marched quietly behind a black-clothed tractor with fluttering pennons. Behind the driver, hoisted up on the rails lay the body of an Uzbek Kolkhoz official, clad in a long white shirt, his bewhiskered, rash-covered face with open eyes still looking alive as if he were supervising the tearless peasants till the last moment of his earthly existence. As Marek passed the procession and overtook the caravan, the funeral drums rolled more vigorously. He looked over his shoulder and saw Kisielev with his wife and child at the station's exit, raising his hand to the visor of his cap to salute the dead.

New gusts of wind again whistled between the huts, carrying the sound of camel-bells across the deserted streets. Outside the Tajik's shop stood two sanitation men wearing aprons, hand-sprayers in their hands, waiting to enter the steam-filled premises for additional disinfection. The empty bus drove through the street towards the station on its last useless ride of the day. In the middle of the road, a few mongrels took a brief, bored interest in Marek, then became excited at the sight of approaching camels. Grey shadows were beginning to veil the road and soften the contours of the houses. The czaikhana was open, but there was no one in it except the manager warming his hands by his ever-steaming samovar.

Marek crossed the street to the other side where a few men stood, keeping a safe distance from each other. Together with them he read a black-margined obituary posted at the barber shop, signed by Kisielev in the name of the Party, Konsomol and Town's Council. As he was about to enter Achum Baba-yeffa Street, he heard a voice calling, 'Hey!' From the darkening street emerged an arba driven by Ulug Beg. As Marek began to approach the cart, the old Uzbek drew in the reins. His jaws rapidly chewing tobacco stopped when the donkey halted. His voice faltered when he asked. 'What are you doing here? Didn't you go with Hamlat?'

'No. My brother fell sick with typhus the day we were to leave.'

Ulug's red-rimmed eyes blinked nervously. 'I just drove Aka to the hospital,' he said, looking at Marek with a miserable expression as if summoning his help.

'Typhus?' Marek asked. The old man nodded. A picture of the merrily smiling girl in the white-walled courtyard came to Marek's mind.

'She was seized by convulsions and vomiting. A red rash broke out all over her skin. I immediately knew it was the spotted fever. I wish her father was here. How is your brother?'

'Very bad.'

The Uzbek's eyes roamed over the men who were commenting sympathetically on the barber's death. He sighed and shook his head. 'Good night.' His jaws resumed the tobacco-chewing as he plucked at the reins and drove away.

For a moment Marek stood in the middle of the road, absently watching the cart disappearing behind the approaching caravan. And suddenly the resignation that had dulled his mind until now gave way to a wave of panic that stirred him and made him walk quickly home, past a trotting water-carrier, past a wall with a sum of probate debt carved near the entrance by a creditor, past washing set out to dry on a line across the street, and past the palm in his courtyard rustling in the dusk.

In the lit window he saw Ajmi sitting with hands folded pensively under her chin. She gave a start and leaned forward, her eyes anxiously following his figure. As he laid his hand on the door-knob, he heard the hurried clatter of her wooden sandals. She opened the door, her slanted eyes looking at him with an alert inquiry. 'Anything wrong?' Marek stared blankly at her slightly flushed high cheeks. Her lips were dry and her long, fine nose quivered for a moment. 'Well, what is it?'

A few seconds passed before his mind focused back on his brother. 'He doesn't recognize people any more.'

'Come in.' He followed her slender grey-robed figure into the room. She pointed to the settee and he lowered himself into it. There was an air of intimate conspiracy between them as she approached the window and glanced out of it, then turned to him and waited for further news.

'The doctor told me I must get adrenalin to save him.'

'Adrenalin?'

'Yes—adrenalin injections. One could get them on the black market in Bokhara or Samarkand.'

She stared at him gravely and thoughtfully for a second, but then turned to the window and shielding her eyes, peered outside through the window pane. 'My husband is coming,' she said. As she passed him on her way to the door, the sweep of tawny skin in her low neckline irresistibly drew his eyes.

Ibram entered the room in his old outgrown suit, carrying a carton with refuse of cotton seed and a bottle. His face was spattered with the unpurified black cotton oil. 'Good evening,' he said to Marek. 'Have you any news about your brother?'

'I just came back from the hospital. He is almost unconscious. His heart hardly beats.'

Ibram frowned. Ajmi took the carton and the bottle from his hands and as she walked to the kitchen, she gave Marek a glance from the door. 'What did the doctor say? Can't they give him some stimulant in the hospital?'

'They don't have any.'

'Didn't they get medicine from Moscow?'

'No.'

From the kitchen came sounds of water running into a basin, then Ajmi called, 'Your water is ready!'

'Excuse me for a moment.' Ibram left the room. Marek approached the window. The sombre ceiling of the sky was closing in from above. Sharp staccato wind-squalls drummed against the house walls, and further away in town an evening concert of brays, neighs and bleating was starting.

After a while Ibram reappeared in the door, wiping his face with a towel. 'It's cold,' he said to Ajmi. 'Light the fire. You'll eat with us, Marek.'

'Thank you, but I have to go. I must do something about my brother.'

'What can you do? If they can't get medicine in the hospital, you certainly won't get it. What medicine is it, injections?'

'Yes, adrenalin injections. One can get them in Bokhara or Samarkand, the doctor said.'

Ibram glanced at the dark window. 'It's too late for a Bokhara train.'

'I tried to go but now one needs a permit from the Health Department to be able to leave the town.'

Ibram put the towel on the settee. 'They wouldn't give you one?'

'No, not for another week. They say two weeks have to have passed from the time of my brother's admission to the hospital. . . . If I don't get adrenalin, he . . .' His voice broke suddenly and he turned away to hide his emotions.

'Where does one get these injections in Bokhara? In a public pharmacy?'

Marek glanced at Ajmi, carrying into the room a basin with brown splinters of brittle saksaul wood, topped by the cotton refuse. 'No,' he said, his still strangled voice dropping hesitantly. 'On the black market.' From over the basin came a quick, startled flash of frightened black eyes. Ibram said nothing. With his lower lip pushed thoughtfully out, his hands folded behind him, he watched the saksaul splinters breaking like glass, in the fire that his kneeling wife was building up. After a while, the wood picked up the flame from the cotton and began to burn noisily. As Ibram lifted the rug from the low table and placed the basin in the oblong space sunk in the floor, Ajmi's disturbed face turned to Marek with a wordless inquiry.

'Make supper for three of us,' Ibram said, turning to her. Marek unclenched his hand in a gesture of protest and apology, but he noticed the deep sunk elongated eyes of Ajmi focused expectantly on his face. An encouraging smile crossed her lips. With a worried frown still wrinkling his forehead, he slightly bowed his head. Ajmi immediately dashed to the kitchen.

Marek looked at Ibram. He was at the window watching a single star struggling with the black depth of the bitter night. Through the open door came the sounds of the sizzling kerosene stove. 'It will be two weeks tomorrow since I took Raim into hospital. I could leave right after my work. Is there any train returning before seven in the morning?'

Marek's throat tightened abruptly. He stared at Ibram's figure at the window, unable yet to believe that he had offered to go to Bokhara, spend a sleepless night and take upon himself all the risks involved in dealing with blackmarketeers. 'There is a train arriving at Kermine before dawn,' he said in a slow, hushed tone, as if afraid that Ibram might change his mind.

Ajmi entered the room and laid the table with a fresh white cloth, put brown clay plates and cups for her husband and herself and a white plate and a cup for Marek. She placed pillows on the carpet around the table, then returned to the kitchen and immediately came back with bread and salt shaker, a saucer with pickled onions, tomatoes and raisins and a bottle of cottonseed oil that her husband had brought home. Ibram turned from the window and motioned Marek to a seat. The two men sat cross-legged on the pillows. The warmth of the basin-fire beneath the table pleasantly warmed his feet, as Marek stared with silent gratitude at Ibram's head bowed over the bread he was slicing. He finally managed to open his lips and say a few clumsy words of appreciation. Shukunov waved his hand, dismissing the subject and pushed the saucer towards Marek. 'Help yourself. My wife can pickle vegetables and fruits like no other woman in town.'

Marek smiled and, as he munched a small pickled tomato, he nodded and granted his approval. Suddenly he felt very hungry and for the first time he realized that he had barely eaten during the past week. Longingly, his eyes flickered towards the kitchen door through which hot, heavy smells of cooked cabbage blew into the room. Finally Ajmi emerged with a bowl of steaming soup and put it on the table. As she took Marek's plate, her narrow eyes swept over his face and she noticed with surprise that it did not wear signs of his previous nervous anxiety. Then as she took her husband's plate she saw a little smile playing over his lips. Her hand with the spoon halted in the air and she looked from one to another. 'What is it?' Her voice rose in curiosity.

'Your husband has kindly offered to go to Bokhara,' Marek said, looking at Ibram, 'to buy medicine for my brother. I don't know how to express my thanks to you both.'

Ibram bit into a piece of bread. 'If I were in your place, wouldn't you do the same for me?'

'Oh, I would!'

'Well now, how about the soup?' Ibram suggested and raised a hot spoonful to his mouth.

Ajmi filled her own plate and sat on her pillow. From the kitchen came the sizzle of oil and onions in the frying pan. Marek's face turned to the chest where a shining samovar and set of white bowls suggested the memory of the familiar dining room in Brest Litovsk. As he spooned up his soup, his eyes travelled slowly over the table with its dinnerware, over Ajmi's bare shoulders and naked throat to her face. As she lifted a piece of bread to her mouth, her eyes fastened on him with merry, benevolent affection. Marek grinned at her, drew himself up and began polishing off the thin cabbage soup which he thought was the best cabbage soup he had ever eaten.

When they had emptied their plates, Ajmi brought in a big steaming bowl. She took Ibram's plate and began to fill it with fried onions. 'They have been asking about you and your brother,' Ibram said. 'They asked me whom you knew in town, who was visiting you.'

'Who asked you?' Marek blinked nervously and his voice sank.

'The NKVD. They were particularly interested to know if a man called Hamlat had ever been here. Or someone from his family.'

Marek swallowed. 'What did you say?' Ajmi put a hot plate in front of him, glancing into his face. The strong smell of onions drifted into his nose.

'I said I'd never seen anyone. Just Marusia. They knew about her anyway.'

'Thank you,' Marek mumbled.

Ajmi sat down. Ibram began to pile onions on his fork. 'Where is Hamlat now?' he asked, his face fixed on his plate. 'I know he isn't in town.'

'I don't know.'

'I was thinking he went over there maybe.' He looked up and his close-set eyes narrowed meaningfully.

'Where?'

'There, where you want to go.'

Marek twitched in his seat. 'I don't know what you mean,' he said, his voice hushed and uncertain.

'I saw Hamlat's daughter coming to see you twice. Then this inquiry about Hamlat followed. I just put two and two together. I assume that now with the war, since the Russians send anyone able to carry arms to the front, the border watch has been slackened. Maybe my time has finally come. I have

144

been waiting for it for years.' Marek opened his mouth and gaped at Shukunov with astonishment. 'Maybe we could go together,' he heard Ibram continue. 'When your brother returns from the hospital. All four of us.' He was leaning forward, crossing his arms on the table. Once or twice he glanced at the window and at the door as if wanting to make sure that no one was listening to him. 'I have been saving up for years, but I still don't have enough. We will pay less if we go together in a group. Also . . .,' his eyes moved tenderly to Ajmi, 'with a woman among us, it would be better if there were more men. One never knows what may happen. . . .'

Marek turned his head to Ajmi. She lifted her face and returned his look. From her unwinking candid eyes he read that he could trust her husband. But there was still a touch of caution in his voice when he asked, 'Why do you suppose Hamlat is a smuggler?'

'I don't suppose, I know. Years ago he got my whole family abroad so they could get to Palestine. I was serving with the army and they could not wait for me. They were among the very last who escaped before the Russians tightened the border guards.'

18

THE HOT GUSTS THAT FLUNG restlessly about the courtyard rattled the glass of Marek's window. The wind swept into the room through the cracks and blew out the kerosene stove. Marek glumly peered out, scrutinizing the thick inky coat of clouds that a few hours earlier had veiled the eerie, yellow-brown sky with a menacing, premature twilight. The day had suddenly turned into night as if there had been a total eclipse of sun. The temperature that usually dropped in the late afternoon had suddenly risen and the torrid hard-blowing windstorm had heaped up dust and filth and sand and whirled it into the air. The streets had been quickly deserted as people scurried for shelter, traffic had halted and all the corner-lamps had gone on.

Marek pulled a box of matches out of his pocket. Only one match was left. Cautiously, he cupped the flame and lit the stove again and put a kettle on it. He wiped the sweat from his face with a towel, then rolled himself a cigarette, lit it from the flame, and sat on the stool by the dark window, waiting for the water to boil for tea. In the flickering light the flimsy pieces of furniture reflected the pale, curious shadows. Uneasily Marek listened to the wind's gasps and whistles, to the noise of a water bucket clattering over the courtyard, to the palm's loud rustle and the terror-stricken voices of the animals in the neighbourhood. The warmth clung to his body, and he thought longingly of the brisk, cold Siberian wind.

Suddenly from behind the wall a song came. It was nostalgic and remote and the words were lost from time to time in the wail of the wind. Marek rose from his seat and knelt on his bed, putting his ears to the wall. The wind breathed a hot wave of air into the room, again blowing out the stove flame, throwing the room into the darkness. Marek rubbed the sweat from his face, and lay down on the bed, dangling his feet over the edge. He stared at the unseen wall behind the bed, the tip of his cigarette glowing in the darkness. The melody was now rising, now floating away.

Suddenly the howling of jackals broke through the wind, like the desperate cries of abandoned children, and when it ceased, no tune was heard. Marek raised his head, propping himself on his elbows and waited for the song to drift back, but he heard only the violent wind squalls that rose in intensity and billowed among the mud huts. His clothes were glued to his body, he felt hot, and thirsty, and restless. He leaped from his bed and tumbled out of the room.

The wind hurled its fury into his face, and blew out his cigarette, scattering the sparks into the air. A thick crust of sand knifed into his eyes and set them aflame. Wedging his way into the wind with lowered head, he struggled down to Shukunov's window, and looked inside the room. Ajmi was at her settee, her hands clasped, staring glazed-eyed and open-mouthed at the blustering waves of dust in the courtyard. On her knees lay her forgotten knitting needles, a skein of wool and the unfinished blue sweater.

Marek pounded a few times on the door before she heard him and opened it. Her eyes squinted at his half-blurred figure in the darkness. The frown left her low forehead and her voice rang with a pleasant tone of welcome as she said, 'Come in quick and shut the door.' As he smoothed his rumpled hair, matted with dust, and kicked the dirt off his shoes, his eyes, burning from wind, followed Ajmi's light, unaffected walk, with the faint swaying of hips under her domestic grey robe. An embroidered, home-made sash accentuated her slender waist. She sat back on her settee and took the skein in her hands. 'How is your brother?' She pulled on her thread and hooked it into the needle.

'The same as yesterday, no improvement. I'm sorry that Ibram had to go in such weather.'

She glanced with distress at the window. Marek guiltily looked around for a place to sit down. 'I left some soup for you.' Ajmi put aside her skein and walked out of the room. The wind brought a sinister groan of electric wires on the main street. In the kitchen the puffing primus stove made a final gasp. Ajmi was back in the room, carefully carrying a full bowl of steaming soup and a piece of bread to the table. She turned to him and waited. The unwinking serious look of her eyes focused on his face aroused a strange feeling in his chest. A drop of sweat stood out on her perspiring forehead, that shone from the dim light of the oil lamp hanging from the ceiling. There was no pillow by the table to sit on, and with a half-apologetic, half self-scolding grin Ajmi darted to the bedstead and brought one for him. Marek looked at the red beet soup flavoured with boiled sour milk that brought memories of home to his mind. He threw her a contented boyish smile and lowered himself neatly into his seat. As he began to drink the hot liquid, slowly quenching his terrible thirst, Ajmi sat on the stool by the window. 'The buran will go on all night,' she remarked, with her sleeve wiping her face.

'What were you singing before?'

She threw him a quick, sidelong glance and her shoulders rose in a quiet shrug. 'An old, native song about Prince Farrad.'

Among the noises of the windstorm, the clanging of spoon against the bowl and the sucking sounds of drinking a hot soup were heard in the room. The smothered howling of dogs came from the street, followed by the loud banging of the shutters in the neighbouring house. A pensive, far-away gaze clung to Ajmi's profile. After a while she raised her head a little, gasped for air, and went to the kitchen to get a glass and poured herself some water from a jug standing in the room's corner. She swallowed the drink and wiped her mouth. 'You want some?' she asked, panting. Marek nodded. She gave him a glass of water, and as he was drinking it, she brought him a dish of red currant jelly.

He looked at her when she put the saucer in front of him. 'Why are you so good to me now? You were different before?' An anticipating smile crossed his lips.

A draught sneaked into the room and sent the oil lamp rocking back and forth, reflecting a gleam of light in the whites of Ajmi's eyes, before her heavy lids fell over them. He followed her back as she walked across the room in her felt shoes, sat on the settee and picked up her needles. Outside the window, the blizzard propelled the gale-strength waves of air clogged with driving sand against the hut's walls and roof. The dust began to seep into the room, slowly covering the window-ledge. On the chest of drawers the white festive tea cups rattled in the draught. 'Because I'm no longer afraid of you,' she said slowly, her eyes focused on the floor. 'Because you are in need of help. Because I remember what typhus is like.'

Marek raised his head from the dish. 'Thank you, Ajmi.'

She looked at him. 'I've a feeling your brother will be all right. I'm sure he will.' He read a rising confidence in her voice, he saw her lips crinkle at the corners, saw the smile grow on her lips and expand over her face. 'Do you play fox-and-geese?'

Marek smiled. 'Indeed I do.'

She put her needles briskly aside, bent down at the chest of drawers and drew out a checker-board and white linen bag. Her lips parted and a glow came into her face as she grabbed another pillow from the bedstead, came to the table and sank down on to the pillow. Vigorously she pushed aside the plates and pulled a black fox figure and four little yellow goose pawns out of the bag. She shook a pawn and the figure behind her back and stuck out her clenched fists. Marek touched her right hand. Her skin was soft and warm and it was a long moment before he remembered that she had unclenched her hands and said gaily, 'You're the fox.' He had never seen her so self-abandoned, buoyant and girlish as now when she was sitting near him, at his right, arranging her four pawns on the dark squares of her first row and placing Marek's figure for him in the opposite corner of the board. 'You start.'

They smiled at each other with a sort of secret glee like school children who have run away from classes for the day and must consciously enjoy every second of their freedom. They became oblivious of the epidemic, the sick brother in the hospital, the husband possibly exposed to the buran on a street of Bokhara. Even the windstorm which roared with a rising snarl and drummed bigger and bigger grains of sand against the window pane was somehow forgotten in the struggle of four geese trying to corner the fox before he has a chance to break through their lines. Ajmi smelled young and scrubbed, and every time she leaned forward to move a pawn, the long lines of her body pleasantly rearranged themselves in shadows under her thin cotton dress. Absently playing the primitive game, Marek shortly found himself with only three squares left on which to move his figure. Ajmi drew in her knees in a playful hug brushing her slanted triumphant face over her knee-joints. Marek's eyes sneaked a glance at the thin bone with taut skin between the redness of her felt shoe and the hem of her pulled up dress. He jiggled with his figure for awhile before retreating again. Her hand, thin at the wrist, hung in the air hesitantly for a second, then her long fingers slowly shifted one of her pawns to the next square. Biting her lips, she studied her position thoughtfully, as if she could still lose the game already won. Marek's disobedient eyes were on her hips, slender and vibrant under the thin cotton of her dress. As she finally, after a little satisfying nod to herself, turned her face to Marek, his eyes flickered back to the board and he made quickly his last, hopeless move. Ajmi jubilantly struck her fists under her chin, grasped a pawn and cornered the fox. 'I won!' she cried, throwing her head back and laughing. 'You want a revenge? I'll be the fox now, all right?'

She knelt on the pillow and eagerly pulled the chess-board closer to herself. As she was arranging the pieces on the black squares, she asked, 'Tell me about Poland. What's the name of your town?'

'Brest Litovsk.'

'Brest Litovsk,' she repeated elaborately, listening to how it sounds. 'Is it like Kermine, or bigger?'

'Bigger.'

'Like Bokhara?'

'Not quite.'

'Are the streets and houses the same as here?'

'No. It has cobblestone streets and brick houses, some two-storey ones. We lived in a three-storey house, the tallest in town.'

Ajmi pushed out her lower lip with admiration for Marek's apparent former wealth. 'All of your houses are brick ones?' Her voice arched high in disbelief.

'Yes. And all of them have electric light and running water.'

Her lips smacked enviously. 'Like Bokhara, eh?'

'Have you been there?' She shook her head. 'Oh, I forgot you told me you never left Kermine. You start the game now.'

She gave a gasp and as if she hadn't heard him, went on asking, 'Did you go to school?'

'Yes. My brother even went to University. I studied at bookkeeping.'

'Is that what you plan to do when we get abroad?'

Marek smiled with an inward sadness as his mind turned

to his sick brother and the imprisoned smuggler. He moistened his scorched lips, once again vowing to himself to go to Ulug Beg after Victor's recovery and to ask him to find someone else to take them across the border. 'You could come to Palestine with us,' Ajmi went on. 'Ibram's family would help you to settle there.' Her heavy eyes looked earnestly into his face.

'We will probably join the Polish Army in England.'

'Army? And what will you do after the war?'

'After the war we will go back to Brest Litovsk.'

Her eyes lowered to the tip of his nose. 'Oh, of course. . . .' She turned her attention to the board and made her first move. For a moment they played quietly. After a while she looked at the window through half closed eyes, a curious smile growing from the corners of her lips. 'Brest Litovsk . . .' she repeated, amused, shaking her head. She began to play aggressively, biting her lips in delighted enjoyment any time Marek paused before making a move.

'You're good at this game. Do you play it often with Ibram?'

'Oh, I never do. He thinks it's childish.' She pouted slightly and Marek's lips twisted into a pleasurable smile.

Waiting for her next move, his eyes wandered to the skein of wool and knitting needles abandoned over the unfinished sweater. 'Why didn't you want to be my friend, when I suggested it? We could have played fox-and-geese many times.'

He saw her almond-shaped eyes elongate even more with a reflective squint and her slim shoulders rise in her habitual dismissing shrug. 'Your turn,' she said, advancing her figure and straightening her back.

For a while Marek fumbled distractedly with his pawns, adjusting them neatly in their squares, then his fingers tightened around one of them, as if he intended to move it forward, but he didn't. Her small tawny face with eyes veiled by long eyelashes regarded him wonderingly. 'It's a difficult position,' he said, feeling her glance on his face, and quickly moved one of his geese forward. Resting her finger-tips over the edge of the table, and roguishly running her pointed tongue in brief jerks over her upper lip, she examined the position. After a while, she crossed her arms on her chest, bending over the board. A slow flush rose in his face and stained it bright red, as he noticed the firm olive sweep of her bosom in the low neckline. The damp skin pulled tight on his forehead and a curious pain ran down the veins of his arm. As he heard the rising intake of his own breath, he bit his lips hard and forced his head to swing away towards the room where the dust that filtered remorselessly through every crack of the window and door, covered part of the floor with a thick coat. 'God, what weather!'

She followed his glance and shook her head in agreement. Behind the window the drifting yellow sand completely blotted out the night blackness. Ajmi looked again at the board and as he looked back at her, he knew from the smile that crossed her dry lips, that she was about to make a particularly clever thrust. But as she picked up a pawn, the door swung open and a blast of air blew a cloud of sand into the room. The light instantly went out, the glass, swept off the table, shattered on the floor, and figures on the checkerboard scattered, With eyes and mouth full of sand, Marek groped to the door, jammed it back and locked it.

'Do you have matches on you?' he heard Ajmi's excited voice in the darkness.

'No'.

A moment later he heard the noise of pots and plates in the kitchen. 'I can't find them! Aren't they on the settee?' He found his way to the plush surface and rummaged over it. His finger came across the needle, got hurt and jerked back involuntarily. He heard the soft sliding sound of Ajmi's felt shoes and knew she was back in the room, but he didn't see her until he bumped against her in darkness, his chest touching for a split second her little breasts, his nose and lips brushing over her cheek. 'I'm sorry,' she said, quickly stepping back. 'Don't you have any matches in your room? I can't find mine.'

'I just lit my stove with the last match and the wind blew out the flame.'

'I had a whole box of matches when I lit the stove.' His eyes became accustomed to the darkness and he saw her silhouette receding towards the window. The warmth of her cheek lingered on his lips and the smell of her moist skin still drifted in the air. The memory of the soft girlish bosom pressed against him drew him irresistibly to the blurred figure at the window. He came close to her and stopped. 'It's late,' she said, without turning to him. He wasn't listening; he stared at the hardly discernible contours of her long body. He saw her turn to him and in the darkness the whites of her eyes gleamed momentarily. 'We'll play another game tomorrow. . . . Good night.'

'Good night,' he mumbled listlessly, his voice sounding hoarse and foreign, and then suddenly he found his arms seizing her head, pulling her to himself and his lips furiously thrusting into her mouth. He closed his eyes, oblivious of anything else but this moment he had yearned for so long. Only when after a while he tasted blood, did he realize that she was biting his lips and, pulling at his hair, struggling vehemently to break the circle of his arms. But when, his mouth swollen and hurt, he was about to let her break loose, her hands left his hair and slid limply down and she was completely inert, as if life had suddenly left her. Then her body shivered against his. Across her small bosom he could feel her heart beating, and when he kissed her again, her lips were open and passive, the tears trickling down her face, wetting her already moist lips.

The fullness of feeling came on him, swelled in his throat, pulsed in his head. He grasped her in his arms and threw her on the bed, his lips biting into her throat, his hand hungrily darting into her low neckline. She gave a short painful cry, as his palm squeezed the warm pliant flesh of her breast, but her body remained impassive, her left hand impotently hanging down from the bed. From her breasts his fingers slipped recklessly down, feeling possessively her belly, haunches and hips, brushing over the lines of her limp legs, and then got lost under her robe, drawn by the velvet, fiery skin of the thighs. His breathing was laboured, and his heart pounded, as if it would break out any second. Then he knew nothing, felt nothing, but the raging fires racing all over his body, burning him mercilessly. He pulled up her robe abruptly and fell upon her. A convulsive spasm went through her benumbed body and she gave a cry and suddenly became alive and wedged her shoulders between him and her, pushing him away with all her strength. But it was too late. As he entered her, with a smothered gasp her face jerked towards his, her arms fell over his neck, her mouth opened wide and her teeth struck against his throat with brief spasmodic cries. In the darkness he could feel her lids and brows tighten, her little face taut from ecstasy. Her fingers dug into his body, clutched handfuls of flesh and pulled it ferociously, as if she wanted to tear him apart. Then with a savage scream, she twisted her arms and legs around him, her open mouth went against his, her teeth struck his teeth, seized his tongue and bit it. The spasm kinked his stomach and the darkness of the room turned around him like the whirlwind beyond the window.

Then they lay quietly, united, their breaths still laboured, their hearts hammering against each other, the delayed spasms occasionally shaking their shoulders and faces. Marek took her face between his palms and kissed her on the eyes. They were open and flickered under his lips. He drove little grateful circles of kisses on her flaming cheeks, then stretched out on the bed, pulling her face close to his, and in affectionate silence lay by her side, happy and peaceful.

After a while he raised his head and looked at her unseen face. His lips moved, but could not find words, so his hand caressed her cheek and nose and forehead. When his fingers touched her eyes, they found them still open. And suddenly she drew away from him, covering her face with her palms, violent sobs shaking her body. 'Please don't cry,' Marek said. 'Please, Ajmi!' He forced her tear-stained face back to his and smothered it with kisses. Under his lips her mouth throbbed with strangled spasms of weeping, until her head fell limply on his shoulder and then with a huge, shuddering sigh she quietened down. He closed his eyes and reassuringly stroked her hair, his hand moving slower and slower, as he fell into the bottomless pit of sleep.

He woke up with a start. Violent howling squalls of wind lashed into his face. The open door banged loudly and the glass shattered on the brick floor. There was a nauseating stench of kerosene in the room. Frantically, Marek's hands groped over the bed beside him. The girl had gone.

He sat up abruptly and called her name. At the same time he remembered he had locked the door, and leaped to his feet. An instant recollection of Hamlat's wife setting fire to herself in the desert after her disgrace struck his mind. Seized by panic he bolted to the door and dashed out into the courtyard.

The whirlwind swept about him, coming at once from all directions, making it impossible for him to move. It seemed to want to pull him off the ground and drag him along its shrieking path, but it kept him in one place, taking his breath away, swallowing his desperate shouts of Ajmi's name. Suddenly a new billow came, strongest of all, and hurled him towards the courtyard's exit. On the road in the dim-light of a street lamp, among the high drifts of sand whipped up during the night, he found the vanishing footprints. He plunged into the darkness and storm, following her trail, time and again lost under a fresh sand layer. His eyes, mouth and nose were choked with sand, but he struggled on among the deserted, wind-swept roads, his face becoming numb with the monotonous heavy whistling in his ears. In the courtyards terrified horses and donkeys neighed and brayed for help. Birds under the roofs whined dolefully. Sparks flickered up high under the torrid wind from the electric wires at Shadiva Street. His legs grew heavy and he panted for breath as he edged against the storm waves with his back to the courtyard walls, praying that he wouldn't lose her track and would soon spot her silhouette.

Achum Babayeffa Street narrowed and passed into a path curving between the walls and opening up into the desert. As he followed the fresher footprints, a heightened fear cried in his mind that Ajmi had found the matches and, hysterically, on the spur of the moment, had run into the desert to follow the centuries old custom of taking one's own life after committing adultery. He wished he had never come here, had stayed away from the border, which instead of freedom had brought the NKVD's inquest, his brother's disease and this terrible night that might end in disaster. 'Ajmi!' he yelled with anguish into the veil of night. His feet splashed through a puddle and mud was blown up into his eyes.

He finally reached the desert, but all the way up the slope of the hill he saw no one. As he fought his way over the scooped topsoils stripped away from roots, a flock of eagles came out of the dust cloud, circling confusedly in the air. Suddenly one of the birds fell like a rock straight down at his feet, and he saw it was dead with its bill and throat packed with dirt.

On the top of the hill Ajmi's trail was suddenly lost. A hard, parched rocky ground stretched away with a few saksaul trees shaking violently in the raging storm. His burned swollen eyes squinted against the sandy wind, searching the terrain, until they made out a group of people and animals inertly clinging to the ground. As he staggered towards the group, the deafening roar of swaying branches of saksaul trees and the terrible rattle of wind-swept pebbles tingled mercilessly in his ears. When at last he reached the group, he noticed it was a stranded caravan that had lost its way in the storm. Engulfed by blinding dust, not realizing that they were close to a town, people huddled under blankets behind the unruffled camels and reinforcing screen of snatched-off saddles. The men with their heads bundled in blankets did not see or hear Marek, only the animals turned their long necks towards him, surprised that, defenceless, he dared the storm in the desert. At that moment a branchy saksaul tree toppled noisily and it seemed to him it exposed the flitting shadow of a girlish figure. 'Ajmi!', he yelled as loud as he could above the noise of the wind, and ignoring the bearded faces that popped out of the blankets, he dashed forward. Through the sand drifting in the air, he could see her figure looming ahead only to be swallowed by darkness a moment later. Then in an instance he saw her face distinctly, as it swung back towards him to see how close he was. Marek came within thirty metres of her when he saw her run to a tree, fall on her knees and strike a match between her cupped palms. 'Ajmi, don't do it!' he screamed, flinging off his jacket. The wind blew out the match, but a new flicker of flame darted out from her hands, and to his horror, picked up the hem of her robe, reaching up over the material sprinkled with kerosene. With his open jacket he threw himself at her body, smothering the flame as closely as he could, paying no attention to her screams and blows. The flames died at once. 'Let me go!' Ajmi shrieked as he twisted her hand, forcing her to throw down the box of matches. She kicked him and struck her fists at his eyes and nose, and when in spite of her resistance he lifted her from the ground, she frenziedly dug her nails into his face. With a strength that surprised himself and with the incessant blizzard blowing behind him he carried her towards the town despite her savage struggles and screams. His eyes burned, inflamed by the wind. He was bleeding and he faltered with his burden, his hair was rumpled, trousers torn, and his jacket had been forgotten in the desert, as with Ajmi sobbing hysterically in his arms, he descended the hill and staggered back to Achum Babayeffa Street.

When he reached her home, he groped through the darkness until he felt his knee touching the hard bed frame. He put her on the bed, knelt on the floor near her and began to stroke her face and kiss her softly, pleading with her to calm down, Suddenly she threw her arms around his neck, pulling him close. Her moist mouth rubbed against his face with spasmodic, wild bites at the flesh of his lips.

19

A HARD RAPPING ON THE door awoke him. He rubbed his face, uncertain whether it wasn't a dream and as, still dizzy from heavy sleep, he listened dully for further sounds, his eyes ranged over the hardly discernible contours of the room. It took him a long time to realize it wasn't his. Then his eyes darted fearfully to the bedstead and detected Ajmi's silhouette under the blanket. Suddenly he saw a blurred figure approaching the window and his stomach tightened. He buckled his belt hastily around his waist and slipped through darkness to the opposite wall. With his back glued to the door, he anxiously watched the shrouded face flattened against the window pane, trying to peep inside. A fly buzzed somewhere under the ceiling. From across the room Ajmi's heavy breathing was audible. A drop of sweat slowly broke out on Marek's forehead. Then a small match flame sprang up outside the window and Marek gasped with relief. The man wasn't Ibram.

Quickly he unlocked the door and stepped out into the wind that had eased up considerably during the night. 'Who is there?' he asked in a low, tense voice. Then as the lanky figure with the bony, dust-splotched face loomed out of the darkness, he recognized the hospital's orderly, Misha. His legs instantly became heavy and a pang of terrible fear ran through him. 'What has happened to my brother?'

'I thought I wouldn't find you. Citizen Doctor said to tell you that you should go to the station and as soon as the medicine comes, rush it to the hospital. You should not lose any time. Every minute is important, the doctor says.'

Marek's jaw pulled and his Adam's apple twitched nervously in his throat. 'Is he conscious?'

'He is in agony,' Misha said. The white courtyard whirled around him and Marek had to look at one of the walls to make it stop. Unable to gather his thoughts, he moved a few steps towards his room, came back and turned to Shukunov's home, then stopped again and glared helplessly at Misha. 'The train is coming in half an hour,' the orderly said. 'Let's go.'

'All right, just a second.' Marek scurried into Ajmi's room, halted in the threshold, unable to plan anything. He wanted to run immediately to the station, but he had a hollow feeling he should do something before leaving. Then suddenly he knew. He rushed out again. Misha was sitting on the bench by the rustling palm tree. 'Give me your matches for a moment, please.' Misha handed him a box and Marek returned to the room and lit a match. He approached Ajmi. In the flickering light he saw her face, her hair tousled from the storm. She slept a hard and deep sleep. Her raised eyebrows were slightly tightened and the skin on her cheeks was warm and flushed. The match blew out, but the picture remained in Marek's mind as he clumsily fumbled with the box to get out a second match. By its light he gathered the shattered glass from the dusty floor and put it in his pocket, then threw the game pieces into the bag and dropped it and the board into a drawer. Then he entered the kitchen where a fly now hummed in a dark corner. He had left a small window open during the night and the kerosene smell had gone. He straightened the overturned primus stove and returned to the room. In the light of a new match he inspected it again, and when he found everything in its place, like a burglar who blots out all marks of his night visit, he tiptoed out of the room. The wind blew into his face. It was no longer thick with sand grains nor hot. He took a shuddering sigh of air into his lungs. 'Come, let's go,' he said. Misha rose from the bench and they left the courtyard.

The storm was spending itself as they made their way across the mounds of sand and heaps of loose branches. The narrow streets of the town, plagued by the twelve-hour long buran, lay asleep in the pre-dawn darkness and scouring whistles of wind. Marek's ears were still ringing, his eyes burned, his throat was dry and his face felt numb. 'The doctor himself doesn't feel too well,' Misha said, shuffling along in his high rubber shoes. 'He has hardly had any sleep since the epidemic broke out. He isn't young, you know.' Marek nodded absently. 'Fortunately, a medical student and a young nurse arrived last night from Tashkent. It will be a lot easier now.'

Marek sighed, his thoughts away in the hospital, as he pictured to himself Victor's red spotted face, the agonizing throbbing of lips that gasped for air, and his delirious, hoarse cries. The silhouette of a night watchman emerged from the side road, moving slowly, banging a cudgel against the courtyard gates to let the people know that storm or no storm they were protected from thieves. As he walked, Marek turned his pocket inside out, getting rid of the glass.

They reached Shadiva Street where the lamps burned, still hardly visible through the slow plumes of dust. A few figures were already at work, tirelessly sweeping away the sand from shop entrances with rude brooms of branches. In Makul Ol Square, the news-stand was overturned with magazines blowing around, the wine store had its roof ripped off and a tree had been pulled out of the ground. The dark clouds in the sky rode by majestically, pierced by the criss-crossing beams of the searchlight from the prison tower. Suddenly a prison car with armed NKVD men standing on its steps skidded noisily around the corner and sped towards the station. A moment later two motor cycles roared out of the same corner, following the police car, their glaring headlights sweeping the street. Marek glanced at Misha and Misha glanced back at Marek and they both said nothing.

Festoons of scrambled wires packed with sand blocked the road at the old mosque. The sidewalk was shining with black water that trickled from the canal. When they passed under the torn banner calling the proletarians of all the world to unite, they saw that the police car was still at the station square, with the NKVD men, the rifles at the ready and bayonets fixed waiting for an order. Unshaven faces of prisoners peered out through the bars. 'Good-bye,' Misha said, and tipped his skull-cap in salute.

'Good-bye. I'll be there soon.' Marek made a cautious détour around the car, but when one of the guards focused his eyes on him, he stopped circling and with as little concern as he could muster walked up the steps and sat on the bench in the dimly lit station-hall. A few minutes later a group of six prisoners, flanked by four uniformed guards with rifles ready to shoot, burst into the station building. As the ragged swooning prisoners were led across the hall, Marek spotted among them the huge broad-shouldered figure that he could not mistake. With open mouth, he watched Hamlat until he disappeared behind the narrow door of the station's NKVD office.

Marek's eyes scrutinized the hall. An Uzbek family was sitting on the floor in the corner, the bearded man regaling his wife and children with clay cups of boiling water and handfuls of raisins out of the bag. A Russian fireman in uniform was sleeping on a bench clutching a steel-helmet in his arms. At the platform exit a paunchy ticket-taker was rolling a cigarette. From his place Marek could see the stooped figures of men shovelling the sand mounds from the tracks. His heart was drumming dreadfully as he got up and asked the ticket-taker whether the train would arrive on time. The loose jowls of the fatherly-looking man shook as he nodded. 'Just a short delay. Do you have a permit?'

'I'm waiting for someone.'

He returned to his bench, leaned the back of his head against the wall, and closed his eyes, breathing stertorously and trying hard to doze to avoid the haunting visions of the hospital barrack. But sleep wouldn't come and his mind powerlessly would turn back to his sick brother. He began nervously to twitch and squirm in his seat, rock back and forth and mumble to himself. Then as the long clock hand moved ahead uninterruptedly and no approaching sound of the train was heard, his panic boiled to an intolerable height and he found himself folding his hands and gasping to God feverish prayers for the medicine to arrive and to arrive in time. Tears welled up in his throat and he had to shut his eyelids tight and bite his thumb hard to halt them. When, after a long while, he opened his eyes, the black curtain outside the building was paling and a bluish light began to descend into the town, awakening it delicately from the slumbrous violence of the night storm. Across the tracks the tops of the mountains were slowly outlining themselves on the horizon.

The cold draught brought the click of telegraph keys into the hall. The fireman woke up, yawned, and looked dumbfounded at the clock. 'Hey, what happened to the train?' he yelled to the guard in the exit.

'Hasn't come yet, but should be in shortly. The buran slowed it down.'

The guard stepped back from the exit to give way to a young man rushing excitedly to the NKVD room with a cable in his hand.

The shutter of the ticket-window banged up and steel-rimmed spectacles and a bundle of grey hair appeared behind the counter. 'Line up for the tickets, Citizens,' the ticket-taker ordered. The noisy grunts of sipping tea ceased in the corner and the father of the family rushed to the counter. The fireman patiently walked to join the two-man queue. From the NKVD office the young telegraphist scurried out back to his own office. Right behind him a uniformed NKVD man dashed across the hall to the street. A motor whirred outside and with a heavy throbbing beat rambled off in the distance. Through the half-lit exit to the street, Marek could see above the flat roofs a spot of dense scarlet composed of countless shadows growing slowly over the greyish sky. Into the hall rolled the rotund figure of the station-master, trimming his red visored cap and stretching his uniform jacket for duty. The door of the NKVD office was flung open and another guard slid to a halt at the sight of the station-master. 'I was about to get you. The Bokhara train must stop here. A special train is coming from Tashkent.'

'Special train?' The station-master's voice rose high in astonishment.

The NKVD man man threw a glance at Marek and shooed the station-master in the direction of the NKVD office.

With misery gnawing at his heart, Marek froze his eyes on the clock, stretching his ears for any sounds. He rose and walked nervously back and forth across the hall, then returned to his place and fell back on to his bench. A charwoman entered the hall and went to the women's lavatory, marked by a painted hen. A second later she was back in the hall with a can and broom, spilling the water over the floor and sweeping away the wet mounds of dust. From the street came the roar of an approaching motor cycle. A streak of light pierced through the door as the wheels of the machine skidded to a stop with a squeal. Then the motor died and a second later Kisielev appeared in the hall, busily rushing to the NKVD office, followed by the NKVD guard who had gone to fetch him.

Marek's eyes focused on the tracks outside, where the men had stopped working and with their shovels moved back to the platform. The ticket-taker stepped out on to the platform and leaned forward, staring into the dark distance. With a rasp, the loudspeaker went on, a man's voice announcing the imminent arrival of the train. The door of the NKVD office opened and the prisoners were ushered out by their armed escorts. Instinctively Marek turned his head away, but when he heard their thudding steps receding towards the platform, he sneaked a glance over his shoulder and saw the tall figure of Hamlat, with his erect head rising above the heads of the other prisoners. At the platform he stopped to adjust his unwrapped rug over his shoe and immediately he received a booted toe in his buttock. Marek saw his tight face glance at the guard with such loathing as if he were about to crush him in a moment. The guard stepped back and cocked his gun. Reluctantly and slowly Hamlat walked away.

The rattle of the train was distinct now, growing louder every second. A whistle of the locomotive resounded in the distance, drowning out the renewed click of the telegraphic keys. The station-master stepped out on to the platform and the ticket-taker called to the Uzbek family wrapping their cups in their bundle and the Russian fireman sitting back at his bench, to get their tickets and permits ready. As they queued up at the exit, the station-master appeared in the doorway and advised them to relax because the train would be detained in Kermine for a couple of hours before proceeding to Tashkent.

As the people moved disappointedly back to their places, another NKVD guard scuttled out of the office with a cable to the telegraph office. On his way he glanced quickly at Marek, and the sudden thought brushed the surface of Marek's mind that Kisielev had released him only in order to put him under observation to trace other smugglers whom he might contact. Instantly he felt that probably all the guards knew of him, and he rose from his bench and went out of the station to wait for Ibram in the dusky street.

He heard the squealing of wheels against the rails and watched the cars popping out from around the bend of the hill, and after a while disappearing beyond the brick station building, slowing to a halt behind the heavily-panting loco-motive. In the long minutes of waiting, Marek clenched his fists nervously until the knuckles showed white. Finally, among the passengers that thronged out of the station build-ing, he saw the familiar short-sleeved figure of Ibram, his hands in his pockets as he walked briskly down the steps. Though Marek had promised himself to wait for Ibram in his place he sprinted to him across the square. 'Have you got it?' he gasped, in trembling tones.

The close-set eyes, red from lack of sleep, blinked nervously and Ibram hushed him up. 'Come with me.' They walked across the square among the people there. Marek's eyes fastened prayerfully on Ibram's lips. 'How did you get through the buran?' Ibram asked.

'All right.'

'No harm done to my house?'

'No.' Marek's brows shot up with unbearable tension. 'Do you have it?' he whispered pleadingly. Ibram nodded quietly. 'Thank God,' Marek breathed. He slowed his pace, to let the other passengers pass them by. 'He is dying,' Marek said with harsh impatience. 'Give it to me quickly.'

Casually, Ibram looked back over his shoulder and seeing no one behind them walked closer to Marek, pulled a small package out of his pocket and passed it quickly to him. 'I got five grams,' he whispered, watching the backs of the people in front of him. 'Enough for five injections.'

'Thank you,' Marek murmured and stopped.

'It's the first time I've done such a thing. I never dealt with black marketeers because it would be silly to get caught, put in jail and lose the chance to get out. But it wasn't too bad, really.'

'I'm very grateful to you . . . I'd better rush to the hospital.'
As Ibram gave him a little farewell smile, Marek avoided his
eyes, looking down at the toes of his shoes. 'Are you going
straight to work?'

'I think so. I don't even have time now to get a quick wash.
Hope the injections will help your brother.' He slapped
Marck's arm sympathetically and walked away. Marek raised
his head, looking after him as if he wanted to say something,
but then turned and began to run towards the hospital.

Across the festoons of barbed wire hastily put out to protect
the tracks from the mass of drifting earth, Marek could see the
last car of the train, a prison car, its door and window strength-
ened by iron bars. He hopped over the uprooted chunks of
earth, his feet sinking into the mud or sliding over dry branches
torn off the trees by the storm. He clutched the package hard
against his chest, afraid of dropping it in his hurry. Squalls
of birds hummed above him, flying out of their night refuge
for a refreshing gasp of air. When Marek had made half the
journey he thought he wouldn't be able to move any farther.
His legs throbbed and his heart hammered and pained terribly.
Suddenly he noticed in front of him a human silhouette, lying
by the road. As he came closer to it, he saw it was a lifeless
body clothed with dirt. From unhealed bruises on the rash-
covered face trickled a little stream of black blood, swarming
with flies. With a gasp of repulsion, he turned his head away,
and, with all the strength he could muster, he spurred forward,
his eyes wandering over the sky, his lips muttering short,
frantic pleadings. The low humming wind sang in his ears,
swelled by occasional train whistles. On the hill he saw many
lights blinking dimly, and as he approached and saw the
blurred tombs, he knew that the candles were burning in the
Uzbek cemetery. In front of him he heard a squeaking sound,
and shortly after from the slowly shrinking night shadows
an arba emerged with two hospital helpers. The driver drew
in the reins and shouted to him, 'Have you seen a body lying
by the road?'

'Yes,' Marek yelled back, not stopping. 'It isn't far from

here, on your left. You can't miss it!' Suddenly the dreadful thought crossed his mind that he might come too late, and he feverishly dashed forward to forestall implacably moving time. The yurt of the Khirgiz shepherd had gone, but by the railway tracks, under a sharp-thorned saksaul tree, a sheep lay dead, mudballs plastered over its face. Above it in the sky, black silhouettes of vultures wheeled silently. Finally the gravelled road opened to his left, with a sign 'Kermine Hospital No. 1.' As he sprinted over the last part of the way, the multi-shaded scarlet of the sun rose, widened and diluted, revealing the reddish contours of the hospital barracks with armed soldiers by the barbed wire. His shirt soaking in sweat, and almost completely out of breath, Marek reached the administration barrack and then stopped abruptly. With sudden panic, he raised the package to his ear and shook it gently. The ampoules were intact. Gasping relief, he bolted to the door and thrust it open.

Behind the table sat an unfamiliar young man with sunken cheeks and severe dark eyebrows that shot up in an annoyance at Marek's abrupt intrusion. 'Can't you knock? It's not your home, you know.'

'I'm sorry,' Marek panted. 'Where is the doctor?'

'I'm a doctor.'

'I mean Pavel Stepanovicz,' Marek said, guessing he was facing the medical student from Tashkent.

'Who?'

'Dr Bunin.'

'He is sleeping. Are you sick?'

'No, I must see him. Immediately!' Marek's voice rose excitedly.

'Shhhh! . . . He sleeps there!'

Marek's eyes darted to the plywood screen. 'Please wake him. It's very urgent!'

'I won't, he needs a rest, too. Now, please go out!' He rose from behind the table.

Marek retreated a step and then shouted, 'Pavel Stepano-vicz!'

'How dare you! Get out at once!'

The young man dashed at Marek and as he tried to collar him, a heavy grumble came from behind the screen followed by an annoyed, 'What the hell is going on there?'

'It's me, Marek Sobel!'

'Oh. . . . Leave him alone!' Hasty shuffling steps were heard and Pavel Stepanovicz came out, be-aproned and shoeless.

'I wanted you to get a rest, Comrade Doctor. I was sent here to relieve you.'

'Boil me a syringe.'

The medical student glanced at Marek, then at the doctor, and without a word went behind the screen. 'How is my brother?' Marek asked, his voice tense and trembling.

'I'll be right with you.' The doctor left Marek waiting in the room, quivering from the unanswered question. While behind the plywood the primus stove sizzled and the sluggish grunts of a struggle to put on shoes were heard, Marek nervously walked back to the door, opened it and stared at the window of the barrack, behind which he knew his brother was lying. On the horizon the bright yellow sun rose. An arba drew slowly past the road towards the office. 'Well, I'm ready, Sobel.' The doctor, with the help of the medical student, wrapped the syringe in a clean towel. 'Let's go!'

They walked out. A short distance from the office the cart was parked, the donkey stupidly searching for grass among the pebbles. In the cross-legged figure sitting at the cart, Marek recognized Ulug Beg. The old man had his eyes focused on the doctor, with a painful wordless inquiry. Pavel Stepanovicz glanced at him, but said nothing. Ulug Beg's red-patched eyes followed the doctor's figure until it disappeared inside the barrack.

As they entered, Marek's eyes darted to the part of the room near the central window. There was only his brother in the barrack and a blurred emptiness around him, as Marek neared his bed. He lay on his back, his eyes glazed and immobile, his damp cheeks pimpled with fever, and the ten-day growth of beard plastered by sweat. The rash that had spread all

167

over his face, chest and even shivering hands, had become very dark. Through dry swollen lips, glued to his teeth, between laboured panting, words came spasmodically, 'Don't take me to the hospital . . . I'm all right . . . I must make the train . . . I must make the train! . . . I must make the train!'

With a heavy heart, his throat closed with unshed tears, Marek gazed at the eyeballs, white as marble, sunk in the deep sockets, framed by the lashes heavy with yellow matter. The doctor took the package from Marek's hand, unwrapped the box and took out one of the five adrenalin ampoules wrapped in cotton. 'Nurse!' he called, and as Marek followed the doctor's look, the rest of the barrack came into focus and he saw four long rows of iron beds with the typhus-stricken, sunk in numbed stupor, muttering to imaginary persons, or moaning painfully among violent tremors. Appalling salty odours mushroomed in the room, stinging the eyes like the vapour of sheep urine. A ginger-haired, freckled girl approached the doctor and glanced at Marek, breathing a well rehearsed sigh of sympathy. She corrected her severe hair bun, as she waited for the doctor to finish examining Victor's pupils. 'Get me some alcohol, please,' Pavel Stepanovicz said to her.

The nurse walked to a medicine chest in the barrack's corner and returned with a bottle. As she was helping the doctor to turn Victor on his side and roll down his pyjama pants, Anna Matviejevna entered the barrack and came to the doctor. She whispered something into his ear; Pavel Stepanovicz glanced at the next bed where the Polish boy was lying with open eyes, and nodded after a few seconds. 'But do not let him get too close,' he said to the nurse as she walked away. The young nurse moistened a piece of cotton in alcohol and rubbed Victor's thigh. Pavel Stepanovicz blinked annoyedly, and grunted under his breath. He raised the ampoule against the light, flicked its top with his fingers to free it from the liquid and cut it off with a little blade enclosed in the package. As he was drawing the adrenalin into the syringe, Anna Matviejevna passed them, holding the little blond boy by the hand and stopped at the next bed. 'Here is your brother,' she said.

The two boys looked at each other for a long while, then the sick brother said in Polish, 'Hallo, Piotrus.'

'Hallo, Franek.'

'Will you rub his skin now, Nurse,' Pavel Stepanovicz said to the young nurse.

'I did, Doctor.'

'Do it again.' The doctor's puffy fingers handling the syringe trembled nervously. 'Didn't they teach you in Tashkent that alcohol evaporates quickly and that the dust particles settle back on the skin?'

The nurse bowed her head, embarrassed, and obeyed the doctor's instruction. He waited for his hand to stop trembling and then, with one energetic move, thrust the needle into Victor's flesh. As if the sudden pain surprised him, his lips stopped moving deliriously, and the gaping mouth revealed a thick tongue covered with ulcers. Marek stared into his face with dismay, praying that the injection would bring about a sudden miraculous recovery. But though the nurse rolled up the pants of Victor and covered him with blankets, the chilling spasms shook his whole body anew, his lips bit hungrily at the air, and then he began to mutter to his brother that because of the Polish-Russian war alliance, they would soon be released from the labour camp. Marek looked at the doctor, trying to read a verdict in his eyes. The young nurse left to go to an old Uzbek, wailing savagely like a deadly hurt animal. 'Now all you can do is pray,' Pavel Stepanovicz said slowly, holding Victor's wrist. 'I've forgotten how, but you may still remember.'

'I do,' Marek gasped earnestly.

'He has a very rapid lysis,' the doctor said to Anna Matviejevna. 'Remind me to give him the next injection in two hours.'

'All right, Pavel Stepanovicz. Now, please go back to bed.'

'I will, I will!' the doctor grumbled and took the box with injections to the young nurse. Shreds of Polish dialogue now came to Marek's ears, 'Kiss our parents for me when you find them. . . . Keep on looking for them, Piotrus . . . I have five roubles in my jacket and two pencils, one coloured, take all that. . . . Eat well, Piotrus, and in the evenings wrap the scarf around your neck, as Mother told you. . . .' The younger boy kept staring at his brother with open mouth, and then as he understood, his lips closed and the tears trickled down from his big blue eyes. Somewhere in the barrack a sick man was seized by a piercing fit of coughing. On the other side of Victor's bed, a bewhiskered old Russian peasant began to cross himself, pound his chest and call upon the Holy Virgin. Pavel Stepanovicz returned and stopped at the bed of the Polish boy at the sight of his perspiring, solemn face and the tear-blurred face of his younger brother. 'Take the boy out now, Anna Matviejevna,' he said, pulling at the white flakes of his brows.

'Good-bye, Franek!' the boy sobbed and made a step to his brother, stretching his arms to him.

The nurse gently took him by the shoulders. 'I can't embrace you, because you might catch typhus!' Franek said, with an adult effort, managing a little smile. 'Keep looking for our parents, remember. . . .'

'Come!' the doctor said to Marek, who stood frozen at Victor's bed with his eyes glued to his brother's mouth, throbbing in delirious spasms. 'It takes some time for adrenalin to take effect. I'll let you visit him again in two hours.' Reluctantly, he turned towards the door.

The sick Russian suddenly sat up in bed. 'Doctor!' he yelled drunkedly after him, 'I want a priest! I don't want to die without the last sacraments. I want a priest!'

'Nurse!' Pavel Stepanovicz called. The young nurse quickly rushed to the patient. 'Give him a sedative.' He took off his spectacles and cleaned them.

'Aspirin?'

'Yes!' He walked to the door. 'I'd rather get some medicine than this sort of help!,' he mumbled to Marek. He turned at the sounds of struggle in the barrack and rushed back to the sick Russian, whom the young nurse and Anna Matviejevna tried to keep from leaving the bed. 'You go!' the doctor called to Marek. 'And I don't want to see you here for two hours.'

Marek walked out of the barrack. Ulug Beg sat in the same

cross-legged position as before on his cart opposite the office. At the noise of the steps, his eyes darted to the barrack's exit, but as he saw Marek they turned away in disappointment without recognizing him. Marek stopped at his cart and the red-patched eyes looked up at him, dully. The old man's wrinkled cheeks had lost their flesh, reduced almost to skin and bones. 'Oh. . . .,' he said. 'How is your brother?'

'Unconscious. The doctor just gave him an injection. Maybe it will help. I hope it will help.'

The yellow lids shot up excitedly. 'The injections have arrived?'

'I managed to get some for my brother. From Bokhara. How is Aka?'

Ulug Beg shook his head miserably. 'The doctor said today will decide if she will live. I wish her father were here. He hasn't come back yet, you know.'

Marek lowered his head, mumbled a word of comfort to the old man and walked away over the gravelled road of the hospital. The sun was shining radiantly. The wind had passed into a soft, pleasant morning breeze. In the air, birds chippered merrily.

'Sobel!' Marek turned at the sound of the doctor's voice. At the sight of Pavel Stepanovicz's long stooped figure walking to him hurriedly, his heart stopped beating, and he began to run to the doctor. 'What happened, Doctor?' he shouted.

Pavel Stepanovicz waved his hands. 'Oh, nothing, nothing to your brother. It's about this Polish boy. I want to ask you a favour. Could you spare a gram of adrenalin for him? I want to save that boy.'

'He's completely conscious. Not like my brother.'

'His lungs have developed a gangrene.'

Marek rubbed his face and sighed heavily. 'Will the four grams be sufficient to save my brother?'

The doctor spread his hands and shook his head. 'I don't know. Maybe the injection I made now will be sufficient. Or maybe even five grams won't help him. I can't tell. I can't assume the responsibility, I can only ask. It's up to you to decide.'

Marek felt his skin instantly tightening over the bones of his face. He gulped and said, 'I can't take the risk, Doctor. When you'll know for sure that my brother will recover, you may use the spare adrenalin for this boy.'

'Then it will be too late. And who knows,' the doctor sighed, 'maybe they could both pull through, who knows. . . .'

Marek looked apologetically into doctor's pale blue eyes. 'I've only this one brother, Doctor. Please understand me. I wish I could say yes, but you can't give me any assurance. . . .' He broke off, for from the hospital barrack the old nurse came gently pushing the blond boy forward, his little knuckles digging into his weeping eyes. The doctor turned and together with Marek they saw the boy parting with Anna Matviejevna, walking slowly towards them, without seeing them, dragging his big rugged boots with crude, unfastened socks falling down over them. Suddenly he stopped, wiped his eyes and quickened his pace, all his attention now focused at the loud whistles and noises of the passenger train that was coming to a stop some half-way between the station and the hospital. Marek looked for a second at the distant train and then again at the boy as he passed them by, crumpling a visored cap in his hand. 'Go ahead, Doctor,' he said. 'Take that gram for his brother.' Without a word Pavel Stepanovicz dashed back to the barrack. 'Piotrus!' Marek called after the little boy, but he didn't hear him. At the end of the gravelled road, Piotrus stopped, and as he looked at the barrack again, a short smothered sob contorted his small face. Then he began to run to the train, which might have brought his lost parents, and the parents the boy knew could rescue his brother from any sickness.

Marek sat at the big stone by the road. He saw old Ulug Beg's stooped figure at the cart benumbed in helpless awaiting. From the distance the breeze carried the train's whistles and the tumult of voices. For a long while Marek gazed at the barrack behind the barbed wire enclosure, guarded by armed soldiers. Then he lifted his eyes to the clear, peaceful sky, and began to pray.

20

MAREK RAISED HIS HEAD AT the sound of a train whistle. In the distance he saw a crowd that had bivouacked by the tracks quickly climbing into the cars. An arba wheeled past him, with an Uzbek and a moaning woman, its way marked by a tiny streak of blood on the gravelled road. Marek got up from his stone and walked towards the hospital. The train, after a few short warning blasts, began to move slowly from its unscheduled halt behind the station. The young medical student stepped out of the office, raised the blanket from the sick Uzbek woman, and began to examine her. A moment later Pavel Stepanovicz came out, a bundled towel in his hands. He gestured to Marek not to follow him and walked into the hospital, past the cart where Ulug Beg sat cross-legged, silently waiting for the outcome of Aka's crisis, disturbing no one with a single word of inquiry. As the train, its window filled with curious heads, rattled by a few hundred metres away, Marek recalled that people in town had been saying that displaced persons from occupied territory were being evacuated to Central Asia. His throat trembled as he stopped at the barbed wire, opposite the central window of the barrack where the blurred faces of the doctor and the young nurse moved over the unseen bed. When after a while the faces disappeared, Marek knew that the second injection had been given to his brother. The doctor came out of the barrack, wearily rubbing his small, red-rimmed eyes. Marek rushed to him. 'How is he now?' he asked tensely. 'Any change?'

'No. You'd better take another walk and come back later.'

'Can't I sit by him?'

'No, he needs some quiet now.' Pavel Stepanovicz joined the medical student, bewildered over the sick woman, her gaunt aggrieved husband standing by, shaking his head at the sight of the growing puddle of blood under the cart. The doctor raised the blanket and scrutinized the woman's face and body, then, disregarding his young colleague, called Anna Matvie-jevna from the office and told her that the woman had had a miscarriage as a result of typhus infection. The nurse nodded and instructed the orderlies to take her to the women's barrack. As the doctor retreated into his office, the young student trailed behind him into the office, explaining vehemently that he had been unable to detect the symptoms because he had never dealt with a pregnant woman before.

Marek circled around the enclosure and stopped, as he had many times before, opposite the central window of Victor's barrack and peered at it from the distance, though he knew it was impossible to see him. After a while he forced himself to leave the barbed wire and began to walk across the hard desert ground covered with pebbles, promising himself to stay away from the hospital, knowing he wouldn't be able to do so for long. He ambled down the hill and again up the hill, dizzy from the sleepless night and the time-killing walk. He saw the track running nearby, winding up through the distant mountains. Marek sat on the railway embankment, thinking about his brother, conjuring up wishful images of his recovery, mingled with frightening visions of his death.

The rail whined, and as Marek looked at the Kermine station, he saw a smoking train running through without a halt, past the Tashkent-bound train that was still there. He rose and began to descend the hill. With the approaching wheels' clatter a bawdy song came to his ears. The cars whipped by with fleeting glimpses of hazy faces in the windows. The song drifted off in the distance, and after a while only purple smoke was moving slowly on the horizon. Marek turned towards the hospital and walked quickly until he reached the top of the hill. As the hospital barracks loomed up in front of him he began to run.

A small throng of relatives were assembled outside the barbed wire, men and women sitting crosslegged on the ground, talking to the guards, accosting the passing nurse for a bit of news. From his cart Ulug Beg gazed cloudily at Marek, and a wretched little smile passed between the two men, so close now in their common vigil. 'Sobel,' Marek heard the Uzbek's voice behind him, when he had already reached the entrance to the barrack. The old man beckoned to him. When Marek came to his cart, he handed him a newspaper wrapping. 'I have been carrying it with me all the time and always forgot to give it to you,' he said guiltily.

'What is it?'

'The money. You didn't go, so I'm giving it back to you.'

'Oh, well, thank you.' Marek put the package into his pocket, then glanced at Victor's window and entered the barrack.

From the threshold he saw the doctor with the help of the young nurse making a lumbar puncture on the apple-cheeked NKVD guard. He walked to his brother's bed and stopped there, miserably watching his face, all streaked with runnels of dried sweat, his blotched lips trembling in a low muttering delirium, 'I'll take care of him, Mother. . . . Just don't worry. . . . Don't worry. . . . We'll keep together. . . .'

'Victor,' Marek sighed, 'I'm here, near you ! . . .' His eyes travelled to the doctor, pleading for help. He was still bent over his patient. As Marek turned back to his brother, his eyes froze. The bed on which the Polish boy had lain in the morning was empty. Marek swallowed hard. After a while heavy steps sounded behind him, followed by the doctor's voice, 'I told you there is no point in your coming in. Nurse!' he called to the young woman helping the patient to lie down. 'Please take his temperature.'

'I did it two hours ago. I took the temperatures of all the patients.'

'I know. Please give him a thermometer and do it every hour.'

'What happened to the boy?' Marek asked.

He saw the doctor's Adam's apple bobbing up in his throat. A vague mist shrouded his pale blue eyes. 'There was no need for your injection. When I came back, he was gone.'

Helplessly, Marek saw Piotrus rushing to the train in hope of the miraculous arrival of his parents to save his brother.

Then as the nurse put a thermometer under Victor's arm and the doctor with the stethoscope in his ears leaned over his brother, Marek's mind flashed back to the summer seashore vacation when he and Victor, aged seven and eleven, were building a train in the sand. He blinked, and his attention snapped back to the present, for the doctor began to listen to Victor's heart. 'How is it?' Marek asked impatiently, peering miserably into the doctor's face. Pavel Stepanovicz hushed him up, listened for another while, then with the same instrument examined Victor's chest. When he finished, he pulled the thermometer out from under his arm and read it at the window. 'It's subnormal already,' he said, slightly surprised.

'What does it mean? Is it good or bad?'

Pavel Stepanovicz shrugged. 'I can't tell yet. We have to watch for further developments.'

'Can I stay here?'

'No, I'd rather you left. You can inquire again in an hour, but I don't want to see you here until then.'

'Thank you, Doctor.' Pavel Stepanovicz walked to a patient groaning loudly in the third row of beds. Marek listened for a moment to his brother's gasping whistles and spasmodic words that now became incoherent, then strode to the exit. When he reached the chart on which the nurse was scribbling Victor's latest temperature, he turned and walked back to the doctor. 'There is an old man outside,' he said. 'He has been there since dawn. How is his granddaughter, Aka?'

The doctor looked up at him, startled. 'Oh. . . . Her crisis also came today. She's unconscious. . . . Why?'

'If you think a gram of adrenalin can help her, please give her the gram that you didn't use for the Polish boy.'

'It would certainly help, but . . . there are so many it would help. Are they friends of yours?'

'I owe a debt . . . to someone in her family.'

The doctor's eyes measured him for a second, then he nodded, and gave the nurse orders to sterilize the hypodermic syringe. He looked over the faces of a few patients around him, then gestured to Marek to stop staring at his brother across the room and to go. The moment the doctor had left, Marek's eyes roamed again to his brother's head near the window. He walked back to him and sat beside his bed on the stool. Victor's face wasn't throbbing now, but his lips were drawn over his mouth and his eyes were shut. Marek looked around the barrack and he saw the young nurse helping the patient in the second row, groaning painfully among the abrupt fits of coughing. Victor's neighbour, who had called for a priest in the early morning, had now lapsed back in numbed stupor with an appalling grimace on his lips, drawn back over his gums. His features were wrinkled in a sort of carnival laugh. Through the open window came a breeze of refreshing air. Folding his hands limply on his knees, his back stooped, Marek watched his brother with an uneasy wrinkle of his forehead.

In the next bed the man opened his eyes as if he had wakened up. Marek glanced at him, and saw that his glazed eyes looked drunkenly at the ceiling. His breathing became suddenly very rapid and the skin on his face and hands moistened. 'Nurse!' Marek called across the room. 'That man needs your help!'

The girl looked hesitantly at her patient whose coughing had now developed into vomiting, then laid him back down in his bed. She glanced at Victor's neighbour, then bolted for the door. In a moment she was back with the doctor. Pavel Stepanovicz leaned over the man. His chest was no longer rising and the flickering in his eyes had gone. 'Why didn't you call me earlier?' the doctor asked the nurse, angrily.

'I didn't know. . . . I cannot look after forty men all at once. . . .' She began to weep softly. 'This is the first time I've been assigned to a hospital. . . .'

'Call the orderlies.'

The doctor approached Victor and took his wrist and for a while listened to his pulse. Then he let his hand go, walked to the medical chest and brought a thermometer. He put it under Victor's arm, then once again with his stethoscope listened to Victor's heart and chest. As Marek peered into his face, trying to read his reaction, the doctor nodded a few times to himself, then began rolling up the stethoscope. 'How is he?' Marek asked impatiently.

Pavel Stepanovicz pulled the thermometer from under Victor's arm and took the reading. Two orderlies came into the room with a stretcher and put Victor's neighbour on it. The doctor looked after them reflectively, as they staggered to the exit with their heavy burden. The man's groans from the second row became louder now with each spasm and made a continuous complaint. The doctor smoothed his grey beard, looking into Marek's face. His eyes were veiled with a faint mist. 'Your brother is yours,' he said.

Marek opened his mouth and gaped at the doctor with disbelief. 'But he is still unconscious, Doctor.'

Pavel Stepanovicz smiled with faint inner humour. 'He sleeps,' he said. 'He just sleeps.'

The tears instantly forced their way into Marek's throat and he was unable to halt them. 'Thank you, Doctor,' he mumbled, and, ashamed, turned his eyes away, wiping them with his palm. 'I'm sorry, Doctor . . . I just couldn't any more . . . I couldn't . . .'

Pavel Stepanovicz glanced at him benevolently. 'His temperature has stopped falling. In fact it has begun to pick up and will soon return to normal. Hope there won't be any complications.'

Marek raised his head. 'What do you mean?'

'Sometimes after typhus, pneumonia sets in from the long stay in bed. But we moved him from side to side frequently, and his lungs seem to be all right. Sometimes a patient gets meningitis. If when he wakes up he doesn't have a stiff neck and can move his head, there is nothing else to be worried about. Though I must warn you that he may lose some hair, have trouble with hearing, remain in a state of apathy or be generally weak, but none of these after-effects last long.' He covered Victor gently with a blanket. 'I think he will pull through all right. The worst is over. He is yours now.' He glanced at the orderlies leaving the room with the dead. He sighed, 'I wish I could have fulfilled that man's last wish and got him a priest.' Again he turned to Marek. 'I will let you wait until he wakes up, but that will be your last visit.'

'Why?'

'Your visits to him have helped to strengthen his will to live, and his will helped his heart. There is no need for you to take any further risk, though I must say you have behaved with as much caution as anybody.'

'But, Doctor, you know I had typhus when I was a child.'

The little blue eyes squinted humorously. 'Did you really think I was an old fool.'

'But, Doctor . . .'

'Okay, okay. . . . The last time, remember!' He quickly scrutinized a few damp faces pimpled with typhus rash and left.

Marek remained on the stool, his eyes focused on his brother. As the time passed he thought that the rash somehow seemed to have paled and Victor's lips and lids weren't inflamed any longer. His chest was rising evenly and the hands lay peacefully over the blanket. New patients were brought in and put into the beds on either side of Victor. Through the open window Marek saw tents being raised in the hospital area. Among the people bivouacking on the ground he saw Ulug Beg, asleep in his cross-legged position, his bony little head hanging over his chest. Suddenly he heard muttering and his eyes moved back to Victor. He stirred a little in his sleep, then his lids fluttered and opened slowly. For a long time he stared emptily at the ceiling. Marek leaned towards him and looked expectantly into his face. Victor's eyes flicked to his brother's face. 'Marek,' he said with a drowsy voice.

'Yes, Victor?'

He saw his brother's forehead wrinkle thoughtfully, then with difficulty he breathed, 'Did you take the money from my trousers? We'll need it when Hamlat comes back.'

'I have it, don't worry. . . . You won, Victor! The doctor said everything is over now.' Marek leaned back in his seat, hoping for Victor's head to turn to him. But it did not move.

His brother closed his lids for a moment, sighed deeply, but said nothing. Unhappily fixing his eyes on Victor's stiff neck, Marek went on, 'Ibram went to Bokhara and got adrenalin for you—in time. Your crisis came this morning. It is all over now.' He drew a long breath and said loudly, as if he was afraid Victor didn't hear him all this time, 'In a week or so you will be strong again and leave the hospital, and then we will go abroad.'

A whole minute passed before Marek's words reached Victor's mind. And then, as Marek's eyes fixed anxiously on his brother's head, he saw a tiny, nostalgic shadow of a smile throb on Victor's pale, narrow lips, and then his head slowly turned and he looked through the open window at the distant mountains glittering under the bright, peaceful sky.

21

IT WAS LATE AFTERNOON WHEN Marek finally started back from the hospital towards the town. Over the writhing road, shimmering in the sun, an intangible film of dust floated in the sultry air. With the buran that had come and gone, it was now another hot November day. On the hill black-robed workers were digging a row of graves in advance. Several lighted candles shone among the barrel-shaped tombs. As Marek walked quickly over the uneven ground, rutted by cartwheels, he tried to imagine his home in Brest Litovsk some years from now. He anticipated the warm atmosphere of evening and saw his parents, their faces beaming, listening to Victor's story of how, during the week of his brother's illness, Marek had matured from a weak, indecisive boy into a man. There was one more thing to be done, he thought, to justify Victor's future statement, and that was why he was now going back to town. He began to rehearse the words of regret and apology. From the desert a Kirghiz nomad was walking towards the road, his dead sheep, killed by the storm, slung across his back. Two lumbering ox-carts passed Marek, carrying piles of tents and folded iron beds to the hospital. It wasn't just that she was married, Marek reflected; what was worse was that she was married to a man without whose help Victor wouldn't be alive. The despair of the night, the uncertainty of dawn, and the morning prayer had bred in him a feeling of deep indebtedness to Ibram. There was only one way out, Marek was telling himself, looking at the approaching Uzbek matrons, jogging along on their ponies—to move from the Shukunovs' house to another room and never show up in their part of town. Perhaps in time Ajmi would forget that night, and perhaps Ibram would never find out about it.

The breeze brought with it a rumble of voices from the busy railway station. A train had just arrived, and over the brick building Marek could see the clouds of steam fading away into the sky. As he passed the window of the dining hall, he saw two railwaymen flanking Marusia at a table laden with vodka, herring and bread. Her head propped on her palms, she stared at her half-filled glass, indifferent to the loud singing of her red-faced companions. Through the door of the waiting hall Marek's eyes roamed absently over the crowd of passengers when he suddenly noticed the little figure of Piotrus. He was moving among the men and women, peering up into their faces, touching their arms with the same question on his lips. Invariably they shook their heads, but the boy, never giving up hope, continued his routine check for his lost parents.

The square in front of the station filled with riders of tiny donkeys. They tethered their animals to the poles and thronged into the waiting hall. Marek walked into Shadiva Street, forcing himself to keep his mind busy on the affairs of the town so that there wouldn't be room left for any hesitation before he carried out his decision. He passed the old mosque in which the town's only 'bus', requisitioned in a hurry and freshly painted grass-green, was drying before its despatch to reinforce the front. The be-aproned sanitation men came out of one house carrying their disinfecting sprinklers, crossed the street and entered another. In Makul Ol Square the many-braided women in colourful paranjas waited in line for their bread, standing at a cautious distance from one another. The white circle was still painted over the closed storefront of the Tajik craftsman. From the entrance of his shop the grocer snapped his fingers at the sight of Marek. 'Wait a second!' He rushed into the store and came back with a small parcel. 'A pound of flour. I'll get the other rations in a few days.'

'Thank you,' Marek said with grim humour, taking the package.

'Did you hear the latest communiqué?'

'No.'

'The Germans have bombed the morning passenger train to Tashkent. There were many killed and wounded.' It wasn't until a whole minute later, when Marek passed squatting Uzbeks in front of the closed barber shop, that he realized the bombed train was the one that had carried Hamlat and his fellow prisoners to Siberia.

Turning into Achum Babayeffa Street, Marek slowed his pace and his heart quickened. He entered the familiar white-edged gate and looked at the Shukunovs' window that shone in the sunlight, reflecting the courtyard walls. Above the house purple smoke was rising from the red-brick chimney. Slowly he approached the door, and as he put his hand on the knob, he already knew that he would not be able to say any of the words he had so carefully planned. Angrily, he turned away and crossed the stony pavement to his unlocked room.

While he rapidly packed his belongings, determined to leave without talking to the girl, Marek forced himself to think about his brother, Brest Litovsk, the distant radio music, anything but the small tawny face framed by two thick braids. When he had finished pushing Victor's and his belongings into the knapsacks, he threw a final all-embracing glance around the dust-filled room, grabbed the knapsacks and left. But as he approached the exit, he found his pace slackening until he stopped at the gate. He looked at the outhouse, the bench under the palm and the near well under the stiff dwarf cactus tree with the dirt still floating over the water. The radio in the distance was shut off and the slumbrous silence that followed was broken only by the buzz of a fly. Suddenly sweetness and sadness of memory mixed nostalgically in him as if he had already left. And as he couldn't tear himself from the courtyard, he made a compromise with himself, yielding to one final quick look into the house.

Slowly he approached the window, and because of the reflection of the sun he could see only fragments of the floor and the contours of the table. Screening the light with his palms, he flattened his face against the pane. Something moved by the left wall of the room. On the settee was Ajmi, her head turned to him, her big dark eyes regarding wonderingly his distant face beyond the window. The skein with needles and the unfinished blue sweater lay at her feet on the floor. Marek's whole body went limp, and in that instance he realized what he had known deep in his mind all along—that he would not be able to leave. Abruptly he detached himself from the window and staggered for his room. He threw the knapsacks into a corner, sunk heavily on to his bed and dropped his face into his hands.

He didn't know how long he had been sitting there, but when he raised his head he saw a silhouette flitting past his window. A moment later his door was flung open and Ajmi was there, her hands resting against the doorframe, as if she had suddenly come to a halt. Her mouth was open, her breath laboured and her dark eyes fixed on his face. Helplessly, he kicked the door shut and took her into his arms.

Her small breasts lifted hard against his chest as she threw her head back pulling away from him. But as his lips reached hers, her resistance melted. She pushed her teeth against the flesh of his mouth, and gripping his head tightly, cried with whispering violence, 'Let's go away from here before he comes back!'

'They won't let me leave the town, Ajmi!'

She drew away, facing him with an angry flash of eyes. 'I won't stay under the same roof with him! Not after what happened!'

Marek had to struggle to break down the barrier of her stiffened arms before he could again lock her in his embrace.

'We will go abroad,' he found himself saying in subdued, comforting tones. 'As soon as my brother returns from the hospital. And when we get there, you'll leave your husband.'

'Why not now? I cannot . . .'

'Because only this morning he saved my brother. I can't pay him back in such a way. Let him go with us, so he can join his family. This is the least we can do for him.'

Her tight lips quivered and her chest heaved with a sigh. A sullen resignation came into her voice. 'When shall we go?'

'Victor should come back in a week.' With a soothing caress Marek ran his fingers through her hair, then kissed her delicately on the mouth. Frenziedly she twined her arms around his waist and buried her face in his chest. Behind the window the long palm leaves drowsily fanned the hot pavement of the courtyard. The light flickered in small bright stains among the branches of cactus as the red disc of sun sank fast to the horizon.

22

THE TABLE WAS COVERED WITH a white cloth. A tall clay vase with showy cactus flowers towered over numerous saucers with pickled cucumbers, peppers and green tomatoes, grated radish and slices of white onions soaked in cottonseed oil. A basket with black raisin bread, still warm from the oven, filled the room with a pleasant scent. A bowl of apricots, plums and grapes added colour to the table setting. In the kitchen the fat sizzled in the pan, and whiffs of the frying of seasoned eggplant drifted into the room and mingled with the aroma of bread. Marek shook his head with admiration at Ajmi's and his own work, then picked up a pile of white plates and cups from the chest of drawers and began to set them on the table. He heard a noise of footsteps in the courtyard and with a start turned to the window, disturbed that Victor might have come before they were ready. But it was Ibram, jovially carrying two bottles of hard-to-get white wine, hanging on a string across his neck as if the bottles were buckets, the wine water and

he himself a water-bearer. He stopped on the threshold, regarding the table with approval. 'Very beautiful,' he said, his
loud voice complimenting his wife in the kitchen.

'He got the wine,' Marek announced.

'Good, I'll be right in.'

For a moment Ibram fumbled at the table before he finally
found a space for his two bottles. He brought glasses from the
kitchen and a piece of cloth and began to wipe them clean,
examining them against the window light, nodding with
satisfaction only when they reached the brilliance of crystal.
Ajmi entered the room with a jug of water and put it in the
corner. Her hair was tied in a severe knot and she wore a white
apron over her festive paranja, the same that she had worn at
the anniversary of the Great Revolution. As she approached
the table, Marek looked at her with a smile of gratitude. 'Is
there anything more I could get in town?' Ibram asked. Under
the simultaneous looks of both men, her eyes wavered. She
stooped to pick up pillows.

Ibram went into the kitchen to wash his hands. Marek
stared pensively at Ajmi's back, as she bent down, arranging the
pillows for seats around the table. Slowly he walked to the window and peered outside. 'Victor should have come by now.'
He felt her gaze on the back of his neck, but as he moved his
head around, he saw her lids quickly shutter her eyes. She
turned to the door and vanished into the kitchen. The clatter of
her sandals died out in the noise of Ibram's washing.

Suddenly a squeaking of wheels was heard from the road.
Immediately Marek dashed out of the house. There in front of
their courtyard was an arba with a bewhiskered Uzbek driver,
a home-going, cured patient, wrapped in a blanket, and Victor,
who was clumsily sliding down from the high platform. When
his feet touched the ground, his face turned to Marek with a
greeting smile. On the sight of his brother's emaciated, sunken
cheeks and his lips gasping from the effort, Marek's eyes
shrouded with a vague mist and he rushed to Victor and embraced him tightly.

'Come on, let's go home,' Victor said, giving him an embarrassed slap on the shoulder. 'Give the driver a tip, will you?'

Marek pulled out the money and gave it to the Uzbek, but the man smacked his lips in dignified refusal and then swished his reins. The cart bumped off over the uneven dirt road.

Victor trudged into the courtyard and looked around with a little smile of recognition. His roaming eyes stopped at the sight of Ibram's and Ajmi's faces, their noses curiously pressed against the window pane. He waved them a salute, and when a moment later they came out, he slowly approached them, as if he had just learned to walk and shook hands with them. 'Please come in,' Ibram said, flashing Marek a conspiring glance.

'I have to get a wash now. I'll visit you later.'

'For a moment only. We want to show you something.'

'What is it?' He entered Shukunovs' home and stopped in the door at the sight of the set-up table. 'It isn't for me, is it?' A slow smile grew from the corners of his mouth as he looked at the grinning faces behind him. 'You shouldn't have troubled, really. . . . Thank you very much. . . . Well, now I shall certainly have to get a wash.'

'Of course,' Ibram said. 'Come as soon as you're ready.'

Victor waved away Marek's assisting hand and walked to his room. The filled basin was waiting for him on a stool. Marek helped him to pull off his shirt and then rub his back with soap the way he used to do when his brother would embark on a holiday scrubbing. As Victor's head loomed out of the towel, a fresh shirt was awaiting him in Marek's hands. His face contorted into a happy grin, 'Well, luxury again. . . .' He put on the shirt, and as he was buttoning it up, the smile disappeared from his face, and it grew serious. And then came the question Marek had all the time been expecting. 'Is Hamlat back in town from his trip?'

'Hamlat was caught on the border. With the three Polish boys.'

For a moment Victor looked blankly at him as if he didn't understand. His voice caught a little as he finally asked, 'How do you know?'

'Kisielev confronted me with him in the prison.' He saw

186

Victor's brows shoot up in alarm. 'Don't worry, he didn't give us away and I admitted nothing.'

Victor's back arched. His eyes focused emptily on the floor. After a while he raised his head and Marek thought he heard him swallow hard. 'All the time I was in the hospital I hoped that as soon as I got out we would leave.'

'But we will, Victor! I'm sure Ulug Beg can find another man for us. When you feel well, I will go to see him.'

'I feel all right.'

'You can hardly walk.'

'In a few days I will feel fine. It will take time to get prepared so let's not waste it. Go to him tonight.' A frown emerged on his forehead. 'What about the money we gave to Hamlat's daughter.'

'I got it back.'

'Good. . . . Maybe this man won't be satisfied with what we can offer him. Hamlat agreed to a thousand roubles because he also got the three Polish boys to pay him.'

Marek approached the window. The golden light of the sunset lit his face. The shadows of the palm and the cactus lengthened and deepened. 'I know some people who have money and will want to join us.'

'Who? . . . How do you know we can trust them?'

'It's Ibram and his wife.'

He turned and saw Victor's lips pressed into a tight line. 'You couldn't keep your mouth shut, you fool!'

'Ibram was questioned about Hamlat. Also, he saw his daughter here, remember? All his family was smuggled abroad by Hamlat, so you don't have to worry.'

'How can we be sure he is telling the truth? You can't trust anyone here.'

'He could have got several years for getting medicine for you in the black market.'

Victor glanced at Marek and said nothing. After a while he rose slowly from bed. 'Come, they're waiting for us.'

As they entered Shukunovs' home Ibram stepped down from a stool from which he had just been lighting the oil lamp that hung from the ceiling. After calling his wife from the kitchen, he once again shook Victor's hand and said, 'It's good to have you back.' Waiting for his wife, he rubbed his hands in pleasant anticipation of the dinner, then as soon as Ajmi entered, he motioned to the table. 'Please sit down.' The men took their places and Ajmi began serving eggplant covered with fried onions.

As Ibram was pouring wine into their glasses, Victor picked up a tomato and, munching it, asked with a grin, 'How come you don't like it here?'

Marek caught Ibram's quiet look before he answered his brother. 'I don't like it for the same reasons you don't.' Then he added after a while, 'I hope you don't mind if we all go together?'

'I think it is a good arrangement.'

'Well then,' Ibram said, raising his glass with a broad smile, 'Let's drink to our trip.' He drank the full glass in a few thirsty gulps, then looked at the brothers slowly sipping their wine. 'Oh no, drain it! For good luck!'

'Give me time,' Victor said. 'I just got out of the hospital.' Then he eagerly resumed the topic. 'I used to live in a different world, so it's hard for me to get adjusted, but you . . . you were born in Russia, weren't you?' He scooped a few onions from the top of the eggplant and chewed them.

'No, I was born in the Emirate of Bokhara.'

'Then you too knew a better world.'

The shadow of a smile crossed Ibram's face as he poured himself half a glass of wine. 'In Bokhara every Jew had to wear a cord around his waist so that if he cheated a Moslem, he could be hung on the spot. If he stole, however, he wasn't hung. He was pushed off the Death Tower.'

Marek looked at Ajmi. A short movement went through her stiff figure and he knew she was conscious of his stare, but would not lift her eyes from the plate. He heard Victor's voice continuing the conversation. 'So actually the Revolution brought a change for the better for you and your family?'

'Yes. Still, all my relatives preferred to leave Russia.'

'Why?'

Ajmi raised her head and she looked up at Ibram, as if she had suddenly become interested in the talk. 'In spite of the persecutions in the Emirate, they could pray to God. They couldn't after the Revolution. Besides, they began to hear about Jews re-establishing their own country in Palestine. The Bible said, "You will return to Zion on the wings of an eagle".' With each sentence of her husband, Ajmi nodded as if agreeing with everything he said, but Marek knew she wasn't listening.

'I didn't know you knew the Bible,' Victor said.

'I went to a religious school when I was a child. . . . Why don't you eat?'

Victor looked down at his plate and fumbled with the egg-plant. 'I'm sorry, I am not really hungry.'

'You must eat,' Marek interjected with a gentle but firm tone. 'You will need all your strength if you want to go. You know that.'

A wan smile passed over Victor's face. 'Those words sound familiar. I used to say them to you before I myself landed in the hospital.' He shook his head as if fighting a hard battle with himself, then cut a piece of eggplant and forked it into his mouth. As Victor ate, Marek looked at him with tenderness, happy that they were together again. He had a strange feeling, as if a transition had occurred during Victor's illness and that now he, Marek, had become the older brother and that to him his mother had entrusted Victor's health and his father the completion of Victor's education. While he lifted the wine-glass to his mouth, Marek looked sidelong at Ibram. There was a genial grin on his face, the contented expression of a man who enjoys being hospitable and kind.

Ajmi got up from the table and Marek's eyes followed her, but, aware of the presence of others, stopped at the window. Outside, the courtyard walls reflected sombre tints from the sun's afterglow. 'Tell me,' Victor asked Ibram. 'You don't think Kisielev and the others know about your family?'

'No. When I was demobilized and returned home to Bokhara and found that they had gone, I came to settle here. All they ever knew here is that I had served in the army before. I had a good record. I left with the rank of lieutenant.'

'Oh, congratulations.'

'Thank you,' Ibram said with wry humour.

Ajmi brought a dish with bouillon and floating pastry stuffed with rice and eggs. As she took Marek's cup, their fingertips involuntarily touched and their eyes met for a split second, only to flicker away immediately. 'I wonder,' Marek heard Ibram say, 'whether Hamlat is back in town.' He turned to Victor and the two brothers exchanged glances.

'His daughter pulled through,' Victor said, changing the subject. 'She left the hospital yesterday.'

'Oh, good.'

For a while Marek sat at the table with eyes half closed in thought as he ate pieces of pastry, swilling them down with the hot liquid. He noticed Victor taking a few spoons, then pushing his cup away and spreading his hands apologetically. Ajmi showed the fruit bowl to him and he picked up a plum. 'Well, that was a good meal,' he said.

Ibram rose. 'The best is coming now. Bring the pirogue, Ajmi. I'll help you with the tea.' He went to the chest of drawers and began to fill the white cups first with the dark tea essence from a glass pot, then with the boiling water from the samovar. Carefully he carried the cups to the table. Ajmi reappeared at the door of the kitchen with a big plate of pirogue. They all looked reverently at her hands as she picked up a knife and cut slices of the boat-shaped pie, revealing its filling—mashed sultanas. 'How about a cigarette with your tea?' Ibram proposed.

'That's a good idea,' Victor said. Ibram handed him a square piece of newspaper and his pouch. Victor made himself a cigarette, then took a sip of tea and a spoonful of pie. 'Wonderful!' he said to Ajmi, laid his cigarette aside and put another spoonful of pirogue into his mouth. Under the contented eyes of Marek and the flattered smiles of his hosts he finished the whole piece in no time. Only then did he light his cigarette. 'I want to thank you,' he said to Ibram, 'for getting me the medicine in Bokhara.'

As the rosy blush on the fringe of the sky above the outside walls began to fade quickly and the darkness descended on the courtyard, Victor and Ibram smoked cigarettes, sipped their tea and discussed their plans for the journey abroad. Marek and Ajmi sat throughout the evening, rarely opening their mouths, elaborately avoiding each other's looks.

23

WHEN THEY RETURNED TO THEIR room, Victor hurled himself on to the bed. 'God, I'm tired.'

Marek began to put on a sweater. 'You'd better go to bed now and get some sleep. You've done enough for your first day out of the hospital.'

'I will wait for you.'

'I think you'd better go to bed. I won't be long.'

'Be careful. Don't enter his house if anyone is around.'

'I won't, don't worry.' Marek turned to the door, when through the window he saw a girl's silhouette slipping quickly into the courtyard, then fearfully peeking out as if she were followed.

'What's the matter?' Victor asked, noticing his brother staring out. He came to the window, and as the girl, after a moment's hesitation at the gate, began to approach their room, they both recognized Marusia.

'Didn't expect her here,' Marek murmured.

'Why not?'

He could not answer because there was a shy knocking on the door and he had to open it. His voice arched high with surprise as he said 'Hello.' He could see the whites of Marusia's eyes darting to Victor's figure bent over the kerosene lamp. The light went on, and as it slowly lit the small room, it enveloped the girl at the door saying 'Good evening' in an uncertain voice. Victor turned to her from the lamp and a slow smile spread over his face as the gratifying recollections of the pre-typhus days awakened in his mind. 'Hello, Marusia.'

'I saw you pass the station in the cart and I came as soon as I was free, to find out how you were. You are well, aren't you?'

'Oh yes, thank you. Sit down.'

She looked out of the window. 'I can't stay long.'

'Something bothering you?'

Marusia glanced at Marek, then sat down at the stool. 'She was questioned by Kisielev,' Marek said.

'Oh, I see. . . . What did he ask you about?' Victor's voice betrayed nothing but a casual curiosity.

Her face lifted up. It was drawn taut in distress and unhappiness. 'He asked me everything I knew about you. And whether you ever told me you wanted to . . . ' her voice rambled off to almost a whisper, ' . . . cross the border.' She grabbed Victor's hands. 'Please don't ever tell him that, please! I'm so scared! But I had to see you, Victor. I'll never come again, but this time, once more I had to see you, so that you'll understand why I won't come again. I love you, Victor, believe me, but I'm terribly afraid!' Her hands and her eyes held Victor's, pleading with him to understand and forgive in advance for her disloyalty. But he just gazed into her face, and a new flood of words sprang from her mouth. 'In Vladivostok there was a girl living next door to my house. They arrested her boy friend, a sailor from the cruiser *Alexander Nevski*, and two weeks later they arrested her. I'm sure she hadn't done anything and I don't think he did either. Someone probably said something about him and that was enough. But you don't have enemies, do you?' Marek walked out. As he was closing the door behind him, he heard the question in a voice that prayed for denial. 'You don't want to leave Russia, do you?'

The roads were very dark and even the street lantern on the Achum Babayeffa street shone dimly as he walked to the house of Ulug Beg. He watched the lonely star that broke through the sky and listened to the sound of his own footsteps, the chirping of crickets and the distant, faint voices of the town.

When he entered the street on which Ulug Beg lived, he quickened his pace, time and again looking over his shoulder to make sure that no one was walking behind him. Soft nostalgic music broke from a courtyard, followed by an accompanying chant. As Marek was approaching the end of the road, the song of the blind story-teller slowly faded away until the crickets' noise dulled it out completely. Once again Marek glanced behind him and, seeing no one, quickly lifted the rug and scurried into the courtyard of Ulug Beg.

A dim light was burning in the windowless house. Through the door he noticed black-robed Addin's Mother weaving a reed mat. At the sound of approaching steps she lifted her head and he saw her olive wrinkled face turn into the room with the announcement of his arrival. From the shadowed corner the stooped figure of the old Uzbek rose to welcome him. His bearded chin interrupted its rhythmical tobacco chewing. He shook hands with Marek, then peeked out. 'Did you see anyone on the road?' The woman returned to her job of fastening reeds with red and blue thread.

'No, no one. Why?'

'We might be watched.' The red-rimmed eyes blinked worriedly and a long dark spittle of tobacco juice landed on the ground.

Marek's eyes, adjusted to the dim light of the oil-dish, discerned bedding improvised on the floor under the wall on which hung the pieces of old armament. A small many-braided head rested on a cushion in a soundless, peaceful sleep. 'Aka?' Marek asked.

'Yes. Thank God she is back. Her father doesn't know she was sick.'

'My brother came home, too.'

'Good. Hamlat will be very grateful when he learns that you gave her medicine. I'm going to tell him about it tonight.'

Marek turned abruptly and gaped at the old man with disbelief. 'What do you mean "tonight"?' The wavering light played on Ulug's wizened face curled into a small smile. He motioned Marek to a seat and himself sat crosslegged opposite him. 'Where is he?' Marek asked with such loud impatience in his voice that the old man had to hush him up. He gestured to his wife to keep watch on the gate.

His voice lowered to a whisper. 'He is hiding in the house of a friend.'

'Here in Kermine?'

'No, in the neighbouring village.' Ulug opened his leather pouch and tapped a fresh pinch of the mixture on to his palm. With a quick movement of head and hand he deposited it between the lower lip and gum. 'He was caught at the border, but escaped from the train when it was bombed. I got a message only this afternoon.'

From the matting enclosure where Uzbeks usually store their milk products a baby's cry was heard. The woman put aside her mat and disappeared. Marek was oblivious to the weird falsetto of a lullaby struggling with the cry. 'You know why I came here? I wanted to ask you if you knew someone else to help us to get out of here. Do you think Hamlat may want to go again?'

'I don't know. I know he can't come back home. They might be waiting for him.'

'When are you going to see him?'

'In about an hour. When everyone is asleep.'

'Will you ask him if he would be willing to go?'

'I will.'

'You know the Shukunovs—the people where we live?'

'Sure, I sent you over there myself.'

'They want to go, too. We could pay two thousand roubles together.'

'They've been wanting to leave for a long time. Hamlat smuggled Shukunovs' family abroad, you know?' Marek nodded. Ulug Beg leaned forward. His eyes swept from the gate to the sky. 'You'd better go now,' he said. 'It's getting late.'

'All right.' As Marek got up and glanced once again at Aka, he noticed she wasn't sleeping any longer. Her open eyes were focused on him quietly. 'Hello,' he said. 'How do you feel?'

A little smile softened her earnest look. The baby's cry and the song ceased and the large woman reappeared in the room and bent laboriously over her work. 'How will you notify us?' Marek asked.

'Don't come here. I won't go to you either.' For a second Ulug twirled his short beard reflectively, then snapped his fingers. 'Addin's Mother picks cottonseed refuse for fuel from the cotton mill in which Shukunov works. I'll send her there with the message first thing in the morning.'

Marek approached the old man and shook his hand. 'Thank you very much,' and then he heard the words 'Thank you very much' repeated like an echo of what he had said. With a smile he turned to Aka.

'We told her about the medicine from you,' Ulug Beg explained.

'How do you feel?' As he bent over the girl, he noticed the old woman's face lighting up and her wrinkled chin nodding gratitude.

'I'll be all right,' the girl said in faint tones. She pulled her tiny hand out from under the blanket, clasped Marek's palm and leaned forward. As her lips brushed awkwardly against his fingertips, he quickly withdrew his hand. Embarrassed, he playfully stroked her braids and said a loud goodnight.

The old man motioned to his wife to inspect the road. On the threshold Marek waited until he saw the woman nod the all-clear. Then he left the house.

Once on the street he began to walk briskly, eager to bring the good news home. He moved quietly in the shadows of the courtyard walls. When he reached his house, he looked behind him and then quickly entered the courtyard. On the bench under the palm tree sat Ajmi, her long hands folded limply between her knees. 'What are you doing here?'

She shrugged. 'Just getting some fresh air. I felt hot inside.'

'Where is Ibram?'

'In the house.' She saw Marek's eyes darting to the light in his window. 'Marusia is still there.'

'Hamlat is back,' Marek said, sitting down beside her.

Her hand reached out impulsively and tightened around his. 'So now we can go! Did you see him?'

'No, he's in a nearby village. He is afraid that his home may be watched. Ulug Beg will see him tonight and will try to arrange for us to go. I hope he will succeed.' They spoke in soft whispers, their heads close together, aware of the nearby road.

'Oh, I do hope he will!' Suddenly her hand crushed his, and as she shook her head, her face wrinkled in an almost agonizing grief. 'I can't stand it any more, I can't!'

'But, Ajmi, please. . . .' He gripped her shoulders, but she shrugged his arms off and hid her face in her palms. 'It won't be long now. A few more days. We have to go through with it.' He kissed her repeatedly, softly talking to her. Her eyes wavered blankly over the light in Marek's window. When under his lips her face finally relaxed, his mouth slid down to hers. But her parted lips were inert and her dark eyes gazed at him straight and quiet. She pulled away and measured him from a distance. A tiny smile grew from the corners of her lips and she lifted her hand and delicately stroked his cheek. An image of Anushka from the hospital camp flashed through his mind. 'Marek . . . ' she whispered. It was the first time she had said his name. His eyes narrowed, Marek stood motionless, afraid that his slightest move would break the spell of this moment, unknown in their relationship before. Ajmi's eyes shone in the darkness and her lips moved with a few silent, unpronounced words. Then stretching on her toes, she kissed his cheek and ran away into the house. Marek watched her enter the door and saw her shadow pass behind the transparent curtain at the window. He sat in darkness under the rustling palm tree and stared at the light in her house until it went out.

24

VICTOR SAT ON THE STOOL, comfortably propped against the wall, his eyes shut as he bathed in the warm sunshine of the morning. Out of the room came Marek, carrying a cup of tea for his brother. 'There is sugar in it and even a piece of lemon.' Victor groped for the saucer, too lazy to open his eyes. Marek sat on a stone by his brother. He looked up at the sky, then at the gate, restlessly rubbing his palms against his knees. When he glanced at Victor, he saw him still holding the cup in his hand. 'Why don't you drink? Thinking about Marusia?'

Victor shrugged. 'What time is it now?'

'She will come again tonight.'

'She won't. That was goodbye.'

'Scared?'

'I guess so. What time is it now?'

'I think it is about ten.'

Victor opened his eyes, took a sip, then glanced at the gate. 'It will be two more hours before Ibram gets home.'

'Seven, I'm afraid.'

'What do you mean seven?'

'They have cut the lunch break to half an hour. He doesn't get back home now until after work.' Victor shook his head in irritation at the new war-time regulations. 'I think she is in love with you,' Marek said, trying to while away the time.

'Who?'

'Marusia.' Victor shrugged again, but after a while a contented smile slowly spread over his face and Marek knew his brother had quickly readjusted himself to life. 'Drink your tea.' He waited until Victor lifted the cup to his lips and went on drinking, then he got up, walked to the gate and inspected the road. On his way back he glanced at the Shukunovs' window, but the sun was in his eyes and he could see only the hazy outline of the curtain. He sat back on the stone, collecting small pebbles around him and passing the time by throwing them at various objects in the courtyard. A feminine song floated from the Shukunovs' kitchen, lost from time to time in the sound of water running into a basin. Victor finished his tea and put his cup on the ground. 'I don't think it will do us harm if I go to see Ibram,' Marek said, aiming a little rock at the can on the edge of the well. 'I go through hell sitting here and waiting!' The noisy rattle of the overturned can followed his successful throw.

'Oh stop it, will you?' Victor shouted, irritated. He wiped the sweat from his throat and face. 'Actually,' he reflected after a while, moistening his lips, 'people know we live at the Shukunovs'. I don't see how anyone could suspect something if you dropped by at his place of work.'

Marek sprang to his feet. 'Of course not. I could safely go there.'

'Okay.'

'Will you be comfortable?'

'I'm comfortable.'

'If you need something call Ajmi. She's at home.'

Victor nodded. His fingers flitted momentarily across his face and then he impatiently waved his brother away, 'Go now!' Marek entered his room and picked up his skull-cap.

Achum Babayeffa Street was deserted and he reassured himself that no one was watching them. The day was warm and the sky cloudless. On Shadiva Street the barber's shop was open and a new young barber with oily hair and long side-boards waited in the door for customers, scrutinizing the hair and faces of passers-by. As Marek crossed the street, the fat manager of the czaikhana, swishing his flies away, nodded to him. Behind him a group of goateed elders sat in circle with their tea-pots and towels, discussing the town affairs in serious undertones.

Marek passed near the cinema with a picture display and a torn poster of 'Merry Comrades' that had played before the theatre closed on the orders of the Health Department. Never had he gone that far down Shadiva Street. Behind a few shacks that hugged the road, and a tumbled-down deserted mosque there was a little czaikhana and an ancient roofed bazaar of dyers, weavers and cord makers. Suddenly the medieval tranquillity of this old quarter of the town was broken by the squeaking of pipes and thudding of kettle drums. A two-men orchestra was introducing a magician. Children excitedly rolled around in the dirt, put out their tongues and jeered at their mothers when they tried to keep them away from the expected crowd. Behind the market was a fenced courtyard, covered by skins of karakul drying in the sun, and behind the courtyard was the long white building of the Uzbek Cotton Mill No. 17. Under the wall stood a row of huge cauldrons with yellow oil, purified by caustic soda. Over the entrance hung a huge banner announcing the employees' decision to work once a month on their rest day without pay for as long as the war lasted.

Marek entered a bookkeeping office. Through the small door he peered into a large hall where a series of circular saws, ranged alongside each other, separated the seed from fibre under the severe scrutiny of white-aproned workers. 'Yes?' Marek heard and turned to a bespectacled little clerk with a crew cut. 'You want to see someone?'

'Yes, Comrade Shukunov.'

'Oh, he's working. He finishes at five.'

'I know, but it's quite urgent.'

The man gave him a searching look. 'Well, I'll make an exception. Just for a few minutes.'

Impatiently Marek squirmed in the door, eyeing that part of the hall where, behind a glass screen, presses extracted the oil from cottonseed. He finally saw the clerk beckoning to him. A face smeared with coal black oil peeped out through the glass. Then a moment later Ibram came out and as he walked towards him across the hall, Marek read from the hidden smile in his eyes that he had good news. 'You couldn't wait, eh?'

'No,' Marek admitted.

Ibram glanced around, then nudged Marek into a corner where a hot water fountain stood. He picked up a glass from the shelf and filled it. 'All is arranged,' he whispered, offering Marek a drink and picking up a glass for himself. 'He has left but will be waiting for us in a yurt in the mountains.'

'At the forester's yurt?'

'Yes.'

'We can't go yet. Victor isn't well enough.'

'Neither is his daughter. He wants his children with him. He is not coming back.'

'I see. . . . Couldn't he wait in this neighbouring village?'

Ibram looked over his shoulder and saw the clerk appearing in the office door, his expression showing that the few minutes had passed. Ibram drank the hot water until the man gave up and went away, then he leaned over to Marek. 'He couldn't stay there. It was too risky. He just came to pick up his children. He didn't know Aka was ill and couldn't go right away. We will have to get her and the baby to him.'

'How shall we go? They may be watching the station.'

'The Uzbek with whom Hamlat stayed will drive us to the next station. When we reach our destination, the forester will pick us up.'

'How will he know when to expect us?'

'He will meet every train until we get there.'

A worker, his overall smudged with black oil, approached the fountain and picked up a glass. In a suddenly changed, light voice Ibram added, 'Well, see you at home.' They both re-entered the office and shook hands. Ibram gestured to the clerk that he was through with the conversation and was reporting back for work. With a happy smile Marek walked out straight into a dense cloud of dust whipped up by the huge wheels of a cart, as its driver spurred his shaggy steppe pony to a trot.

In front of the bazaar children were romping, imitating the magician who was swallowing nails and broken glass and burning charcoal and walking smilingly over the glowing iron. Only a few curious ones assembled to admire his skill, for the population was instructed by posters and word-of-mouth not to gather in crowds.

Walking quickly, his cap perched on the top of his head, his mind filled with plans for the trip, Marek soon found himself back on his street. There was Victor in the gateway, waiting restlessly, examining his face from the distance just as Marek had earlier examined Ibram's.

Marek shooed his brother into the courtyard. 'Better come

inside.' On his way, he glanced at the Shukunovs' window. Now it was open. The breeze rustled the curtain and shook the glass pane in which the cactus tree was outlined.

In the room, Marek reported all the arrangements to Victor. His brother's emaciated face broke into a smile. He flopped on to the bed, crossed his arms under his head and dreamily fixed his eyes on the ceiling. 'As soon as we get over there, we'll find ourselves a nice room with running water. And we'll buy ourselves suits, and once a week we'll go to a bathhouse, and get ourselves a steady girl. And I'll enrol at a university and finish my studies.' In his voice Marek read the same pre-war determination that had made him so successful with his studies and his girls. He was well on the way to complete recovery.

'I hope we can leave in a week or so,' Marek said.

'Don't be silly. We can go in a few days.'

'You won't be strong enough.'

'I will. I'll sleep as much as I can and eat as much as I can.'

'You hungry?'

'No, but I'll take a nap.'

'Okay. I'll go now and tell Ajmi everything. Goodnight.'

Turning to his side, drawing circles on the wall, Victor went on thinking up details of everyday life after their border crossing. Marek knew that not for a moment would he permit himself any doubts. A vision of mountain trails, frontier guards with bayonets and ferocious dogs came unbidden into Marek's mind, but with a vigorous slam of the door behind him, he shut the images out of his thoughts. He crossed the courtyard and knocked at Ajmi's door.

'Who is there?'

'Me, Marek.' Simultaneously he pushed the door open and saw her sitting on her settee, grey-robed and barefoot, her hair yet unbraided, appraisingly holding the blue sweater in front of her. It was finished now. 'I just saw Ibram. All is arranged. We're leaving in a week.'

She dropped the sweater on the floor, closed her eyes and held her breath for a moment. Never before had he seen her face so expressive as now with her eyes shut. He approached her, pulled her to himself and kissed her eyes. She threw her arms around his neck, pressing her whole body against him. The warmth of her hips and bosom and the aroma of her skin made him instantly dizzy. He closed his eyes in anticipation of the softening of her lips, tightening of her eyelids and fierce striking of her teeth against his flesh. But he felt her hands suddenly pushing him away, and when he didn't let go of her, her elbows wedged between him and herself to break the circle of his arms. 'Someone is outside!'

Immediately he freed her and swung his head to the open window. A man was standing in the road, holding a stack of cards, comparing the address on one of them with that of the entrance. Marek and Ajmi anxiously watched him crossing the courtyard. Ajmi peeked out. 'What is it?'

The man approached the window. His long severe face was covered by pock marks. 'Does Ibram Shukunov live here?'

'He is not home now.'

'Are you his wife?'

'Yes.'

'Please give this to him.' He handed a card to Ajmi and turned to the exit. The card was red and had a bold-lettered imprint on its top, 'Draft Call.' With alarm Ajmi looked at Marek. His eyes raced down the card where over the printed dots a date was inked. 'Sunday 4 p.m.,' he read. 'It's Wednesday today. I didn't think they would draft a man in his age.'

'He is a reserve officer. . . . What are we going to do now?'

Nervously Marek ran his hand over the stubble on his jaw. 'I don't know. . . . It's only four days. We couldn't leave that soon. Victor and Aka won't be strong enough.' And suddenly he put his palm over his mouth and his eyes grew wide. He looked up at her and she looked back at him and both had the same thought. 'No, Ajmi!' he said after a while, shaking his head vigorously; and as if there were still need to convince himself, he added a few times, 'We can't do that, we can't leave him here!'

She looked away and guiltily bowed her head. 'Victor and

Aka will have to make an effort. We will leave the night before the draft call.' Without looking up she nodded obediently. Helplessly, Marek's eyes travelled to the floor where lay the blue sweater of Ajmi's husband.

25

THE TOWN LAY IN DARKNESS and the silence of sleep. A few stars and a pale moon looked down at the two shadowed figures coming out of the narrow, ill-lighted streets and starting to climb the slope. They walked over the buran-scarred topsoil, until they reached the crest of the hill. Then they turned for a last look at the town. The mosque cupola and wooden lookout post of the prison towered over the hive of mud huts pressed so tight together that it looked as if there were no roads dividing them. 'Let's go,' Victor said. 'They're waiting for us.'

'Don't you want to rest a bit?' Marek asked.

'Don't be silly. I've forgotten that I was ever ill. Come on.' They walked across the hard rocky ground that opened up in front of them, among the sharp-thorned saksaul trees jutting out of the desert. In the distance several little huts revealed themselves in the darkness. 'I see no one,' Victor remarked. 'Ibram and Ajmi must have reached the village.' As they stepped up their pace, little pebbles under their feet began to crunch noisily, so they slowed down again. 'I hope everything is arranged so that we can leave at once.'

Cautiously they entered the village's single street, moving along the crumbling walls and houses until they reached a little tumble-down mosque. They began counting the gates and stopped at the fourth one. Victor lifted the rug, peeked inside and from his nod Marek knew they were in the right place.

Under a courtyard wall stood a cart with a harnessed horse, munching tufts of hay from a sack. As they entered, the animal raised his head, stretched his ears, but after a sidelong scrutiny of the newcomers, returned to his meal. In the door of the hut appeared a tall, lean Uzbek with sunken cheeks and a round shaven head. He shook hands with them and beckoned them into the room. 'Let's not waste any time,' Victor said.

From the hut came Ibram and his wife, then Aka and finally old Ulug Beg carrying the basket with Hamlat's baby. The men helped the women climb on to the tall platform, then they jumped aboard the cart. Ulug Beg leaned over the basket and kissed the baby and then entrusted it to Aka, placing it on her knees. As he reached out in an unfinished, awkward gesture and stroked the girl's cheek, she threw her arms around his neck. The driver smacked his lips, urging the horse to a start. The cart wheeled towards the large opening in the side wall, with old Ulug Beg trotting behind it. It reached the road and moved quietly away, leaving the small stooped figure at the gate, his hand raised limply in a silent farewell.

From the little shacks and hovels hugging the dirt road, the paneless windows gaped like sightless eyes at the laden horse-cart, its crooked shadows outlined in the pale moonlight. At the end of the deserted village a patient donkey trod a circular path, turning the wheel of an irrigation pump.

From his seat in the rear of the cart, his legs dangling down, Marek looked over his shoulder at Ajmi, sitting by her husband. At the same time she lifted her head, and as their eyes met for a second, a furtive smile passed between them. Then she looked down as Ibram put a blanket over her knees and offered her his shoulder to lean against and sleep. She shook her head, glanced at Marek, and turned her attention to the road that opened up on a plateau covered with great broken boulders.

The driver raised his head, observing with concern that the moon brightened with every minute, whitening the few nearest clouds. As the cart reached the bottom of a long incline, his back straightened and he began attentively peering at the blurred road in front of him. Shortly before reaching the hilltop, he pulled the reins and halted. 'What is it?' Victor asked.

'They put up a road block after the epidemics started. I'll

drive alone and meet you about a kilometre from here at a deserted shack. Be sure you make a wide circle before you get back to the road.'

'You're sure they will let you pass?'

'They know that my married daughter lives in the nearby hamlet and that no one in my family is ill.' He took the basket from Aka's knees and held it until the girl reached the ground and picked up her brother. The men jumped down from their seats. As Marek helped Ajmi, she squeezed his hand hard without looking at him. They began their long walk into the desert, with Ibram carrying the basket. The cart moved over the hillcrest and disappeared.

'You feel all right?' Ibram whispered to Aka. She nodded, and he turned to Victor. 'How about you?'

'I feel fine.'

As they left the road, their feet began sinking into the sand, slowing their pace, but they continued until they had covered a good distance. The slope slanted down, opening up a long view of the desert. Suddenly Victor, who was walking ahead, dropped to the ground and they all followed him. A remote but strong flashlight pierced the night and a breeze brought with it far away voices.

After a moment the light went off and the whole group crawled along until they reached the cover of a hill. With Victor walking in front and Ibram behind him carrying the baby, they worked their way around the inspection post. Then as they returned to the road, the road wasn't there. In front and behind them there was nothing but the shifting dunes, peacefully silvering under the wan starlight. As his eyes probed the surroundings, Marek in a sudden panic, imagined miles and miles of desert just as he used to dread the endless stretches of snowfields when he dreamed of a never-attempted escape from a Siberian camp. Ajmi came over to him and as she walked beside him, glanced into his face, searching for reassurance. 'Listen!' Ibram said, halting suddenly. They all paused. A remote pounding of many hooves came to Marek's ears. Far on the horizon he saw a herd of gazelles sprinting across the desert. 'There must be hard ground and probably the road.'

As they began walking in that direction, Marek said to Ibram, 'Let me carry the baby now.'

'It's all right,' Ibram said. 'It isn't heavy.'

The moon now gave a clear, even light, helping them back to the hard ground. The wind brought with it a horse's whinny, and following the sound they presently saw the walls of a deserted shack, white against the dark sky. With a sigh of relief Marek saw the cart waiting for them, the harnessed horse peacefully munching his hay again.

'God, where have you been?' the Uzbek driver asked as they emerged from the dark desert.

'We lost our way.'

'We'd better hurry if we want to catch the train.' Hastily, he helped them climb into the cart and then he himself jumped on to the front seat. Moments later they were entering a small hamlet of a few huts plastered with mud, hidden behind the tall walls. At the sight of the cart, mongrels that were chasing a cat began to bark at the horse. The driver slapped the reins, hurrying the bouncing cart through the village. The dogs were soon left behind, barking at the moon in frustration. Victor lay on his back, his head on his crossed arms. 'You'd better sleep now,' Marek said.

'There is no point to it. We'll soon be at the station.'

Propping himself on an elbow, Marek turned to his brother. 'Are you thinking about Mother and Father?' He suddenly wished to talk about home, about the Christmas tree in the dining room, about the bicycle rides on summer Sundays, and their parents' private dancing lessons when the tango became a refinement and refinements came to Brest Litovsk.

But Victor said, 'I'm thinking about the university. I could finish it in a year, if I work hard at it.'

'I'm sure you could. By the time we get home, you might already be an engineer.' Marek smiled in the darkness as he thought again about their home-coming, flattered at the thought of Victor surprising his father with a University diploma.

Over the road swirled clouds of sand. The wind brought a shrill cry from the desert and then dozens of gleams appeared in the dark curtain. Victor sat on the platform and listened. 'Jackals,' they heard Ibram's voice behind them. The pack passed them by; then the quiet night settled in again, but the image of the howling animals remained in Marek's mind bringing with it the unwanted vision of frontier watch-dogs. To elude it Marek's thoughts snapped to the approaching time, maybe only a day away, when after crossing the border Ajmi would leave Ibram, and become his, only his, looking into his eyes, stroking his cheek, and sleeping on his shoulder every night, betraying nobody, hurting no one. He saw it all, there in the Persian mountains, Ajmi taking Ibram aside and telling him everything, and then Ibram rejoining the group with Ajmi, her head bent, following him from a little distance. He tried to figure out what Ibram would say—would he shout at him, strike him, or maybe, what would be the worst, say no word at all. As Victor lay on his side, closing his eyes, Marek turned his head, looking behind him. Aka napped with her face on the basket and the driver dozed, his head jerking over his chest. Ibram's eyes were lowered and tender as he watched Ajmi in his arms, overcome by heavy, irresistible sleep. Helplessly, Marek thought of the words Pavel Stepanovicz had spoken in the hospital, 'Your brother is yours.' Thanks to Ibram he had not lost his brother; but there, across the border, Ibram would, thanks to Marek, lose his wife. For a long moment Marek watched Ajmi and her husband, then lay down by his brother. His pensive eyes were on the stars above him.

26

BEYOND THE TRAIN WINDOW THE low drifting mist began erasing the glittering images of the stars. The dawn unveiled the stretches of sand among the cliff rocks. Slowly the far distance revealed the hazy outlines of the mountain slopes clothed with green forest. From his shirt pocket Marek pulled the cardboard-framed photograph of his mother and father sitting on chairs in front of their sons. Again with the familiar spasm of pain and delight, he tried to picture Victor and himself knocking on their door on a quiet evening, his father's calm, unaware 'Come in,' and his mother's frail figure rising abruptly from the supper table. He kept the photograph in his hand until the daylight, breaking into the compartment, brought the blurred faces of his parents into focus, and then he still held it a little longer before putting it back into his pocket. His eyes slid down to Victor's face on his knees, a little pale with sunken cheeks and unhealthy lines between the nose and the open mouth that breathed heavy sounds of sleep. Marek lifted his head to the opposite bench where Ajmi was resting on the shoulder of her husband, who slept in the corner by the window. Under Marek's silent gaze the girl's heavy lids quivered and then opened. In the curious light of her eyes Marek read the soft pleasure of seeing him the first thing in the morning. She turned to the window and at the sight of the sun showing its edge above the earth, a slow recollection of where she was reached her mind. She raised her head, looked up at sleeping Ibram as if surprised to find herself using his shoulder, and then sent Marek a little smile of good morning. Marek felt his throat tighten, and after his lips twitched in an uneasy return smile, he looked away out of the window.

The basket on the bench swayed and the baby's whimper came from it. Glancing helplessly at Aka, hunched on the bench, Ajmi bent over the child, and with unpractised hands rocked the basket. The baby uttered a loud cry, now awaking everyone in the compartment. Aka drowsily staggered to her brother and pushed a rubber nipple into his mouth. 'He won't cry later, don't worry,' she whispered apologetically to Ibram. 'We will see to it.' A native couple rubbed their eyes and stretched. Yawning loudly, a red-bearded Turkoman, who for the night preferred the roomier space of the floor, stumbled back to his seat near Aka. 'I reckon we should be in shortly,' Victor said, blinking his tired, glazed eyes. 'You didn't sleep, did you?'

'I'll have all day to sleep. Let's have some fresh air here.' Marek opened the window and a gust of wind refreshed the stale, thick air of the compartment. It brought with it a clamour of passengers' voices and the noise of the locomotive.

'Did you sleep?' Ibram asked his wife.

'Yes, thank you.' Ajmi leaned towards the window, eyeing a distant forest she had never seen before. Her eyes shone happily and for a moment she forgot why she was on the train. She gave Marek a sidelong smile reminding him of their talk about forests and meadows.

The door opened and a conductor looked inside. 'Anybody getting out at Dushak?' There was no answer and he moved to the next compartment with the same question. Behind the wall resounded a gramophone record. A hoarse bass voice began to sing 'The Little Blue Handkerchief', apparently unsatisfied with the recorded voice of the singer. The Turkoman woman with silver breast ornaments and a big pregnant belly began to unpack bread, dates and a bottle of fermented milk wine. From his flowing caftan her husband pulled out a knife and cut the bread, and offered a hunk, a few dates and a swig to the red-bearded Turkoman. The man thanked them for their hospitality, then the two men lifted their eyes heavenwards, touched their lips in a word of prayer and began to eat and chat.

'You didn't say goodbye to Marusia, did you?' Ibram asked Victor. 'I didn't see her around the last few days.'

'After her last visit she said she would come the next day, but she never showed up.'

'Oh, some women are like that.' He looked at his wife, his warm smile betraying his gratitude that she wasn't like that. 'I hope you aren't sorry?'

Victor gave his shoulder the usual unconcerned-about-women shrug, and then looked out where trees, bushes and tufts of grass began to appear, breaking the desert monotony. The mountains that were outlined sharply against the leaden sky seemed to grow every minute. The train passed a nomadic camp with morning fires built under tripods outside the yurts, and then a string of tawny camels plodding silently on a path along the tract. In the next compartment the duet came to an end, but after a short break, the same tune started all over again. This time a few more voices joined the recorded vocalist in singing 'The Little Blue Handkerchief'. The Turkoman finished eating and as the woman rose to pack, her casual meal companion respectfully tapped her on the belly and raising his hand in a salute, complimented her and her husband on their fertility. The wheels began to clatter and the cars to jerk as the train suddenly ran on to a second track. In the corridor was heard the conductor's voice announcing the approaching station. Outside, a town appeared with clay houses shadowed by trees, boasting a few buildings of burned brick and a mosque with a towering minaret. The train slowly came to a halt in front of a two-storey railway station. Passengers, already riding on the steps, with cans and pots in their hands, lined up outside the boiling water faucet. Through the door of the station hall a throng of tall, broad-faced Turkomans in flowing caftans and enormous sheepskin shakos came on to the platform and boarded the train. As Marek looked into his compartment, he saw that the native couple were gone and two of the Turkomans sat in their places, talking animatedly with broad gestures. The portly station-master shouted orders, walking up and down the platform with bulky strides, swinging his hands back and forth with authority.

A whistle sounded, the flock of passengers with their cans leaped back on to the steps, and the train began to move. 'Next stop,' Ibram said. Through the window Marek caught glimpses of two men squatting near a wall, obligingly helping each other with hair cuts, a saddled oxen dragging logs with a man riding oxback, and then a herd of fat-tailed sheep tended by a shepherd. Suddenly he realized that the train wasn't picking up speed. Uneasily he glanced at the others. Ibram and Victor wore the same bewildered expression. The

Turkoman in the corner, relieved that the concert behind the wall had come to an end, pulled his sheepskin shako over his eyes and dozed again. The car came to a stop outside a small wooden shack. Marek's legs went limp as he read the Russian sign, 'NKVD Control Post', then saw a uniformed man with a cartridge belt around his waist and a rifle across his shoulder leap aboard their car. Another NKVD man boarded the next car. The wheels began to roll quicker, resuming their steady rhythm, while Marek and his companions sat breathless and speechless, exchanging fearful glances, waiting for inspection. In the distance appeared the twisting blue line of a river glittering in the sun. A string of men was pulling a tow-rope to help a small boat that had run aground on a sand bank. The mountains and forests were immediately behind the river. Ajmi's eyes were on Marek, searching for signs of reassurance which he could not give. The two Turkomans, after several times slapping each other on the knees in dispute, finally clasped hands in agreement. As the train clattered over the narrow iron river bridge, the loud native voices in the next compartment were suddenly quietened by an imperious Russian voice. Then there was silence for a long while, and as Marek and his group fixed their eyes on the door, it slammed open and the NKVD man appeared. His eyes moved slowly over the two benches of people. 'Where are you going?' he asked the two Turkomans who had just come in.

'To Kaakhka.'

'And you?' He looked at Victor, but before he could answer, the NKVD man probed a sack on the luggage shelf with his rifle. 'Whose is it?' No one answered so he shook the sleeping Turkoman. 'Is that yours?'

The native pushed up his shako, drowsily opened one eye, and noticing the uniform, leaped to his feet. 'Yes, it's mine.'

'What have you got there?'

'My belongings.'

'Open the sack.' The Turkoman pulled the sack to the floor and untied the string. After a quick glance inside, the NKVD man dug his hand deeper to the bottom and came up with several karakul skins. 'What are you doing with these?'

The red-bearded Turkoman said, 'They're from my sheep.'

'I don't see a government stamp on any of them. You're selling them on the black market. Come with me!' He picked up the sack. 'Go ahead!' They went out, leaving grim silence behind them.

'I hope he doesn't come back,' Marek mumbled in Polish, his eyes glued to the door.

Suddenly the train began to slow. 'I think this is it,' Ibram said, peering out of the open window, the wind tousling his hair. 'Let's go.' He walked out into the narrow corridor crowded with people. Seeing the NKVD man with the Turkoman and his sack at one end of the car, he beckoned to the others to follow him in the opposite direction.

From the compartment the conductor appeared. 'Getting out at the Red Star Kolkhoz?'

'Yes,' Ibram said hesitantly.

'Tickets, please.' They handed him their tickets and went on, making their way to the door. They didn't look back, but they knew the conductor must have thrown them into his bag, for there was no inquiry as to why the tickets were marked for Kaakhka.

Through the window they saw the forest growing up over the mountainside and then the train abruptly came to a halt. 'Red Star Kolkhoz!' they heard the conductor's voice, and quickly jumped down the steps, mingling immediately with the throng of passengers that walked away from the car towards the scattering of white huts in the distance. As Marek glanced behind him, he saw the NKVD man with his prisoner talking on a field telephone installed on the platform. The train began to move. They all looked in another direction as the cars with the other NKVD man on the steps sped by. On the right side of the track Marek saw a large field with the tractor and people at their work among the scarecrows. 'New?' Marek heard, and turned to a small Russian with a visor cap, who nudged him with the elbow.

'Yes,' he said, not knowing what else to say.

'They sent you from Tashkent?'

'Aha.' Marek looked helplessly at Victor walking some steps behind him, but his brother's eyes roamed around in search of the man who was to wait for them.

'Two weeks ago they also sent some people, mostly refugees from the Ukraine.' Marek noticed a path on his left running up into the mountains. He looked at Ibram and Ibram nodded. 'It's a good kolkhoz. Last year we overfulfilled our harvest plan by thirty per cent. We were second in the Dushak agricultural area. Only Kalilin Kolkhoz topped us.' The man went on talking and Marek not listening until the first hut emerged from behind the trees. Outside it a woman was catching a bridle rein from her husband as he dismounted from a horse. Pretending his shoe strings had untied, Marek halted and bent down. Victor stopped as if waiting for him. The Russian with visor cap turned back, looked over his shoulder, but continued his walk. Then Ibram stopped, put the basket with the baby on the ground and sat on the stone, wiping his forehead. Ajmi and Aka obediently stopped near him. Soon they saw the group in front of them entering the kolkhoz street and break up. No one seemed to bother about them. 'Did you see the forester anywhere?' Ibram asked.

'No,' said Victor.

'Neither did I.'

'We'd better get away from the track and take that path, as Hamlat told us.' Victor turned and in the distance saw a hand-car coming from the direction of Dushak. It stopped, picked up the NKVD man and his prisoner and began going back. When it disappeared, they walked back near the track until they came to the path they had crossed before. Then they began moving up the tree-covered mountainside. Their eyes were raised, hoping that their guide was watching them from some higher point and that any moment now they would hear his voice. But they heard only the rustle of a stream somewhere in the mountains. Suddenly Victor stopped. 'What is it?' Marek asked anxiously, watching him clasp his hand to his heart. He saw him close his eyes momentarily, then swallow hard and resume his walk as if with an effort.

'Oh, nothing, just feeling a bit tired. It is better already.' His lips curled into a smile but his eyes remained troubled. Worriedly, Marck glanced at him from time to time as they climbed up the slope among the trees. They crossed a little brook and paused. A small clearing with a huge rock in the middle opened up a view on the dense pine forest. Ajmi's eyes swept over the green trees with delight. She looked up at Marek, but his face was turned to the mountain ridges that stood out sharply against the dazzling clarity of the sky. There was the frontier.

Suddenly from under the rock's shadow a figure rose. The man was imposingly tall, dressed in green uniform and sheepskin shako. They waited uncertainly. The man approached them, looked them over, then bent down and stroked Aka's cheek.

'Your father is waiting in my yurt,' he said. He turned to the others. 'Follow me.' He took the basket with the baby from Ibram and moved in front of the group, guiding them up the mountain into the forest among the pine trees where there was no path.

27

IN THE YURT THEY SAT in a circle on reed mats around a tripod that supported a pot over the smouldering fire. The glow of embers played on their faces, as they picked up chunks of mutton from towels spread on their knees and leaned forward to dip them in a sauce bowl. Through the narrow low door Marek could see the forester's small son keeping watch among the pine trees rustling under the darkening sky. Beside him, Victor looked calm and rested, as, to finish his meal, he sucked bone marrows, hungry after an all-day sleep in the yurt. The Turkoman forester, with his headgear now removed, squatted by the fire, pouring the boiling green tea from the pan into three tin cups. He called his son, and the boy re-

entered the yurt and collected the towels from the guests'
knees. Then he brought a basin and setting it in front of each
person, he poured over their hands a stream of water from the
long-spouted pitcher. He looked very much like his father,
slim and tall, with a strong chin, straight nose and shaven
head. He was no more than eight years old, and for the first
time he now remained with his father, while his mother and
their sheep moved down to the lowlands for the winter.

Hamlat picked up a cup of tea and took a gulp. 'We will
be leaving soon,' he said in Russian to the Turkoman, for it
was their only common language. 'Please count the money.'
He pulled a wad of roubles from his pocket and laid it on the
mat. The forester passed the two other cups around, advising
the guests to share them, then rose from his seat and walked
to a metal-worked chest above which on the felt wall hung a
rifle and a two-stringed flute. He unlocked the trunk, lifted
its lid and took out a leather pouch. Before sitting down he
stirred the embers with an iron poker. In the quivering glare
Marek saw Ajmi's face, her serious eyes focused on him across
the fire. As the others drank their tea, Hamlat and his friend
made an exchange of Russian roubles for Persian tumans, with
a profit to the Turkoman for his services.

Over the fire Aka warmed up a pan with mare's milk,
poured the liquid into a bottle and bent over the basket to
feed the baby. 'Well, we'd better start,' Hamlat said. He rose
to his feet, while the Turkoman put the money into his trunk
and returned with several pairs of felt slippers. Marek took
off his shoes, hung them by the laces around his neck and slid
his feet into the slippers. He watched Ibram put on his new
blue sweater that Ajmi had made for him, then move into
the shadow of the big trunk, turn to the wall and with bowed
back sway religiously. Time and again he looked at his wife
and Marek knew he had included her in his appeal to the
Jewish God.

Marek walked out of the yurt and stepped into the shadow
of the trees. Lifting his eyes to a star gleaming in the sky, his
lips moved in a prayer that his brother would reach the border

and get safely home to his parents. For what would be the use, Marek continued, in an ardent whisper, of Victor surviving the typhus, if he didn't survive the border crossing? He closed his eyes tight for a moment, the way he used to when as a child he wanted to achieve the closest contact with God. And then a vision of the swaying Ibram glancing at his wife sneaked back into his mind. Any time now when he thought of Victor, the image of Ibram would follow as if the two men were related by some invisible link. Painfully, Marek rubbed his face when behind him he heard footsteps rustling over the pine needles. He turned and saw Ajmi. She asked softly, 'What are you doing here outside?'

'Oh, just thinking.' She came close to him and took his hands. He kept his face away from hers. 'Come let's go back into the yurt,' he said.

She nodded and walked back with him, her eyes focused on him searchingly. And suddenly he turned to her, took her into his arms and pressed her hard to himself. Her hands fell over his neck. Desperately, he kissed her throat and face and hair and then as suddenly as he had embraced her, he tore himself away from her and re-entered the yurt. She followed him a moment later.

All were almost ready for the journey, with their shoes hung across their necks, filling their bottles with water. Hamlat was strapping the basket with the child to his back with leather belts. Ibram approached his wife and leaned over her. Marek saw her close her eyes almost in pain as her husband's lips touched her cheeks. The forester's son carried a little yearling inside the yurt, to show it off to his father's guests before their departure. Hamlat and the Turkoman shook hands. They both were enormous, the forester's height accentuated again by the massive sheepskin shako, which made him look almost like a giant. 'Well, I guess we won't see each other again,' he said. 'May God protect you and your children.'

'May you and your son live in health,' Hamlat said. 'And may your sheep fatten nicely every summer.'

All the men shook hands with the forester, stroked the

yearling's head and the boy's face, and walked out into the night.

The noise of their footsteps was muffled by the felt shoes as they walked in Indian file led by Hamlat. From the end of the line Marek watched Victor's back now disappear, now show itself again among the trees. They climbed up the mountainside that sloped gently, but below it was steep and he could see the distant gleams of the Red Star Kolkhoz's lights in the valley. High overhead the wind shook the frail tops of the pine trees. Stars flickered and the hazy moon whitened a few nearby clouds. A violet sleep enwrapped the forest, stirred only by occasional calls of night birds, the swish of a squirrel, or the remote murmur of a mountain stream. As Marek walked over the ground covered with pine needles, he found himself somewhat reassured by this peaceful, beautiful night.

They came to a clearing, skirted its edge and began climbing a steeper slope, halting now and then for breath. The warm air of the lowlands was giving way to upland air, sharp and cold. Suddenly an owl hooted and as Marek looked up he saw its face with the two beady lights of its eyes following the intruders. The wind brought with it the hoof-rattle of a scared ibex and then again the forest became still.

For a long time they mounted steadily without a trail, zigzagging around the trees, bending under the branches, crossing the brooks, avoiding moss-covered rocks that blocked their way. Finally they came to a large plateau covered with ruins of burial mounds and stone monuments of an ancient nomadic tribe. At the sight of them a flock of birds fluttered away into the safety of the forest. 'We'll rest here,' Hamlat said. He unbuckled the leather straps and put the basket on a stone. As he leaned over it, a smile softened his little grey eyes, for the baby slept calm and undisturbed.

Marek sat by his brother. Victor breathed heavily and his shirt and sweater were both wet from the climb. 'How do you feel?'

'I feel all right,' Victor said between gasps. They spoke in whispers, for in the moonwash the white burial monuments made the area look inhabited. Marek watched his brother take a few thirsty swigs of water. His hands trembled a little as he raised the bottle to his mouth. Aka lay on the grass at Marek's feet, her head on folded arms, her breath laboured. Then as she opened her eyes, she noticed Marek's drawn face above her and sat up with a smile. 'Don't worry about me,' she lisped. 'I won't cause any trouble.'

'We'd better continue,' Hamlat said, 'before Kisielev finds out you've all vanished from Kermine and alerts the frontier guard, as he did the last time.'

Marek immediately rose to his feet. 'Can you walk?' he asked his brother.

'Wait just one more minute,' Victor said, and in the heavy hiss of his voice Marek heard the faint echo of hospital days.

'The moon will soon be clear,' Hamlat warned, worried, watching the sky. 'There is only one cloud bank left. We must cross the river while the moon is hidden.

Marek approached Hamlat. 'Let me carry the baby.'

At the same time Ibram came from the other side and, turning his back to the Uzbek, grinned into Marek's face. 'Hamlat and I have agreed to carry the child in turns.'

'But you've taken care of the child all the way.' Marek's wounded manhood added volume to his voice and Hamlat told him to be quiet, calmly strapping the basket belts around Ibram's back. Marek started to protest, but Hamlat got up from his place with a curt 'Let's go' order. He started up and Aka moved behind him. 'Come on, we're going,' Ajmi said. Ibram winked at Marek and went after her.

'Are you all right?' Marek asked Victor, who got into line ahead of him.

'Yes.'

Behind him Marek heard flapping wings as the mountain birds retook possession of the ancient cemetery. 'Let me carry your shoes.' Paying no attention to Victor's objection, Marek snapped the shoes from his brother's neck and hung them over his own, now bearing both pairs.

The timberland swallowed them up again. Either the forest

was becoming thicker or the night darker, but Marek now had to feel his way from tree to tree, as with a heavy heart he followed Victor's stooped figure now moving now stopping to catch a breath. Once more he began to pray that his brother might reach the border and reach it in time. He was imagining the military police calling on Ibram, then waiting for him at his home, then when neither he nor Ajmi showed up for the night, informing the NKVD. He had a vision of Kisielev crossing the stony pavement of their courtyard, scrutinizing Shukunov's place, then knocking at his and Victor's room and finding that they, too, weren't there. A series of small frightening pictures unrolled in his mind as he walked, and felt his muscles twitch from the steepness of the ascent. The grey-haired woman's face with steel-rimmed spectacles answering from behind the station's ticket window that no, she had not seen them leaving town. The armed NKVD men searching Hamlat's and Ulug Beg's houses. The bent figure of the old man asking their help in tracing the children who had mysteriously disappeared. Kisielev's angry face at the telephone reporting to his superior in Bokhara, the latter's puffy fingers impatiently clicking down the receiver in an effort to get Samarkand, and finally the imagined bulky figure of the Samarkand's NKVD chief alerting by phone the commander of the frontier guard.

The forest suddenly brightened and the pine needles glistened in the darkness. Marek looked up at the sky. The clouds had lifted and the moon shone clearly, but travelling fast towards the other bank of clouds as if ashamed of being exposed. In front of them was a stream and now Marek saw silhouettes crossing the water over the rocks, through the wisp of mist slowly floating away. As he reached the centre of the stream, the rocks ended, and following the example of the others, he took off his felt slippers and socks. He plunged into the water, with bare feet stepping over its gravelled bed, the icy cold current stroking at his feet. On the other bank, everyone was resting, drying their feet, putting socks and shoes on again. Suddenly the baby began to cry and Ibram took the basket off his back. Aka was too tired to attend to her brother, so Hamlat fed him after warming the bottle on his belly. Over the stream Ajmi bent, filling her empty bottle and after drinking thirstily, she offered it to Marek. Absently, he shook his head, his eyes fixed on his brother, sitting on a stone and shivering, limply holding his socks in his hands as if he hadn't strength to put them on. In spite of his protest, Marek raised his brother's feet and rubbed them dry against his own trousers, then he sat by him and put his arm around his shoulder. Victor gave him a wan smile. None of them said a word.

After a while Hamlat, noticing that the baby slept again, looked at the mountain peak. 'It won't be long now,' he said. 'We'd better go.' The mountain crest looked near, but it had seemed so all the time.

Hamlat began to wrap the basket belts around his back. 'Let's wait a bit,' Victor asked. 'I can't walk.'

'You must pull yourself together. Aka was ill too and see how she is taking it.'

'But my brother has a weak heart,' Marek said. 'Aka hasn't. Let him rest a minute, please.'

'We must get to the river before the moon reaches the next bank of clouds,' Hamlat said. 'We'll need every minute of dark sky for crossing the river.' He looked at Victor's whitened face and resignedly let the belts of the basket slip from his shoulders. Again he looked up at the sky, studying the position of the moon and the speed of the clouds. Then he hastily lifted the basket on to his back. 'We must go,' he said, with a tone of urgency. 'We can't waste a minute.'

This time Victor stood up. He stopped shivering, but as they resumed their climb, he moved his heavy legs with great effort, often catching at branches to help himself up. Hamlat came down the line to tell him to keep away from the trees because they were making a noise. In the light of the moon as it shone on his brother's face, Marek noticed him nod, and then, as they started up once agian, he crouched, using the ground instead of the trees. Suddenly Marek saw him halt, lift a hand uncertainly in the air, and then touch his heart. His face turned back to Marek; it was distorted by a grimace. Marek hurried to his brother and, propping his back, whispered encouragingly, 'Come on, we're close to the top.' His mouth open, Victor was swallowing gulps of air as if suffocating. Grief-stricken, Marek peered at Victor's painfully tightened eyelids, when he realized that Ibram was already out of sight. He hissed after him, but only the rustle of branches answered. 'Put your arm around me, come on.' Submissively, Victor laid his arm around Marek's shoulder and they staggered up for a while, but they saw no one in front of them and soon even the faint noise of felt shoes drifted away. 'Wait here, don't move from this spot!' Marek began to run upwards and though lung-aching and leg-dead he didn't stop until he saw Ibram at a standstill, waiting for him and Victor.

'Where is your brother?'

Under the pine trunks that looked black against the glimmering green needles, Marek saw the outlines of Hamlat and the girls sitting on the ground. 'He can't walk any more. We must rest for a while.'

Hamlat rose to his feet. 'We're within two hundred metres of the top.'

'I know, but he can't even make fifty metres. . . .'

'Tell him he must do it. We've no time. Look at the moon!'

'I will go with you,' Ibram suddenly volunteered. 'Come on,' and without waiting for Hamlat's approval, he started down.

Marek passed him to lead the way. His heart drummed painfully for he was afraid that Victor might have collapsed meanwhile, or that they might lose their way back to him. Again he began to pray silently as he ran downhill among the trees that all looked alike.

Suddenly he heard the whispering of his name, and he rushed towards the direction of the voice. Victor was sitting with his back and head propped against a tree, his eyes narrowed in pain. His hand struggled helplessly with the cloth of his pocket, trying to pull out the bottle. Ibram lifted his own to

Victor's lips and he drank the water in great gulps, spilling it over his chin and sweater. 'We're almost there,' Marek said, pleading with his brother. Slowly Victor got up, let both men lay his arms over their shoulders and drag him up the steep ground. Finally they reached the rest of the group.

While lying on the ground, Victor's eyes focused on the mountain top and its nearness gave him a sudden spurt of fresh strength. He got up and they started again. For a while he was able to walk alone, but about fifty metres from the summit, his will-power once more left him. The trees were now so close together, that it was impossible to help him from both sides. Marek called on his remaining energy, threw his arms around Victor's waist and dragged him up, and when completely exhausted, he himself could hardly move, Ibram took over. Finally they reached the crest and sprawled down by the others. At the bottom of the highland dale covered with low bush Marek saw the blue dashes of the mountain river visible between the boulders.

'Victor, look,' he gasped. But his brother lay with his head in his arms, his breathing laboured, the sweat from his face dripping down his arms. Gently, Marek put his hand over Victor's hair. It was wet and sticky. 'Look, the river!' he breathed. Slowly, Victor raised his head, but it was so heavy that his chin fell back on his arm. His narrow eyes remained open though, and in them Marek saw the shadow of a happy smile.

'See that huge boulder,' Hamlat whispered, pointing ahead. 'That's where the canoe is.' He looked at Victor. 'Can you make it?' Victor nodded. 'The canoe can hold only three people. I'll have to make three trips. The women and the baby will go first.' He took the basket down from his back. Holding it with one hand, keeping the other in constant readiness over the child's mouth, the Uzbek moved forward, crouching. Though Marek strained his eyes, he could not see nor hear him among the brushwood. Then Aka followed her father, her palm over her mouth to muffle her gasps. Marek took a deep breath of cold mountain air. It smelled of resin and night dew. He looked at Ajmi, lying on his other side, amazed at her silent endurance. She sent him a little smile and then she also was gone.

Awaiting his turn, Marek lay flat watching the river. He could catch glimpses of the other bank, clothed with shrub and grass. Behind him the thick forest looked like a second night, different from that on the sky. The moon now skirted the first wing of the clouds. When Marek again glanced to his side, Ibram had already left. Victor was lying with his head over his palms, trying to get as much rest as possible in anticipation of the renewed effort, 'It's your turn,' Marek breathed. Victor raised his head, nodded, then got up. Marek watched his figure, bent double, move into the bush. He waited until Victor had disappeared before he himself crouched forwards, maybe a little earlier than advised by Hamlat, anxious to follow his brother closely. Moving as noiselessly as he could, feeling his way from shrub to shrub, Marek finally crawled through the last clumps, and when he emerged from them, there was the river at his feet, slapping sharply against the row of boulders, whipping foam up along the banks. The moon was now hidden behind the clouds. Their legs deep in the water, Hamlat and Ibram were hastily pushing a canoe out of the hidden cave. Marek didn't see the others except his brother, until Aka with her basket loomed from the clumps, and then Ajmi rose from under another cluster of shrubs, following her. He saw her glance back before entering the boat which the two men held with difficulty against the battering current. Aka's face was fixed on the basket on her knees, her palm hung over the baby's mouth. As Hamlat silently jumped into the middle of the canoe and Ibram pushed it away from the bank, Ajmi's eyes swept over the bush, searching for Marek.

Kneeling, Hamlat was stroking the paddle, moving the canoe across the river. It was so small that Hamlat, Ajmi and Aka with the baby filled it completely and it seemed a miracle that it could carry them at all. It swayed precariously among the rocks, the silhouettes above it diminishing gradually and then finally disappearing in the mist that, like a white ghost, floated over the waters.

Marek lay in the bush between Victor and Ibram feeling the grass wet from the dew under his elbows. He smelled the pines and heard the noisy splashing of the water as it swirled between the banks, shining dully under the clouded moon. Over the mist, on the other side of the river, the forest again rose on the slopes. The view reminded Marek a little of the Polish mountain landscape. In the Carpathian mountains there had also been a river, he remembered, though not along the frontier. Strangely, the recollection of the Rumanian border did not frighten him; though it was the first time that it had failed to frighten him. He recalled having heard that soldiers tremble before a battle, but when the guns start blazing they find themselves void of fear. The endless minutes of waiting dragged on while Marek kept watch both on the river and on his brother. He thought he heard the heavy hiss of Victor's breath, and for a second it occurred to him that now when for the first time he felt calm, his brother was feeling afraid.

Then Marek saw the boat emerging from the mist, carrying only Hamlat. He looked up and saw with distress that the moon was more than half-way through the clouds. As the boat approached their bank, Ibram beckoned to Marek and Victor to follow him, then rushed into the water and caught the boat's bow. While he held the canoe, Marek helped his brother climb into it, then waved Ibram aboard. But Ibram shook his head and motioned to Marek to get into the boat. 'Go on with your brother,' he whispered. 'I'll wait.'

'No, you go now.'

Hamlat beckoned, impatient with the men's chivalry. 'Come on quick, either one of you.'

Suddenly Marek heard excited cries approaching the river. He pushed Ibram into the boat, and as Hamlat caught him by the shoulders, he helped the Uzbek pull Shukunov aboard. Marek pushed the boat far into the river and dashed to the deep shadow of the nearest boulder, flattening himself against it. From behind the rock hurtled a uniformed man with a rifle in his hand, followed by another with a field flashlight. 'Light up the river, Kola!' the guard called, raising his rifle. And in that split second before the light could be turned on and reveal the boat, Marek jumped away from the boulder, leaping as noisily as he could over the gravel. 'Look there, Kola!' He felt himself drawn in the flash beam and heard a bullet whistle by, echoing in the forest. The boulders above the bank shielded him from the guard, but he heard their running steps behind him. Desperately, he fought his way among the rocks, taking the men away from the boat. The moon came out now from behind the clouds, and in its glare that cut through the mist, Marek caught a glimpse of Hamlat and Ibram forcibly pulling Victor on to the opposite shore, Hamlat's powerful hand tightened on his brother's mouth. The night was suddenly pierced with the criss-crossing beams of powerful searchlights from the distant watch towers. Abruptly the rocks ended, giving way to unprotective gravel. For an instant Marek halted, undecided, but as the steps thudded immediately behind him, he made a frantic lunge for the river. He had almost reached the water when his figure was caught in the strong beam of a searchlight. At the same time he heard the rifle's crack and felt a warmth and faintness in his leg, followed by a burning heat, and suddenly he could not move his leg. It became numb and heavy as a stone, and he fell, facing the water, his hands almost touching it. From the other bank came a woman's frenzied scream. He groaned under the stroke of a rifle butt, accompanied by an angry curse. A searchlight fell over the opposite bank on the empty rocking canoe, and as the beam slid to the shore, he saw Hamlat dragging Victor and Ibram pulling Ajmi into the bushes. Marek heard the baby's whimper and Ajmi's muffled cry and then finally Victor's shrill call of his name, and then a machine gun from the watch tower laid a short burst of fire on the opposite bank. The bullets hit the empty canoe, then the fire ceased abruptly as if by order. The wind brought with it the voices of men and the barking of dogs, and while both uniformed guards, with their bayonets set, kept watch over

Marek's figure prostrate on the gravel, he once again had a vision of homecoming to Brest Litovsk. He saw his parents welcoming Victor in their arms and then listening to his tale of how during his brother's illness Marek had finally matured into a man. It did not matter, it did not spoil the image at all, that he himself was not there.